A Regrettable Charade

Lords & Ladies of Mayfair

Laura Beers

Chapter One

England, 1813

Harred Woodville, Marquess of Kendal, had a no good, terrible louse of a brother. William had managed to squander through his own inheritance and now he was spending money that he didn't even have.

He held up the bills from the establishments that were demanding to be paid. It was not surprising that they were all from disreputable places, such as brothels and gambling halls. The sum totaled nearly five thousand pounds. If he didn't act quickly, his brother would empty out the coffers and he would be left with a bankrupt estate.

Why had he promised his father that he would always look after William? It was a promise that still haunted him to this day. He was nothing like his brother. He valued duty above all else and William only cared about himself.

They couldn't keep going on as they had. His brother would ruin him, alongside his tattered reputation.

"Mitchell," Harred shouted as he sat behind his desk.

Perhaps the butler could provide him with some insight into where his brother was at this early hour.

The white-haired, narrow-shouldered butler stepped into the study. "What can I do for you, my lord?"

Harred dropped the receipts onto the desk and asked, "Do you know if Lord William has returned home?"

"Yes, he only just arrived and headed straight to the dining room for some breakfast," Mitchell informed him.

He welcomed this news since he had spent the last few days trying to track down his brother but to no avail. With any luck, William would be in the right frame of mind to have a frank conversation. He was never quite sure what state his brother would be in when he returned home.

Rising, Harred said, "Thank you. I think some breakfast will do me some good, as well." He came around his desk. "I intend to go riding after breakfast. Will you see to my horse being prepared?"

Mitchell tipped his head. "Yes, my lord," he responded before he left to do his bidding.

Harred exited his study and headed towards the dining room on the main level. He had no doubt this conversation would be difficult, but it had to be done. His brother couldn't keep going on as he had been. Quite frankly, neither could he. He had more important things to see to than chasing after William.

As he stepped into the dining room, he saw William was seated in a chair but his head was face down on the table. A slight snore escaped his lips as the plate full of food went untouched next to him.

Harred sighed. His brother couldn't possibly be happy with this life, he thought. Drinking, cavorting with women, and gambling were acceptable pastimes for a gentleman for a period, but then at some point, they were forced to grow up and take on some form of responsibility. Clearly, his brother had not reached that point yet.

Coming to a stop next to his brother, Harred placed a hand on William's shoulder and slightly shook him. "William, wake up," he urged.

His brother grunted. "Leave me be."

"We need to talk," Harred stated as he let his hand drop.

"Can't it wait until later?" William asked, not bothering to open his eyes.

"No, it can't," Harred said firmly.

It seemed to take a considerable amount of effort on his brother's part, but William eventually sat up and opened one eye. "Why is it so bright in here?" he demanded.

A footman moved to close the drapes but Harred put his hand up to stop him. "Leave them open," he ordered. "It is hardly bright in here."

"Why are you insisting on being difficult?" William asked with a slight slurring of his words.

"Me? Difficult?" Harred clenched his jaw at that ridiculous question. Did his brother not know how truly infuriating he was? "I have been looking for you for the past few days, but no one seemed to know where you were."

William seemed amused by the smirk that appeared on his face. "That is because you do not frequent the places that I do. In fact, they wouldn't even let you in looking like that."

Harred glanced down at his finely fitted clothes. "What is wrong with how I dress?" he asked. His tailor made sure he was dressed in the height of fashion. Not that he cared about such trivial things.

"You are no fun, Brother," Wiliam replied. "You need to relax and start living life how it is meant to be enjoyed."

"Like you do?"

"Precisely," William said as he turned his attention towards the food on his plate. "I am famished. I don't think I ate dinner last night."

Harred was a smart enough man to know when his brother was attempting to dismiss him, but he had no intention of backing down. "I will not be dismissed," he stated. "This has gone on for long enough and I am putting you on an allowance."

William visibly tensed. "I beg your pardon?" he asked in a curt tone.

"There should be no confusion since I spoke plainly enough."

"You wish to give me pin money, then?" William shoved back his chair and jumped up. "Will you give me enough to buy a nice hat or some ribbons?"

Harred wasn't the least bit deterred by his brother's sharp tone and proceeded with his next words. "It will be a generous allowance, given the circumstances."

"And, pray tell, what are those circumstances?"

"You have wasted your inheritance on your mistresses and gambling," he explained. "Now you are wasting my money and I will not condone your behavior."

William's brows shot up. "How dare you!" he shouted. "You think you can stand there and judge me, but you know nothing about what I have been through."

Harred wanted to laugh at the irony of his brother's statement, knowing William had no one else to blame for his actions but himself. William always tried to shift blame to others. It had been this way since they were young.

Taking a step closer to his brother, Harred asked, "What, exactly, have you been through that isn't of your own making? You have made one poor decision after another and now you are attempting to defend your actions to me."

William brought a hand up to his forehead and winced. "If I didn't have such a splitting headache right now, I would challenge you to a duel for what you just said."

"A duel?" Harred asked. "Do be serious. You can hardly stand up straight, much less hold a pistol."

"When will you accept that I will never be you? I will never be the perfect brother," William spat out.

"I am not asking you to be perfect, but I do think it is time that you find a way to produce an income."

"An income? Surely you are not serious," William huffed. "Father was richer than Hades. Why should I have to work? That is beneath me."

Harred didn't think he had ever met a more entitled person than his brother. But he had made that blasted promise to his father and he intended to honor it. "I could use your help managing the country estate. I would pay you a fair wage."

William's jaw dropped and he looked stupefied. "You wish for me to work for you?" he asked. "What's next? Should I bring you your port in the evening, my lord?"

With a glance at the footmen that were standing guard, Harred said, "You are being utterly ridiculous. If you take some time, you will realize that I am offering you a perfectly respectable form of employment."

"I don't want to think about it. The answer is no," William stated before he started to storm off.

Harred called out after him. "If you don't take this opportunity, then I want you to move out of my townhouse."

William came to an abrupt stop. "'Your townhouse'?" He spun back around. "No, this was our parents' townhouse. You have no right to kick me out of it."

"I have every right, and you know it," Harred said, standing his ground. He had no intention of letting William use their parents' memory to try to win this argument. They weren't here. Not anymore. And it was his job to continue on their legacy.

William narrowed his eyes at him. "You would do that to your own brother?"

Harred gave him a look that he only hoped conveyed compassion. "I don't want to, but you can't keep going on as you have. If you do, you will bankrupt both of us," he said, attempting to reason with his brother. "I can't stand by and let that happen."

William didn't look swayed by his explanation. Why should he? He was living the life that he wanted, without any of the consequences of his actions. His brother came and went when he wanted, giving little heed for anyone but himself.

That ended now.

"I'm sorry, but this is how it will be now," Harred continued. "It is time that you step up and be the person that you were meant to be."

William put his hands out wide. "There is nothing wrong with the way that I am living. You are just jealous of me; you always have been."

"You are just spouting nonsense."

"It all makes sense now to me," William declared. "You aren't happy in your boring, pathetic life and you want to be more like me."

With a shake of his head, Harred said, "You could not be more wrong."

William's stomach grumbled and he placed a hand to it. "If you will excuse me, I think it would be best if I ate my breakfast in the privacy of my bedchamber." He walked over to the table and retrieved the plate. "I tire of your company."

"You can tire of me all you want, but this changes nothing. Take the job or find a new place to live," Harred ordered.

"What if I take a wife instead?" William asked.

Harred resisted the urge to laugh. William could scarcely take care of himself. How could he take care of a wife as well?

William gave him a smug look. "Yes, I will find an heiress and then I will be richer than you."

"I wish you luck with that. I truly do, but what woman would want you, given your dishonorable reputation?" Harred asked as he attempted to keep the humor out of his voice. What respectable young woman would want to marry a rakehell? Who also happened to have not a penny to his name?

"It only takes one," William said, flashing him a smile.

"So you intend to trick her, do you?"

William's smile dimmed. "You think you are so clever, but women adore me. I will have no issue with convincing one to marry me."

Harred was done with this ridiculous conversation. William had a better chance of having a dukedom conferred upon him by the Prince Regent than finding an heiress for a wife. Not unless he abducted her and eloped to Gretna Green. On that thought, he would need to keep a close eye on his brother for the time being. Just in case.

William performed an exaggerated bow with the plate in his hand. "If your lordship is all right with it, I would like to go eat my food in my bedchamber," he mocked.

"Just think on what I said," Harred admonished.

Without saying another word, William departed from the room with a huff.

Harred sat down at the head of the table. It was finally quiet. Just the way that he preferred it.

Lady Octavia Westlake was conflicted. Should she choose what she always went with, or should she be more adventurous? It was a tough decision, for sure.

Her brother's hushed voice came from next to her. "You are holding up the line. Just pick one and be done with it," Fredrick chided.

"That is easier said than done," she replied as she perused the flavors of ice. "What if I choose one that I do not like?"

"Then we can get you another."

Fredrick was so pragmatic but she didn't want to have to

wait in the long line of Gunter's again. She had waited long enough. It was time to make a decision.

"Lemon ice, please," Octavia ordered.

She could practically hear Fredrick roll his eyes at her choice. "You waited this long to order the same thing you always indulge in?" he asked.

"It is safe, and I know that I like it," she defended. "Did you decide on a flavor yet or did you use your time poorly to chastise me?"

With a grin, Fredrick addressed the worker. "The asparagus ice," he ordered.

As their treats were being prepared, they moved up the line to pay for them. It was a moment later when they both had a glass and spoon in their hands.

They stepped outside and walked towards their curricle. Fredrick assisted her onto the bench before he went around to the other side.

Octavia took a bite of her lemon ice and enjoyed the cold sensation in her mouth. It was just as delicious as it always was. She was an adventurous type of person but not when it came to Gunter's. She liked knowing precisely what she was going to get.

Fredrick shifted in his seat to face her. "Is it as good as you imagined it would be?" he teased.

"It is delicious, just as I *knew* it would be." She held her spoon up. "Can I try a bite of yours?"

He shifted the glass in his hand, angling it further away from hers. "This one is mine. I can't have you eating all of it."

"It is just one bite, Brother," she said as she tried to reach for the glass.

Fredrick relented with a sigh. "Fine, but one small bite."

Octavia dipped her spoon into his glass and took a generous portion of his treat. After she ate it, she smiled. "That is delicious."

"I do not think I have tried one flavor at Gunter's that I

haven't liked," Fredrick shared as he took a sampling of her ice. "It is only fair that I have some of yours."

She sat back against the bench and realized that she was happy. It was nice having Fredrick home after so many years of him being gone. He had been fighting in the war on the Continent and he returned home just at the right time to help save her from some bad men that were intent on killing her.

Fredrick gave her a curious look. "You are quiet. What are you up to?" He narrowed his eyes playfully.

"Nothing," she replied. "I was just thinking about how happy I am that you are home."

The humor left Fredrick's face as he said, "I had little choice in the matter. It was my duty to return home."

Octavia was confused by his response. Did he not wish to be home? She opened her mouth to ask him, but he spoke first.

"We should eat before our ices melt," Fredrick advised in a tone that in no way reflected the light tone he'd had in his voice only a few moments ago.

She wondered what had just happened. They were having such a lovely time, but now Fredrick seemed upset. Had she said something wrong?

As she ate her treat, a tall, dark-haired gentleman approached the curricle. He stopped next to it and addressed Fredrick. "Good afternoon, Lord Chatsworth," he greeted with a slight bow.

Fredrick looked displeased by the intrusion. "What do you want, Lord William?" he asked in a dismissive tone.

"Nothing but the pleasure of an introduction to your lovely sister," Lord William replied.

"I do not think that is a good idea," Fredrick said. "Run along."

So this was Lord William, Octavia thought. She had heard of Lord William's dishonorable reputation. In fact, everyone had. He was a rakehell of the highest order. No respectable young woman would be caught conversing with him alone. But no harm would come from an introduction.

Lord William didn't appear cowed by her brother's lukewarm response. "It is just an introduction, my lord," he pressed. "I have no intention of ruining your sister."

That was evidently the wrong thing to say to Fredrick. In a low growl, he said, "I do not want you to even speak to my sister. Do I make myself clear?"

"Shouldn't you let your sister decide that?" Lord William asked.

Octavia could see that her brother's conversation with Lord William was starting to draw some unwanted attention from the other patrons. The last thing she wanted to do was end up in the Society page, especially if her name was associated with Lord William.

Placing a hand on her brother's sleeve, she said, "Lord William is right. It is just an introduction."

Fredrick did not look pleased, but he did as she said. "Lord William, this is my sister, Lady Octavia," he stated in a rushed tone.

Lord William dropped into a low bow. "It is a pleasure to meet you, my lady," he said.

She acknowledged him with a tip of her head. "Will that be all, Lord William?" she asked. "I do agree with my brother and I think it is best if you move along."

To her surprise, Lord William took a step closer to the curricle. "Would it be acceptable if I called upon you later?"

Octavia could hear her brother take a deep breath and she saw him clench his fists. It would be best if she quelled his anger before he did something foolish. "I do not think that is a good idea," she said.

Lord William didn't look too disappointed- or surprised- by her response. He stepped back and smiled. "Enjoy your treat, my lady."

While Lord William walked away from the curricle,

Octavia could see that her brother was still upset. "It is all right. He is gone," she assured him.

"I do not want you to associate with that man," Fredrick ordered.

"I won't disagree with you. I find him to be a despicable man, especially since he took the late Lord Rushcliffe's wife as a mistress."

Her response seemed to appease Fredrick. "I have known Lord William for a long time and he is not honorable. It is a shame that he is related to Lord Kendal."

"I am not acquainted with Lord Kendal."

"Lord Kendal is Lord William's older brother and he is a fine man," Fredrick shared. "We studied at Oxford together."

Octavia looked down at her lemon ice and saw that it was mostly melted. "I blame Lord William for ruining this treat for me," she said, halfway joking.

"It is still edible," he encouraged. He brought the glass up to his lips and took a long sip.

Feigning disappointment, she remarked, "That is very uncouth of you, Brother."

"I have learned to make do ever since I was a soldier. Nothing can go to waste, especially an ice from Gunter's."

"Mother would be mortified at your actions," Octavia joked.

Fredrick winked at her. "Mother is not here, and you are not going to tell her. Are you?"

"No, but that does remind me. We need to purchase a bag of dry sweetmeats for Mother."

"I thought the doctor put her on a restrictive diet?" Fredrick questioned.

Octavia extended her glass to Fredrick. "He did, but Mother enjoys a treat on occasion," she shared.

"How often does she indulge in a treat?"

With a dismissive wave of her hand, Octavia replied, "It is

not important. She is dying and she deserves to eat whatever she wants."

Fredrick grew solemn. "I suppose you make a valid point."

She closed her eyes as she willed the tears away. Why had she brought up her mother on this outing? She couldn't cry here. Not in front of all these people. It would be mortifying and it could cause a scandal. Which is precisely what she wished to avoid.

Her brother reached for her hand and squeezed it. "We will get Mother all the dry sweetmeats that she could possibly eat."

Octavia opened her eyes and met her brother's comforting gaze. "Thank you, Fredrick. It is the one thing I can do for her. It makes me not feel so useless."

"I would be remiss if I did not tell you that Father would be furious if he found out what you are doing."

"Most likely, but I will take that risk."

A server approached the curricle to collect their glasses. "Would you care for anything else?" he asked.

Fredrick handed the glasses to the server and replied, "Yes, I would like a bag of your dry sweetmeats."

"Right away, my lord," the server said before he hurried off to fill the order.

Octavia smiled at her brother. "You are a good brother."

"Better than Roswell?"

A laugh escaped her lips at that unexpected remark. "You both are in contention for my favorite brother."

"I still cannot believe that Roswell is married and is on his wedding tour," Fredrick said. "He did good by marrying Anette."

"I just adore Anette. She is one of my dearest friends." Octavia cocked her head. "Do you intend to marry soon?"

Fredrick bristled. "Where is that question coming from?"

"I am just curious," she replied. "You are Father's heir and will one day take over as Marquess of Cuttyngham."

"That is not a day that I am looking forward to. I want Father to live a long, fruitful life."

"I am not sure how much longer he will survive after Mother is gone," Octavia said. "She is his whole world. I have never met two people that have loved each other so fiercely."

Fredrick looked off into the distance before saying, "It is a rare love, indeed. I just don't see myself ever settling down."

Octavia nudged his arm with her elbow. "I have many friends that I could introduce you to—"

He spoke over her. "No, thank you. If I do marry, it will be on my terms."

The way he said that caused her pause. What terms were those? But before she could ask him what he meant, the server approached with a small cloth bag.

"Here is your bag of dry sweetmeats," he said.

Fredrick removed a coin from his waistcoat pocket and handed it to the server. "Thank you," he responded as he accepted the bag.

Octavia held her hand out. "May I hold the bag?"

"Of course," Fredrick replied.

As she placed the cloth bag in her lap, she untied the string and removed a piece of dry sweetmeat. She then plopped one of the cherry treats into her mouth.

Fredrick chuckled. "I thought those were for Mother," he teased.

"I just had to make sure they weren't poisonous," Octavia replied as she savored the treat. "Luckily, they are not. Now I have no reservations about giving these to Mother."

Reaching for the reins, Fredrick said, "We better get home before you eat all of those and Mother is left with nothing."

"That is for the best," Octavia agreed.

Chapter Two

The fog hung low to the ground as Harred raced his horse in the woodlands of Hyde Park. It was dangerous to do so but he just wanted to feel something. He had spent his life doing precisely what was expected of him, but he wasn't sure what he was supposed to do now that his father was gone.

His father had been his constant supporter and he always knew he had someone to fall back on. But that was in the past. Now he had no one. He was all alone. His brother was useless and an utter drain on his finances.

He wondered if he would ever be able to live up to his father's legacy. Or would he fail? That mere deprecating thought of failure kept him going. He couldn't give up and lose everything his father had worked so hard to obtain.

His father had been a champion of the poor and fought for them in the House of Lords. Through his influence, he had been able to pass many bills that alleviated their suffering. Harred wanted to continue his father's work, but no one would throw their support behind him. He may be a peer but there was a hierarchy to these things. And he was at the bottom.

He wasn't happy right now, but he didn't know if that

would ever change. How could it? His entire life was mapped out. People's livelihoods depended on him and he was so afraid of disappointing everyone, including himself.

As he neared the edge of the woodlands, a rider jumped the hedge and startled his horse, causing it to rear up. He tumbled off the back of his horse and landed on the hard ground.

"This is what my life has become," he mumbled to himself as he laid on his back, staring up at the sky. Could anything go his way? Or was he destined to have bad luck?

The rider approached on her mare and he was able to make out a young woman with dark hair that was tucked under her riding hat.

"Are you all right, sir?" she asked, reining in her horse near him.

Harred wanted to unleash his sharp tongue and tell her what he was really thinking, but as he opened his mouth, his mind went blank. In front of him was a beautiful lady that had delicate features, a straight nose, and lips that were begging to be kissed. He thought he was the type of man to not be beguiled by a pretty face, but he realized he was wrong in thinking so. He was truly, and utterly, captivated.

Knowing that she was still waiting for a response, he replied, "I will live."

"Is anything broken?" she asked, concern etched on her features.

"I don't believe so." Harred sat up and saw that his horse was a short distance away. At least his stallion hadn't abandoned him.

The young woman gave him an apologetic look. "I am sorry about startling your horse. My brother and I race through here often and we have never seen another soul before. If I had known we weren't alone, I would have been more attentive."

There was something about how she said her words that

made him wonder if she meant what she said. "No harm done." He rose and dusted off his trousers. "I'm afraid I am more mortified than anything. I can't remember the last time I was upended off my horse."

"It was through no fault of your own," she said.

He appreciated what she was trying to do, but it was him that was covered in dirt. "You aren't riding by yourself, are you?" he found himself asking.

The young woman turned her head towards the direction she had come from. "No, my brother is coming but his horse isn't as fast as my mare. He left his horse on the Continent and he had to make do with one of the horses in our stables."

"I take it that your brother is a soldier."

"He was," she replied.

The sound of pounding hooves could be heard and it was only a moment later before a familiar rider approached. A smile came to his lips when he saw Lord Chatsworth rein in his horse.

Harred put his hand up in greeting. "Fredrick," he acknowledged. "I have heard rumors of you returning but I wasn't sure if there was any truth behind them."

Fredrick gave him a curious look as he asked, "Why are you covered in dirt? And why is your horse over there?"

He was about to explain but the young woman spoke first. "Rosie spooked his horse when we jumped the hedge and he was upended."

"You jumped the hedge... again?" Fredrick asked with a frown. "I believe I have explained that is far too dangerous for you."

"And yet, I do it every time and I am perfectly fine," she replied.

Fredrick turned his attention back towards Harred. "I'm sorry for my sister. She is usually much better behaved than this." He spoke his words with a serious expression but there was a lightheartedness to them.

"I think your sister is a delight," Harred said. The moment the words left his mouth, he wished he could take them back. What had he been thinking saying something like that? It was much too bold, especially for someone he hadn't even been introduced to.

The young woman gave her brother a smug smile. "Did you hear that?" she asked. "He said I was a delight."

"I wouldn't think too much of it because he clearly hit his head," Fredrick joked before he went to address Harred. "Would you like me to go collect your horse?"

"That won't be necessary. I can see to my own horse," Harred said.

The young woman adjusted the reins in her hands as she remarked, "I do believe an introduction is in order, don't you agree, Brother?"

Fredrick nodded in agreement. "Lord Kendal, allow me the privilege of introducing you to my sister, Lady Octavia."

Harred bowed. "Enchanted, my lady. I'm afraid our introduction is far overdue," he said. "For every time I visited your country estate, you were away at boarding school."

"Well, I do wish I was meeting you under better circumstances, but here we are." Lady Octavia's horse whinnied. "I do believe Rosie wishes for an introduction, too."

Fredrick shook his head. "Rosie is a terrible name for a horse."

"It is a perfectly acceptable name for a horse," Lady Octavia contended.

"My sister is terrible at naming her animals," Fredrick explained. "She named her pet peacock after me and her horse after Roswell. For some reason, she could find no other suitable names for them."

Harred furrowed his brow. "You have a pet peacock?"

"Yes, it was a rather unfortunate purchase," Lady Octavia replied. "I thought Freddy would be somewhat attentive to me, but I'm afraid he hates me. He chases me whenever he has the chance and has a horrible temperament." A smirk came to her lips. "Much like my brother's temperament."

Fredrick looked heavenward. "Why did I agree to go riding with you again?" he asked.

"Because you love me, and you knew I would go mad if I didn't get out of our townhouse," Lady Octavia said.

"One would think you would be nicer to me then," Fredrick remarked.

Lady Octavia laughed. "Why start now?" she asked.

Harred couldn't help but smile at their interaction. It was evident that Lady Octavia and Fredrick loved each other very much. He felt a twinge of envy knowing that he and William had never been close. They had been at odds for as long as he could remember.

Fredrick glanced up at the sun. "We should continue our ride if we want to return home before breakfast."

Lady Octavia perked up. "I think that is a fine idea. I could use a cup of chocolate."

"That is not surprising in the least, considering you can always indulge in a cup of chocolate," Fredrick said.

"It is much better than the coffee that Father drinks," Lady Octavia declared. "I do not care for coffee."

Fredrick met Harred's gaze. "Are you sure I can't retrieve your horse for you?" he asked. "It would be no bother."

Harred gave his friend a grateful smile. "Thank you, but a walk will do me some good. Fortunately, my horse didn't go too far."

"Will I be seeing you at Lady Henwick's ball this evening?" Fredrick asked.

"I doubt it. I would prefer to gouge my eyes out than attend a ball with scheming matchmaking mothers," Harred admitted.

Fredrick chuckled. "I feel the same, but Octavia convinced me to escort her this evening. Apparently, she is bored."

Lady Octavia bobbed her head. "I am. Do you know how

many reticules that I have knitted these past few months? Far too many for any one person to ever own."

Harred had meant his words earlier. He found Lady Octavia to be a delight. She wasn't afraid to speak her mind and he found that trait admirable. Perhaps he could go this evening, assuming he could dance with Octavia.

"If I did go this evening, would you save me a dance?" Harred inquired.

Lady Octavia winced slightly. "I may go to a ball, but I don't actually dance. I just like to watch people and make up stories about them in my head."

Fredrick interjected, "I think it is a splendid idea if you dance with Lord Kendal. I promise that he won't trip you."

"I am more concerned about tripping *him*," Lady Octavia shared. "The dance master once told me that I have two left feet, and under no circumstances, to ever dance in public."

"Surely you can't be that bad?" Harred asked.

"I assure you that I am."

Harred wasn't ready to concede. He wanted to dance with Lady Octavia and he wouldn't take no for an answer. "I daresay that you haven't found the right dancing partner. Besides, I do believe you owe me the privilege since you caused me to fall off my horse."

Lady Octavia looked thoughtful. "I suppose you make a good argument," she acknowledged. "Fine. I will dance one set with you, but it can't be the waltz. My friend says that is the 'dance of love'."

"No one calls it that but Anette," Fredrick remarked.

"But I don't think she is wrong. She danced the waltz with Roswell and now they are married. Coincidence? I think not," Lady Octavia stated.

Fredrick feigned exasperation. "Your logic is faulty, dear sister. I have danced the waltz with young women before and I did not marry them."

"Maybe you danced the waltz wrong?" Lady Octavia asked.

"How can you dance it wrong?" Fredrick pressed.

Lady Octavia shrugged her shoulders. "How would I know?" she asked. "I have never danced it with a gentleman before."

"And with that, we should go," Fredrick said. "I do think we have taken enough of Lord Kendal's time. I am sure he has more important things to do than listening to us bicker."

"We aren't bickering; we are debating. There is a difference." Lady Octavia shifted her gaze towards Harred. "Did we bore you, my lord?"

"Heavens, no. I can't remember the last time I enjoyed such a lively conversation," Harred admitted. And it was the truth. It was far more interesting than sitting in his study as he worked on the accounts.

Lady Octavia smiled, and he couldn't quite seem to look away. "I shall save you a dance this evening."

Harred bowed. "I am looking forward to it."

"Good day, Harred," Fredrick said.

As they rode off, Harred started walking towards his horse. He hadn't been to a ball in quite some time, but for Lady Octavia, he would go and dance. And, for the first time in a long time, he had something to look forward to.

Dressed in a blue ballgown with a square neckline, Octavia knocked on her mother's bedchamber door.

The door was promptly opened and her mother's lady's maid greeted her. "Good evening, my lady," Nancy said, opening the door wide. "Your mother is just having dinner and would no doubt enjoy your company."

Octavia stepped into the room and saw her mother's eyes

light up, which was in stark contrast to her pale skin. "Octavia, what a pleasant surprise."

With a glance at the uneaten food on the tray, Octavia asked, "Are you not hungry?"

Her mother made a face. "Not for whatever that is," she replied. "The meat is dry and the sides are even drier. I do not even think it is edible."

"I'm sorry. I do have something that I think you might like." Octavia walked closer to the bed and extended a small cloth bag. "I picked it up when I went to Gunter's with Fredrick this afternoon."

A smile came to her mother's face as she accepted the bag. "Thank heavens for you, Child," she declared. "How I adore dry sweetmeats."

Octavia watched as her mother retrieved a treat and plopped it into her mouth. She had no doubt that her father would chide her for her actions, but she did not care. Her mother was dying and she deserved to eat whatever she so desired. If it brought her one ounce of joy, it was worth it.

After her mother savored the treat, she said, "You are looking rather nice this evening. I must assume you are attending a social event."

"Yes, I am going to a ball with Fredrick."

Her mother blinked. "Is Fredrick back from the war?" she asked.

Octavia nodded. "He is, Mother. He came home over a week ago." She had lost count how many times she had explained this to her mother, but it didn't bother her. She would do it as many times as it took.

"Did we win the war?"

"I'm afraid the war still rages on," Octavia said. "But Fredrick came home for Roswell's wedding and to see you, of course."

A frown came to her mother's lips. "Roswell is married? I feel like that is something I should have known."

"He married Anette. You remember her, don't you?"

"I do. She is such a pleasant young woman," her mother replied. "I always liked her."

Octavia pulled a chair closer to the bed and sat down. "How are you feeling?"

"I am tired," she shared. "And my mind isn't as sharp as it once was, but I am trying my best."

"We know, Mother, and you don't need to explain yourself. We love you, just the way you are," Octavia said.

Her mother's face softened. "I love you, Child. I want you to know that. No matter what happens, never doubt that you have been one of my greatest treasures."

Reaching for her mother's hand, Octavia responded, "I love you, too, and nothing will ever change that."

"I want you to promise me that you will enjoy yourself this Season," her mother said. "Promise me."

Octavia pressed her lips together. Could she promise such a thing when her mother was lying in bed, dying? The thought just seemed inconceivable to her.

Her mother tightened her hold on her hand and waited until she met her gaze. "I know that look. Stop worrying about me and focus on yourself."

A knock sounded at the door and Nancy crossed the room to answer it. As she opened it wide, Fredrick stepped inside.

Her mother gasped. "Fredrick! You have returned."

He offered their mother a kind smile. "Yes, Mother. I have returned home from the war to see you."

With a wave of her hand, their mother said, "Come closer so that I may have a look at you. It has been far too long."

Fredrick approached the bed. "How are you faring?"

"You don't need to fuss over me," their mother replied. "Since you are home, does this mean the war is over?"

He shook his head. "No, I'm afraid not. But I received permission from Wellington to come home."

"That was kind of him," their mother acknowledged. "Did you hear that Roswell got married to Anette?"

"Yes, I attended their wedding. It was quite lovely," Fredrick replied.

Octavia knew their mother was trying her best and she appreciated her more for it. She wished that there was a way that she could help her.

Their mother perused the length of Fredrick. "You are looking sharp this evening," she said. "You must ensure that Octavia dances with only the finest gentlemen there. No rakes or fortune hunters; you must promise me."

Fredrick tipped his head. "I promise. You need not concern yourself with that. No one that isn't worthy of Octavia will come near her."

His response seemed to satisfy their mother. "Thank you. Now off with you two," she encouraged. "I am going to close my eyes for a spell."

Rising, Octavia said, "Goodnight. I shall visit you tomorrow after my morning ride."

"I shall be looking forward to it," their mother responded before she closed her eyes.

Fredrick took a step back and gestured towards the door, indicating Octavia should go first. "The coach has been brought around front," he informed her.

As Octavia walked towards the door, her eyes remained on her mother. She looked so pale and weak in the expanse of the feather mattress. She knew it was only a matter of time before she visited this bedchamber and her mother would no longer be here.

She stepped out into the corridor and let out the breath that she hadn't even realized that she had been holding.

Fredrick looked at her with concern. "Are you all right?"

"No... yes... I don't know what I am," she admitted. "I just hate seeing Mother in such a state. I just wish there was a way to help her."

"I'm afraid not. The doctor told us that her mind will keep slipping until she dies."

"That is not very comforting," she muttered.

"I am sorry that I haven't been here to help you with Mother," Fredrick said. "I can only imagine how hard it has been for you."

Octavia glanced at her mother's bedchamber door before saying, "Frankly, it has been awful. I struggle every day to maintain some type of composure, but I feel as if I am failing terribly. What is worse is that Father hardly even notices me anymore because he is so focused on Mother. What will happen to him once Mother has passed?"

"I don't rightly know," her brother admitted.

"I wouldn't have made it this far if it wasn't for Roswell. He has helped me tremendously, but I know he is dealing with his own struggles," Octavia said. "I just wish you would lie to me and tell me that everything will work out."

Her brother offered his arm and started leading her down the corridor. "Do you truly wish for me to lie to you?"

"No, that wouldn't help. Although, you should know that Roswell was much better at comforting me," Octavia remarked, feeling the need to lighten the mood. "Sometimes, he even brought a biscuit with him to deliver bad news."

"I did treat you to Gunter's earlier today. Was that not sufficient?" he asked as they descended the stairs.

"I suppose it was."

Fredrick's lips twitched. "Why do I have to work so hard to win your favor?"

"If you want to be my favorite brother, you must go above and beyond," Octavia explained with a wave of her hand.

Fredrick chuckled. "I daresay you have an impossible standard, dear sister." He tipped his head at the butler as they passed through the open door. "I can only imagine what obstacles you will make a suitor go through to court you."

Once Octavia was situated in the coach, she smoothed

down her skirt. "There will be no hoops because I am not sure if I will ever marry," she confessed.

"If you don't marry, what shall you do?" Fredrick asked as he went to sit across from her. "Not that I am questioning your choice. I do not fault you for avoiding the marriage mart."

Octavia was surprised by Fredrick's reaction. She had halfway expected him to criticize her choice, not support it.

Fredrick continued. "Marriage is not something you do on a whim. If you do get married, I want you to secure a love match. That is no less than you deserve."

"Roswell said something similar," Octavia said.

"Good, because we are your family and we will support you in whatever you decide. But rest assured, no matter what happens, you will always be taken care of."

Octavia smiled, touched by her brother's words. "Thank you, Brother."

"I would strongly encourage you not to write a book because I am fearful of what your mind would unleash on this world." He shuddered.

With a laugh, Octavia said, "I have no desire to write a book, but I wouldn't mind doing spy stuff with you."

"What is this 'spy stuff' you are talking about?" Fredrick questioned. "I only ask because I stopped working as a spy once I returned home from the war."

"Do you miss being a spy?"

Fredrick turned his attention towards the window. "I do not miss the war, but I miss the comrades that I made there. I worry about them every day, and I wonder if I made the right choice by returning home."

Octavia could hear the pain in his voice and her heart lurched for him. "For what it is worth, I am glad that you are home."

"My duty to this family comes first," Fredrick stated. The way he said his words made it seem as if he had to convince himself of that.

A silence descended over them as Fredrick retreated to his thoughts. Octavia thought it was best to not press him. He hardly spoke about the war, and when he did, he never went into detail. She wondered what he had seen over there to affect him in such a way.

The coach came to a stop in front of a three-level, white-washed townhouse. It was only a moment before the footman opened the door and assisted her out.

Once she was on the pavement, she took the opportunity to adjust the top of her white gloves. The townhouse was lit up with light coming from nearly every window and a steady line of guests made their way to the main door.

Fredrick came to stand next to her. "It is not too late to depart and pretend this night never happened," he said, a teasing lilt to his voice.

"A ball will do you some good."

"I doubt it," Fredrick responded. "I am an unattached lord. Do you know how terrifying that is for me?"

She patted his sleeve. "Poor lord. What a burden you must bear."

Fredrick sighed. "Let's get this over with," he muttered.

"I could use some more enthusiasm from you," Octavia joked. "I don't want you to appear as if you are going to the guillotine."

"That is asking a lot from me," he replied as she accepted his offered arm and they stepped into the line. It wasn't long before they arrived in the crowded ballroom.

Her eyes wandered around the rectangular hall, and she took in the grandeur of her surroundings. A large golden chandelier was suspended in the center of the hall and it cast a warm glow over the chalked dance floor. The red-papered walls seemed to glow next to the lighted sconces that lined them, and her eyes were drawn to the intricate mural that adorned the ceiling.

Fredrick led her towards the rear of the ballroom and

positioned them near a column. "There are far too many people in here, making it deucedly uncomfortable," he remarked.

"Would you care to step outside?"

"Perhaps in the future, but I can make do for now," he replied. "Do you know if any of your friends are in attendance?"

Octavia went on her tiptoes and her eyes scanned over the room as she looked for anyone that looked familiar. But she saw no one. "I don't see anyone," she admitted.

"Then it is just you and me this evening."

"That isn't the worst thing," Octavia said. "I have been told that I am a delight. Do you not remember?"

Fredrick cast his gaze heavenward. "Yes, I remember a conversation that happened earlier today, and I contend that Lord Kendal was just being polite."

"It doesn't matter why he said it, but he did say it," Octavia said.

The half-orchestra started warming up in the corner and she started to feel the familiar feeling of guilt at enjoying herself. Her mother wanted this for her, but is this what she wanted for herself? To pretend that all was well when everything was falling apart in her life?

Fredrick nudged her shoulder and advised, "Stop worrying and enjoy yourself."

"How did you know I was thinking just that?"

A smug smile came to his lips. "Don't underestimate me," he said. "Now, who will be your first victim... er... I mean dance partner?"

Octavia could feel herself relax. With her brother by her side, she could handle whatever came her way.

Chapter Three

As Harred sat across from William in the coach, he could feel himself growing more irritated by the moment. There was fashionably late, and then there was late. And they were late. His brother had made sure of that by not adhering to their agreed-upon schedule.

And why was William making a weird clucking sound with his tongue? It was starting to grate on his nerves.

"Will you stop that?" Harred demanded.

William's brow creased in puzzlement. "Stop what?"

"Whatever noise you are making with your tongue," Harred replied. "It is irritating and you have been doing it since we left the townhouse."

"I hadn't realized." William crossed his arms over his chest. "I see that you are in a rather cantankerous mood."

"It would appear so." Harred had no wish to discuss his temperament with his brother. It was because of William's actions that he was so bothered.

William sighed. "I know that you are angry that I was late, but I had little choice in the matter."

"What, pray tell, was so important?"

"It wasn't a what, but a 'who,'" William replied with a

smug smile on his lips. "And she beguiled me. I had no choice but to remain where I was."

Harred turned his attention towards the window. He should have assumed his brother had inconvenienced him because of a woman.

"You are wound up too tight, Brother," William remarked. "There is nothing wrong with spending some time with women."

"I have much more important matters at hand, such as keeping our estate afloat," Harred stated. "Speaking of which, have you had a chance to consider what we discussed?"

William bobbed his head. "I have, and I do believe the best course of action for me is to find an heiress. I have no interest in taking a job from you," he said. "Furthermore, I have already decided on whom I will take as a wife."

"Who is the unlucky lady?"

His brother's lips twisted into an obnoxious grin. "The lovely Lady Octavia Westlake," he revealed.

An image of Lady Octavia came into Harred's mind and he felt a fierce protectiveness wash over him. He wasn't entirely sure why that was since he hardly knew her. But there was something about her that made him want to keep her safe. Or it could have to do with being loyal to Fredrick and Roswell. Either way, if he had his way, his brother would go nowhere near Lady Octavia.

"Pick another lady," Harred grumbled.

William gave him a baffled look. "I beg your pardon?"

"I do not want you to pursue Lady Octavia," Harred replied. He knew he needed to come up with a reason other than it was a terrible idea. It only took him a moment to think of one. "She is the sister of two of my friends and I do not think they will take kindly to you coming around."

"I can handle brothers," William said haughtily.

"Not these two. They are protective of their sister and they will know of your real intent in pursuing her."

William uncrossed his arms and leaned back. "Regardless, she is by far the prettiest of all the debutantes this Season and she is the richest, making her the obvious choice."

Harred couldn't quite believe the audacity of his brother. William had no business in pursuing anyone, much less Lady Octavia, when his actions were so dishonorable.

"If you truly want a wife, you should stop your association with other women and at least attempt to be faithful," Harred advised. "That would be the honorable thing to do."

William looked at him as if he hadn't even considered this possibility. "Why would I do such a thing? I am not you," he said.

"Perhaps you should at least try not to be so despicable?"

It was evident that Harred's words fell on deaf ears by William's next comment. "Now, I just have to get Lady Octavia alone to press my suit," he mused. "Will you help me with that?"

Harred stiffened. Why would his brother think he would go along with this madcap plan? He would never stoop so low as to help his brother trick a woman into marriage.

"I will do no such thing," he declared. "Lady Octavia is an innocent and she deserves more than a loveless marriage to you."

William's disappointment showed on his face. "I said nothing about 'loveless.' I could grow to love her, assuming she won't take issue with me having a discretion or two."

"You are an idiot."

"I know why you aren't helping me," William started. "You don't want me to be richer than you. You want me to fail."

"That is ludicrous and not the least bit true." Why did his brother always make it about himself? It was vexing to say the least.

William scoffed. "It is true. You have always been jealous of me."

Harred's eyebrows shot up. "Jealous of you?" he repeated. "What am I jealous of, Brother? Your drunken behavior, your disreputable intentions with women or how you spend more time at a gambling hall than your own home?"

"I am free to live my life as I see fit and you are trapped."

With a shake of his head, Harred said, "I am not trapped."

"You are and you don't even see it," William remarked. "You spend all your time reviewing your accounts and you make time for little else."

Harred stared at his brother in disbelief. How did he think their accounts were paid? It was because he worked hard to ensure their estate had success. He didn't have time to shirk his responsibilities like his brother did.

In an incredulous tone, Harred asked, "Good gads, are you daft? If I didn't work constantly, how do you think we would survive? Regardless, it is far better than what you do, which is nothing."

William narrowed his eyes as the coach came to a stop in front of Lady Henwick's townhouse. He opened his mouth to no doubt say something intolerably stupid but closed it when a footman held the door open.

"We will continue this conversation later," William grumbled.

"I can hardly wait," Harred muttered.

In a swift motion, William departed from the coach and cut the line of guests that were waiting to go inside.

Harred couldn't quite believe the audacity of his brother. The rules of polite Society never seemed to apply to William. He was entirely too entitled for his own good.

As he waited his turn to enter the townhouse, he remembered why he detested social events so much. People. There were far too many people here for his liking. He could only imagine how crowded the ballroom was.

But he was here for one purpose- to dance with Lady

Octavia. He looked forward to the short time that he would be able to spend with her and to hold her in his arms.

It wasn't long before he stepped into the ballroom and groaned at the large crowd that was assembled. The dancing had already commenced but he didn't see Lady Octavia on the dance floor.

He wondered where she was. His eyes roamed over the large, rectangular hall until they landed on the object of his desire. Octavia's dark hair was piled high atop her head and two long curls framed her face. She was wearing an alluring blue gown and a strand of pearls hung low around her neck.

She smiled at something Fredrick said to her and her whole face lit up. Or maybe it was Harred's. All he knew for certain was that his soul had awoken with that smile.

What nonsense was he spouting, he thought. It was just a smile. A smile from a beautiful young woman. So why was he hoping he might be the cause of one of those smiles?

A movement in the crowd caught his attention and he saw his brother approaching Lady Octavia, albeit slowly. William was stopping long enough to smile at each young woman along the path. He was nothing if not predictable.

Harred decided it would be best if he got to Lady Octavia first. He brushed past people as he headed towards the rear of the ballroom.

It wasn't long before he broke through the crowd in front of Lady Octavia and Fredrick.

He bowed. "My lady," he greeted. "Fredrick."

Lady Octavia smiled, but it wasn't as genuine as the one he had seen previously. "Lord Kendal, it is a pleasure to see you again."

"It is about time you showed up," Fredrick said. "I was wondering if you had decided not to come this evening."

"I do apologize, but I made the poor choice of waiting for my brother to ride with me," Harred explained. "He was detained, I'm afraid."

Fredrick did not look impressed by his admission. "That doesn't surprise me in the least. I do hope he will behave this evening."

"One can always hope." Harred turned his attention to Lady Octavia, knowing that time was of the essence. William was approaching and he would no doubt ask Lady Octavia to dance. But Harred needed to thwart his brother's advances. "May I have the privilege of dancing with you for the next set?"

Lady Octavia exchanged a glance with her brother before saying, "I would be delighted." Her words didn't seem very convincing, but he still took it as a victory that she agreed to it.

No sooner had her words left her mouth than William came to stand next to him. He bowed. "Lord Chatsworth. Lady Octavia," he greeted.

Fredrick's jaw clenched. "Lord William. What are you doing here?" he asked in a tight voice. "I do believe I made my thoughts abundantly clear that you were to stay away from my sister."

Not appearing disturbed by Fredrick's less than welcoming reception, William replied, "You did, but I came in hopes that Lady Octavia will dance the next set with me."

"Absolutely not," Fredrick said as he moved to stand in front of his sister. "Run along to whatever sewer from whence you crawled out of."

If Harred wasn't mistaken, William almost looked amused by Fredrick's disparaging remark. "I do believe the lady can speak for herself."

"She can, but there is no need," Fredrick asserted. "My sister is too good for the likes of you, and I will do everything in my power to ensure you stay far away from her."

Harred couldn't help but notice that their conversation was beginning to attract some unwanted attention from other patrons, who were clearly eavesdropping. It seemed prudent for him to step in and advise William to leave before Fredrick challenged him to a duel.

Just as he was about to intercede, Lady Octavia stepped out from behind her brother and addressed William. "I'm sorry, but the next dance is spoken for by Lord Kendal," she said.

William shot Harred an annoyed look. "I hadn't realized you were acquainted with Lady Octavia."

"We just met earlier today in Hyde Park," Harred shared.

"How nice," William muttered. "Perhaps the lady will grant me the privilege of dancing with her on a later set?"

Harred wasn't quite sure how Lady Octavia would respond. Fredrick had already voiced his opinion on the matter, giving her an out. But would Lady Octavia defy her brother and accept his request?

In an apologetic tone, Lady Octavia said, "I'm afraid Fredrick and I are departing after I dance the next set with Lord Kendal."

William bowed, his expression giving nothing away. "Then I wish you safe travels," he stated before he spun on his heel.

Fredrick eyed William suspiciously as he walked away. It was evident that he was not pleased that William was paying attention to his sister. Not that he blamed him. William was a known rakehell and spent his time cavorting from one woman to the next.

The next set was announced and it was to be the quadrille. Harred extended his hand towards Lady Octavia. "Shall we, my lady?" he encouraged.

She placed her gloved hand into his. "I hope you will not regret this," she said lightly but there was a seriousness to it.

"Trust me. I won't let you fall," Harred said.

"I believe you."

And with those three simple words, he was charmed.

Octavia kept her head held high as Lord Kendal escorted her to the dance floor. She couldn't help but notice the people watching them and she wondered if she had done something wrong. Why were they garnering so much attention?

Lord Kendal leaned closer to her and said in a hushed voice, "I'm afraid I must apologize. I do believe that I am causing a stir since I hardly attend these social events."

"May I ask why you came this evening then?"

He grinned. "I came only to collect my dance with you," he replied.

Octavia felt a blush warm her cheeks. Why did she have such a reaction to Lord Kendal's words, she wondered. She had been flattered by handsome men before- and Lord Kendal was definitely handsome- but there was something different about him. His words seemed genuine, as if she could trust his intentions.

With his full, dark brown hair, and straight, chiseled jawline, Lord Kendal's mere presence commanded attention. But it was his piercing green eyes that fascinated her. They held pain, and a part of her wanted to tell him that he was safe with her. Which was just foolishness. She hardly knew him.

Lord Kendal gestured towards the dance floor. "It would appear that someone is trying to get your attention."

Octavia followed his gaze and saw Lady Brentwood waving at her. She dropped Lord Kendal's arm and rushed over to her friend.

"Rosamond," she greeted as she embraced her friend. "What a pleasant surprise. I hadn't expected to see you this evening."

Rosamond dropped her arms and stepped back. "Malcolm was insistent that we come this evening."

Lord Brentwood cleared his throat and stepped closer to his wife. "That is not even remotely true."

Rosamond's smile grew mischievous. "All right, I will admit it. I may have strongly encouraged him to come to the ball, but he is grateful for my insistence."

Octavia remembered her manners and turned towards Lord Kendal. "Are you acquainted with Lord and Lady Brentwood?" she asked him.

"I am acquainted with Lord Brentwood, but not with his lovely wife," Lord Kendal said as he performed a slight bow.

Lord Brentwood took his wife's hand and remarked, "I daresay that we are holding up the dancing. We should get into position."

As Octavia lined up with Lord Kendal, she felt a sense of relief that she was dancing with friends. It wasn't as if she wanted to be a bad dancer but she just lacked the coordination that made it look effortless. But she could do anything for one set. She just needed to focus on the steps and remember to enjoy herself.

Fortunately, Lord Kendal had been true to his word. He was a proficient dancer and he didn't let her fall. It wasn't long before she started to relax as she executed the repetitive steps and she even found herself smiling a time or two.

The dance came to an end and she felt some disappointment that it was over. It had been far too long since she had so much fun dancing a set.

Lord Kendal offered his arm as he asked, "Dare I hope that you enjoyed yourself, my lady?"

"I did," she replied. "It wasn't as awful as I thought it would be."

He gave her an amused look. "That is quite the endorsement," he teased.

Rosamond approached her and said, "I hope you enjoy the rest of your evening. If you have no objections, I shall call upon you soon."

"I always welcome a visit from you," Octavia responded. "Perhaps we can even go riding through Hyde Park."

"That sounds wonderful, assuming you do not take issue with my horse," Rosamond said.

"What is wrong with your horse?" Octavia asked.

Lord Brentwood interjected, "It is a very ugly horse."

Octavia blinked. What did she say to such a remark? Surely the horse couldn't be that ugly.

Rosamond exchanged a loving look with her husband before saying, "Malcolm isn't wrong. Bella is rather ugly, but I will never part with her."

"Nor should you," Lord Brentwood said.

Octavia found herself to be most curious about Rosamond's horse. She didn't think she had ever seen an ugly horse. Their stables were stocked with the finest horses that money could buy. She was a little surprised that Rosamond would have acquired a horse that would garner such unwanted attention, but she wouldn't question her about it. It was her choice and she would respect that.

Lord Brentwood's voice broke through the silence. "It was enjoyable to dance with you, Lady Octavia, but we intend to depart." He shifted his gaze to Lord Kendal. "Harred."

Lord Kendal responded in kind. "I will be seeing you in the House of Lords."

"Yes, you will," Lord Brentwood replied before he led his wife away and disappeared into the crowd.

Lord Kendal extended his arm towards Octavia. "If we don't exit the dance floor soon, we might have to dance another set," he remarked. "May I escort you back to your brother?"

"Yes, please." Octavia accepted his arm.

Once they started making their way towards the rear of the ballroom, Lord Kendal said, "I am sorry about my brother."

"There is no need for you to apologize."

"I'm afraid it is a habit when it comes to him," he acknowledged. "My brother is a rakehell and he has set his cap on you. I tried to discourage him but he is adamant."

"Well, he shall be sorely disappointed. I have no intention of taking him on as a suitor. Quite frankly, my brother would never allow it either."

"You should know that William is not one to take no for an answer. He is stubborn and entirely too full of himself. Your rejection will only seem to encourage him, I'm afraid."

Octavia appreciated Lord Kendal's honesty, but she could handle herself with a pesky gentleman. Once Lord William saw that she was not interested and she had no intention of changing her mind, he would move on.

With a grateful look, she said, "You are kind to be concerned about me, but I will be able to thwart Lord William's attentions rather easily."

Lord Kendal didn't look convinced. "If he becomes too bothersome, please let me know at once and I will speak to him again."

"I do not think Fredrick will let Lord William become bothersome," Octavia said. "He is fiercely protective of me and he does not care for your brother." She winced. "I meant no offense, my lord."

"None taken. I am fully aware of William's shortcomings and reputation," he responded. "I strongly urge you to never find yourself alone with William. I do not trust him, and I worry that he has no qualms with putting you in a compromising position, forcing you to marry him."

"I would never marry your brother," Octavia asserted.

"Good, because he would make a terrible husband."

Octavia found that she rather enjoyed conversing with Lord Kendal. Their conversation wasn't forced and she didn't have to stick to polite conversational topics. How she grew tired when she talked about the weather. No one truly cared to discuss the weather. Frankly, it wasn't that interesting. They lived in England. It rained all the time.

Lord Kendal led her to her brother and dropped his arm. "Thank you for the dance," he said. "I greatly enjoyed myself."

"As did I," she confessed.

Fredrick spoke up. "Did I see you smiling on the dance floor?" he asked, eyeing her closely. "It was so surprising that I feared I imagined it."

A laugh escaped her lips. "I did smile on an occasion or two," she admitted.

"Well, miracles never do cease," Fredrick joked.

With a slight bow, Lord Kendal said, "I do not wish to take up too much of your time, my lady. I hope you have an enjoyable evening."

Octavia dropped into a curtsy. "Likewise, my lord."

While Lord Kendal walked away, Octavia had to admit that she had enjoyed spending time with him. There was a familiarity about him that she couldn't quite explain. It was strange but she found herself being open and honest with him. Something she had never done before with a man she hardly knew.

Fredrick's voice drew back her attention. "Lord Kendal is a fine gentleman."

"He does appear so," Octavia said.

"It is a shame he is related to Lord William," Fredrick remarked. "It is surprising that he hasn't died in a duel yet."

"Perhaps people have finally acknowledged that duels are barbaric, and, more importantly, illegal."

A look of seriousness came into Fredrick's eyes as he advised, "Just be wary of Lord William. He is a man that is not to be trusted."

"You do not need to tell me that. My spy senses already confirmed that to me," Octavia said.

The corner of Fredrick's mouth quirked up. "Your 'spy senses'?"

"I may not technically be a spy…"

"For obvious reasons."

"…but I do believe I have the instincts of a spy."

He laughed, just as she had intended. "I would be remiss if I did not tell you that the first rule of being a spy is that you don't talk about being a spy. Ever."

Octavia shrugged one shoulder. "I would have already learned that lesson if I had been entrusted with being a spy. Unfortunately, your friend, Kendrick, won't give me an assignment."

"Kendrick is not my friend, and he won't give you an assignment since you are not employed by the agency."

"Perhaps I should be a spy for hire."

Fredrick let out an amused-sounding huff. "Dare I ask what is a 'spy for hire'?"

"I do not think I could explain it any more clearly."

"This conversation is going in circles. It would be best if we departed since you informed Lord William we were doing so after your dance with Lord Kendal."

"It was the only way to get out of dancing with him without feeling guilty for refusing him," she admitted.

Fredrick placed a hand on her shoulder. "I'm sorry he put you in such an awkward position, but you handled it with grace. Mother would have been proud of you."

"That is high praise coming from you," Octavia joked.

Removing his hand, her brother said, "Forgive me. I may have drunk one too many glasses of champagne while I waited for you and it is making me too complimentary. I will have to work on that. I do not wish to inflate your ego more than it already is."

Octavia's eyes left his and roamed over the room. "I think it is a grand idea if we left now. I can't wait to take off these uncomfortable shoes and replace them with my slippers."

"Poor thing," Fredrick said. "After you put your slippers on, we could play a game of chess."

"What is the point?" she asked. "I always beat you."

"That is not the least bit true. I am two games ahead."

"For now. But before that, I was on a winning streak and I was five games ahead," Octavia pointed out. "To be honest, I was rather embarrassed for you."

Fredrick shook his head. "That is in the past, and you must focus on the future," he said as he led her towards the front of the ballroom.

"That is rather convenient of you to say now that you are winning."

It wasn't long before they stepped out of the townhouse and started down the line of coaches. Once they arrived at their crested coach, a footman stepped off his perch and opened the door.

Fredrick pointed further up the line of coaches. "It would appear that Lord Kendal is not staying for the rest of the ball either."

She followed her brother's gaze and watched Lord Kendal step into his coach. He had mentioned he had only come to collect the dance with her, and it seemed that he had spoken true.

"Octavia," her brother said as he held his hand out.

Embarrassed that she had been caught staring at Lord Kendal, Octavia ducked her head and accepted Fredrick's hand into the coach. Lord Kendal was an intriguing man, that much was true, but she had no interest in taking suitors this Season.

Chapter Four

As the morning sun streamed through the windows, Harred sat at his desk in his study as he reviewed the accounts. It felt like a never-ending task but it had to be done. If not, livelihoods were at stake. It was a great responsibility that had fallen upon his shoulders, and he hoped he was up to the task.

He couldn't fail. So why did the doubt always creep in? It had become a constant companion as of late, and he would do anything to banish these unwelcome thoughts.

The door flew open and his brother stormed into the room with an irate look on his face. "Why do you insist on ruining my chances with Lady Octavia?"

Harred calmly placed the paper down onto the desk and met his brother's gaze. "I hate to be the bearer of bad news but you have no chance with Lady Octavia; you never did. I tried to tell you as much but you refused to listen."

"You are just jealous of me," his brother shouted.

"Not this again," he muttered. "What, pray tell, do I have to be jealous about?"

William came to stand in front of the desk and glared down at him. "If I marry Lady Octavia, then I will be richer than you. You might even have to come to me for money."

Harred huffed. What a ludicrous thought. He couldn't believe his brother could even say that comment with a straight face, considering how he squandered his money. "I assure you that will never happen."

"Regardless, you will not stand in my way. I will have Lady Octavia as a wife and you can continue on with your pitiful life."

Leaning back in his seat, Harred asked, "Does Lady Octavia have a say in this? I only ask because her brother, Lord Chatsworth, is adamant that she goes nowhere near you."

William's eyes narrowed with suspicion. "What did you say to him?"

"I said nothing that he didn't already know," Harred said. "Your reputation precedes you, especially when it comes to the ladies. No respectable young woman wants to associate with you. Surely you know that."

"If you were a good brother, you would have defended me," William asserted. "You are no better than the gossips that love to wag their tongues."

Harred glanced down at the large stack of papers on his desk before asking, "Is there something that you wanted or are you just here to argue?"

William sat down on the chair that faced the desk. "I need to woo Lady Octavia. You are acquainted with her. What should I do?"

Surely his brother didn't think he would help him. "I only just became acquainted with Lady Octavia. Besides, I will not help you trick her into taking you as a suitor."

"I saw the way that Lady Octavia smiled around you and I want to be the one that makes her smile like that," William admitted. "Frankly, I have yet to make her smile."

This was the last conversation that he wanted to have with his brother. He had no designs on Lady Octavia but that didn't mean he wished ill-will to fall upon her. And that is precisely what would happen if she married William. His brother wouldn't treat her with the love and respect that she deserved.

"I'm sorry, but I think it would be best if you didn't pursue Lady Octavia," Harred said. "She will never sink so low as to accept your offer of courtship."

William jumped up from his seat. "You must want her for yourself!" he exclaimed. "That is the only reason why you won't help me."

"There are many reasons why I won't help you, but this is a natural consequence of your disreputable behavior. Perhaps if you stopped cavorting around Town and became more serious in your nature."

"Like you?" William scoffed. "You work entirely too much and you never have any fun."

"I have fun," he defended. "Furthermore, someone needs to see to all this work. It would go a long way if you agreed to help me with running the estate."

William tilted his chin stubbornly. "I will not lower myself to taking a job like a commoner," he declared in a haughty fashion.

"It is a respectable position," Harred said. "You would bring in an income and start maintaining your own accounts. It is time that you grow up and take responsibility for your own household."

"But it won't be my household, will it?" William asked.

"You can continue living at the estate or live in one of the properties on the land."

William pointed his finger at Harred. "You want me to move out and live in the countryside?" he asked. "This was your diabolical plan all along, wasn't it?"

Harred didn't think he could take any more of this argument. It was ludicrous and he had far too much work that he needed to see to. "There is nothing diabolical about it. I just think you would benefit from leaving London. There are far too many trappings here for you."

"I refuse to leave all my friends in Town to go live at a small cottage near our grand estate," William said.

"Fine. Go to debtors' prison," Harred stated. "Because that is where you will end up if you keep going on as you have been. I refuse to pay any more bills from gambling halls or brothels that come across my desk."

And right on cue, William's nostrils flared slightly. "You think you hold all the power, but Father would never have treated me this way."

"He would have, if he had lived long enough to see what you have become."

Taking a step back, William responded, "You are a terrible brother. I will prove to you that I don't need your help. I can make it on my own."

"Please do," Harred encouraged.

William seethed with indignation before he spun on his heel and departed from the study without saying another word.

Harred shook his head. He didn't think he could have the same argument with his brother, over and over. He had no intention of backing down. It was time for William to become the man that their parents would have wanted him to be.

But he was at a loss as to how to help his brother.

A chime came from the long clock in the corner, alerting him of the time. He would need to depart now if he wanted to arrive at the House of Lords on time.

Harred rose and came around his desk. He exited the study and headed towards the entry hall, where he was met by Mitchell.

Mitchell extended his top hat to him. "The coach is waiting out front for you, my lord."

"Thank you," Harred responded as he placed the top hat onto his head. "I won't be home for supper this evening."

"I will inform the cook of this," Mitchell said as he opened the door.

Harred departed from the townhouse and stepped into the coach. During this time of day, the journey to the House of Lords usually didn't take too long.

As the coach merged into traffic, Harred leaned his head back against the bench and let out the sigh that he had been holding in. How much longer could he keep going on as he had been? Something had to change, but he didn't quite know what that was.

How had his father accomplished all that he had and still managed to make time for their family?

The sweet fragrance of flowers drifted in through the opened window and he realized that he had made a terrible mistake. He hadn't ordered Mitchell to send flowers to Lady Octavia.

He pounded on the top of the coach and it promptly came to a stop in front of a flower shop. Not bothering to wait for the footman to come around, he placed his hand out the window and opened the coach.

Harred stepped down onto the pavement and headed into the quaint flower shop. He saw all types of flowers and different sizes of bouquets. Where did he even begin?

A white-haired woman approached him as she dried her hands on the apron that was hanging around her neck. "Can I help you, sir?"

"I need some flowers to be delivered."

"I can help with that," the woman said. "Do you have a particular flower in mind?"

Harred had no idea what kind of flower Lady Octavia might prefer nor did he have a favorite flower. His eyes roamed over the shop until they landed on a bouquet of red roses. "Those will do," he responded.

The woman nodded in approval. "Excellent choice," she

acknowledged. "Red roses signify love. Your lady must be quite special to you."

"No... er... I have danced one set with her," Harred revealed. "Do you have a bouquet that represents that I enjoyed becoming acquainted with her, but doesn't imply that I have feelings for her?"

She smiled. "I would recommend yellow roses, tulips, or chrysanthemums. Those symbolize joy and friendship."

"Yes, those will all do," he replied.

"I can create a lovely bouquet with those flowers. It shouldn't take too long and I can see to them being delivered to this particular young woman."

Harred removed some coins from his jacket pocket and handed them towards the woman. "Will you have them delivered to Lord Cuttyngham's townhouse in Mayfair? They are for Lady Octavia."

The woman walked over to a table and picked up a piece of paper. "Would you care to send a card with the flowers?"

"Yes, I think that would be appropriate," Harred said.

"What would you like the card to say?"

Harred's mind seemed to go blank. He hadn't sent flowers in many years and he was out of practice. He didn't want Lady Octavia to believe he intended to pursue her but he did want to bring a smile to her face.

A thought occurred to him. "Will you deliver two bouquets of flowers to Lord Cuttyngham's townhouse?"

A line between the woman's brow appeared. "Two, sir?"

"Yes, one for Lady Octavia and one for her mother, Lady Cuttyngham. She is rather ill," he explained. He hoped that Lady Octavia would appreciate his gesture and that she wouldn't think it was too presumptuous of him.

The woman's eyes held understanding. "I will be happy to do so," she replied. "That is most thoughtful of you."

He reached back into his jacket pocket but the woman put

her hand up. "You have sufficiently paid for both bouquets. But we still do have the matter of the card, sir."

"Yes, the card," he muttered. Blasted card. What could he write? And why did it matter what he wrote?

The woman held up the quill. "I daresay that you are overthinking this. What is your first thought as to what you should write?"

Harred bobbed his head. "You are right. Please just inform Lady Octavia that I enjoyed our dance and I am glad that she didn't trip."

"Very good," she said. "And your name?"

"Lord Kendal."

The woman signed his name and asked, "Will there be anything else, my lord?"

"No, but you have been most helpful."

"This lady must be rather special to you since you want everything to be so perfect," the woman mused.

"We are just friends," he rushed to correct. Although, he hoped that Lady Octavia would consider him a friend because he considered her one.

As he departed from the flower shop, he realized that he was smiling.

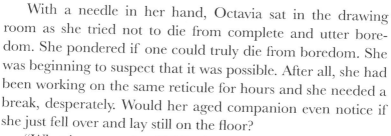

With a needle in her hand, Octavia sat in the drawing room as she tried not to die from complete and utter boredom. She pondered if one could truly die from boredom. She was beginning to suspect that it was possible. After all, she had been working on the same reticule for hours and she needed a break, desperately. Would her aged companion even notice if she just fell over and lay still on the floor?

"What is wrong, dear?" Mrs. Harper asked.

Octavia lowered the needlework to her lap and wondered

if her companion was more astute than she had let on. "I don't think I can do one more moment of needlework," she admitted.

"You just need a change of scenery," Mrs. Harper suggested. "Perhaps we should adjourn to the parlor?"

Much to her disappointment, she had been wrong about her companion. Mrs. Harper was just as oblivious as she always was. "I don't think that will help."

"Shall I ring for a tea service to be brought in for us? Tea has always seemed to calm your nerves before."

"It is not nerves." Octavia leaned forward and placed her needlework onto the table. "I think I will go read in my father's study."

Mrs. Harper went to rise. "I shall come with you."

"No!" Octavia exclaimed, putting her hand up. "I mean… er… if it isn't too much of an imposition, I would prefer to read on my own.

"Very well, I could use a nap anyways," Mrs. Harper said as she returned to her seat. "I will wait for you here."

Octavia offered her a grateful smile. "Thank you. You are very kind."

"Do not dally, though," Mrs. Harper said. "That reticule won't knit itself."

Octavia had no wish to argue with Mrs. Harper, but how many reticules did she need? She already had more than she knew what to do with.

As she rushed out of the drawing room, she let out a sigh of relief. Mrs. Harper was a sweet old woman but Octavia could only take so much of her. There was more to do in this life than sit around and practice their embroidery.

Perhaps she could convince Fredrick to take her riding, she thought. It might be unlikely since they already had gone riding this morning.

A knock came at the main door and Carson crossed the

entry hall to open the door. He accepted two identical magnificent bouquets of flowers.

Carson placed the flowers onto the table before he reached for the card.

Finding herself curious, Octavia asked, "Who are they from?"

After Carson read the card, he extended it towards her and replied, "They are from Lord Kendal. He sends one for you and one for Lady Cuttyngham."

Octavia read the card and found herself smiling. What a thoughtful gesture on his part. A bouquet of flowers would no doubt brighten up her mother's bedchamber. She would have to thank him the next time she saw him, which she hoped was soon.

She placed the card down and admired the flowers. It was common for a gentleman to send flowers after dancing a set with a lady but she was still pleased that he had done so. It made her feel special, and she hadn't felt that way in a long time. With her mother's advancing illness, she was usually overlooked and oftentimes spent time alone.

"Will you send one of these bouquets up to my mother's bedchamber?" she asked.

Carson tipped his head. "Yes, my lady."

With a parting glance at the flowers, Octavia headed towards the rear of the townhouse where her father's study was situated.

She stepped into the room and headed towards the shelves along the wall. She selected a book and sat down on a leather settee.

Octavia had just opened the book when a distinctive tap came on the glass. She looked up and saw Lord William on the other side of the closed window.

Dear heavens, what was he about, she wondered. Fredrick would be furious if he knew that Lord William was here, especially under these circumstances. It would be best if she got rid of him, and quickly. Fredrick's anger was not one that someone wanted to stoke.

She rose, walked over to the window and opened it. "Whatever are you doing here, my lord?" she asked curtly.

Despite her sharp tone, William looked at ease, as if nothing was amiss. "I came to speak to you," he said.

"This is highly inappropriate, and you must leave at once." She paused before asking, "Pray tell, why didn't you come through the main door?"

William shrugged. "Your butler denied me entry. He said Lord Chatsworth said I was not welcome in your home."

"Then what would you have me do?"

He held his gloved hand out. "Come and walk with me in the gardens." The way he spoke his words made it seem like he was doing her some great honor by extending such an invitation.

"I will do no such thing," she asserted. "What you are asking of me could cause a scandal."

With a smile that was no doubt attempting to disarm her, he replied, "It is hardly scandalous to walk in your gardens."

Lord William may be handsome, but his cocky demeanor did not impress her much. "I'm sorry but my answer is no," she said. "My brother would be furious if I spent any time with you."

His smile dimmed but it was not gone completely. "Do you intend to let your brother control you?"

Octavia felt her back grow rigid, knowing that Lord William was attempting to manipulate her into doing his will. "He does not control me nor would I ever feel that way."

"Yet you are letting him dictate your actions?" he argued.

"Lord William, you must know how inappropriate your actions are..." Her words came to an abrupt stop when she heard a low growl coming from the gardens. She knew precisely what was making that sound. She may not care for

Lord William, but she didn't want any harm to befall him either.

In a panicked voice, she said, "You need to leave the gardens now."

Clearly, Lord William did not sense the urgency of her words by his next remark. "Not without you agreeing to a ride through Hyde Park."

Good gracious, was this man daft, she wondered. He was in danger, but he was still trying to woo her. "I think not, but it is for your own good if you flee right now," Octavia explained, her words rushed. "There is a peacock—"

Lord William looked amused. "I can handle a peacock."

What an infuriating man. Why wasn't he listening to her? "No, you don't understand. This particular peacock has an evil glint in his eyes and he has claimed the gardens as his own domain."

Another growl could be heard and it was followed by a rattling sound. "Freddy is coming," she warned.

"Freddy doesn't sound very terrifying," Lord William said.

"Please run, and save yourself," Octavia urged.

Lord William leaned his shoulder against the side of the window as if he didn't have a care in the world. "I would be happy to protect you from this peacock—" His words stopped as he turned his head. "Why is that peacock charging at me?"

"Run to the gate!" she exclaimed.

Lord William finally understood the danger he was in and took off running. In true Freddy fashion, he raced after him with his feathers on full display. The peacock wasn't going to make this easy on Lord William and she appreciated that. For once, this bird came in handy.

Octavia leaned out the window and tried not to laugh as Lord William ran towards the gate along the back wall. She knew she shouldn't find this amusing, but she did. At least, a little bit.

Fredrick's voice came from behind her. "It serves Lord

William right. I can't believe he had the audacity to come into our gardens to speak to you." He came to stand next to her and gave her a pointed look. "You shouldn't have opened the window."

"I know, but I was trying to warn him about Freddy. He just wouldn't listen."

"Most people don't understand how terrifying an attacking peacock can be," Fredrick said. "Luckily, Freddy will give up the fight before he injures anyone."

"Yes, thankfully," Octavia muttered. "I should be grateful that Freddy leaves the servants alone when they tend to the gardens."

"You must be relieved that Freddy takes issue with more people than just you," Fredrick joked.

"On a good note, I have enjoyed updating all my hats with peacock feathers," she said. "They are the height of fashion."

Fredrick closed the window. "If Lord William was smart, he would learn his lesson and never come back here again."

"I don't think he is that clever."

With a solemn look, Fredrick said, "Stay away from him."

"Really, Brother?" she asked in exasperation. "You have already warned me to do so, multiple times, in fact. And I will not fight you on it. I have no desire to have Lord William as a suitor."

"I know, but I do not like the way that Lord William looks at you," he said. "I am considering calling Lord William out for his actions. He crossed the line of respectability and honor by the stunt he pulled today."

Octavia shook her head. "You will do no such thing. I abhor duels and they have no place in a civilized society."

"But Lord William needs a comeuppance for his behavior."

"You aren't wrong but shooting him is not the answer."

Fredrick smirked. "It would certainly make me feel better."

Their father stepped into the room with a concerned look on his face. "Did I hear screaming coming from the gardens?"

"You did," Fredrick confirmed. "We had an uninvited guest visit our gardens, but Freddy ensured he promptly left."

Their father chuckled. "I can only imagine Freddy came as a surprise to him," he said.

The sound of Freddy wailing could be heard in the distance.

"It would seem that someone is proud of themselves," Fredrick acknowledged with a smile.

Octavia turned towards her father and asked, "How is Mother faring today?"

All traces of humor vanished from her father's countenance. "She keeps stopping mid-sentence because she forgets what she was speaking about," he said. "It is not a good day, I'm afraid."

"The doctor did warn us that she would get progressively worse towards the end," Fredrick advised.

"Yes, but we do have a problem," her father remarked. "Your mother is confused and she is adamant that she wants to meet Octavia's new husband."

"But I don't have a husband," Octavia said.

Her father nodded. "The doctor believes that she has internalized Roswell's marriage but has conferred the thoughts and feelings onto you."

"Oh, dear," Octavia muttered. "What are we to do?"

Fredrick's next words were so out of character for him that she feared she'd misheard him. "I think we find Octavia a husband, and quickly," he said.

Octavia placed a hand on her hip. "Pardon?" she asked, daring him to continue. He couldn't possibly mean that, could he?

Her brother put his hand up, no doubt in an attempt to still her anger. "Hear me out first before you reject my idea."

Octavia arched her eyebrow but she didn't say anything.

"Mother is dying and we don't want to upset her in her final days," Fredrick said. "We could ask Lord Kendal to play the part of a devoted husband."

"Why would he go along with such a charade?" Octavia asked.

"If we explain our reasoning, I do believe Harred wouldn't take issue with it," Fredrick said. "Besides, you would only have to meet with Mother on a few occasions."

Octavia bit her lower lip before saying, "I do not like the idea of lying to her."

Fredrick placed a hand on her shoulder. "Just think of it as a tender mercy," he said.

"I think it is a brilliant plan," their father interjected.

"You do?" Octavia asked.

Their father's eyes held a profound sadness to them. "I normally do not condone lying, but your mother's grasp on reality is gone. I say we give her some peace right now."

Octavia could understand where her father and brother were coming from. And she would do anything to help her mother, even if it meant she would pretend to be married to a man that she had only just become acquainted with.

"Very well," she said. "I will do this for Mother."

Fredrick smiled broadly, almost too broadly. What was her brother up to?

Chapter Five

The sun was high in the sky as Harred exited his coach and stood in front of White's. He had received a message that Fredrick wanted to meet with him here. It had better be important because he had much more work that he had to see to. He didn't have time to dilly-dally at a gentlemen's club. If so, he was no better than his brother.

A liveried servant opened the door and allowed him entry. As he stepped into the hall, he saw Fredrick was sitting at a table and drinking a cup of tea. That was an odd choice of drink, especially for this type of establishment.

Fredrick met his gaze and put his hand up in greeting. Harred returned the gesture and headed towards his friend.

Once he arrived at the table, Harred asked, "Pray tell, what is so important that we needed to meet here?"

With a knowing smile, Fredrick replied, "I thought you could use the break from your work."

Harred pulled out a chair and sat down. "The longer I am away from my work, the more it seems to accrue." He paused. "You will know soon enough, won't you?"

"I already have, at least somewhat. My father has asked for

me to become acquainted with the accounts so he can focus his attention on my mother."

"I'm sorry," Harred said, unsure of what else he could say to that. He felt immense sympathy for Fredrick's situation and what he was forced to endure.

Fredrick reached for his teacup and took a sip before asking, "How are you faring?"

"I am well." He hoped if he kept his answer vague that Fredrick wouldn't press him. But he was not so lucky.

"Are you?" Fredrick asked, eyeing him closely. "I only asked because you lost both of your parents not long ago in a carriage accident. That had to take a toll on you."

"I don't have time to grieve because I am dealing with the estate and my louse of a brother," Harred confessed.

Fredrick's eyes held compassion. "I understand, but you must take time for yourself and deal with your emotions."

"Do you understand?" Harred asked, his voice rising. "I only ask because you still have both of your parents." He knew that he shouldn't be so defensive, but he refused to let Fredrick advise him on something that he knew nothing about.

His friend grew quiet. "You are right about my parents, but do not think that I haven't suffered a great loss. I watched my comrades die on the battlefield and I could do nothing about it."

Harred could hear the pain in Fredrick's voice and he knew that his friend did indeed understand the gnawing grief that followed him everywhere.

"I'm sorry for your losses," Harred attempted. "I was wrong to say what I did."

"There is no need to apologize. I just wanted you to know that you aren't alone in your grief. It comes in waves and sometimes the wave comes when you are least expecting it. And it doesn't matter how long ago the loss took place,"

Fredrick advised. "The empty space that loss leaves inside of you is permanent."

"I worry that I won't ever be able to live up to my father's legacy," Harred admitted. "He was a great man, and I feel so inadequate."

Fredrick nodded his understanding. "Your father was indeed a good man, but do not sell yourself short. I have known you for a long time and I know what you are capable of. You will rise to the challenge."

"If I only had to worry about our estate and the House of Lords, that would be much easier. My biggest headache is my brother, William."

"Yes, and he is becoming rather burdensome," Fredrick said. "He snuck into our gardens to speak to Octavia since I ordered our butler to deny him entry in our home."

"My brother is an idiot," Harred muttered. "Please say that Octavia didn't give him any heed."

Fredrick chuckled. "They spoke, but only for a brief moment. My sister's pet peacock chased him out of the gardens."

"Thank heavens for Freddy," Harred said.

A server approached the table and asked, "Would you care for something to drink?"

"I would," Harred replied. "I will have what my friend is drinking."

"Very good," the server said before he departed.

Fredrick gave him a curious look. "Do not let me stop you from drinking. I get terrible headaches from alcohol so I tend to avoid it."

"It is far too early to be drinking anyways," Harred remarked. "At least, it is for me. William has no issue with having a drink or two over breakfast."

"What are we going to do about William? I want him nowhere near my sister."

"Neither do I," Harred responded. "I will speak to him

again, but he has it in his mind that he wants to marry Lady Octavia."

Fredrick did not look pleased by his admission. "If he attempts to ruin her, I will have no choice but to challenge him to a duel."

"I do hope he won't do something so foolish."

"As do I, because I have no desire to kill him," Fredrick said. "But I will do anything to protect my sister and her reputation."

Harred truly hoped that he could get through to his brother before he did something that he couldn't come back from.

The server returned and placed a cup of tea in front of him. "Will there be anything else?"

"Not at this time," Harred replied.

Once the server walked off, Harred picked up the teacup and took a sip. He had to admit that it was nice to be out of his office and speaking to a friend, even if they were discussing his brother.

Fredrick leaned forward and lowered his voice. "I have a favor that I need to ask of you," he said.

Harred had known Fredrick for a long time, and he was not one to ask for help. Which made him that much more curious as to what Fredrick would ask of him. "What kind of favor?"

"As you know, my mother is quite sick and her mind is slipping," his friend said. "She is under the impression that Octavia is married and wants to meet her husband."

Afraid of where this was going, Harred hesitantly asked, "You aren't asking me to marry your sister, are you?"

"Heavens, no," Fredrick said. "I was just hoping that you would play the part of a devoted husband on a few occasions, for my mother's sake."

Harred sat back in his seat as he considered Fredrick's request. He wouldn't mind spending more time with Lady

Octavia. She always seemed to bring a smile to his face. But could he pretend that he was married to her? That seemed like an enormous feat since they hardly knew one another.

Fredrick must have understood his apprehension because he said, "You will have to become more acquainted with my sister in order to make the ruse believable."

"I am not opposed to that," Harred admitted. "But is Lady Octavia agreeable to this plan? I wouldn't want her to do anything that she is uncomfortable with."

"She is," Fredrick confirmed.

Harred didn't have time for this, but he would make the time. The thought of spending time with Lady Octavia was far too appealing to turn down. He found her intriguing, and he wanted to learn more about her.

With a bob of his head, Harred said, "I will do it."

Fredrick looked relieved. "Thank you. It will mean a great deal to my mother," he acknowledged. "Perhaps you could take Octavia on a carriage ride later today so you can discuss the particulars."

Harred fought back the urge to groan. The thought of a carriage ride through Hyde Park, particularly during the fashionable hour, seemed unappealing. He hated being on display and being gossiped about. However, it would give him a chance to get to know Lady Octavia without any distractions. "Very well," he said.

As his words left his mouth, Mr. Caleb Bolingbroke's voice came from behind him. "Good morning, gentlemen."

Fredrick tipped his head. "Caleb," he acknowledged. "Please join us."

Caleb pulled back a chair and sat down. "I am surprised to see you both here, especially at such an early hour."

"It is not that early," Harred said. "I have been up for hours."

After Fredrick took a sip of his tea, he addressed Caleb. "What brings you by White's?" he asked.

"I am trying to avoid my mother," Caleb admitted. "Ever since Anette departed for her wedding tour with Roswell, my mother has been relentless with trying to get me to wed."

"That sounds awful," Fredrick said.

Caleb nodded. "It is, and no matter how many times I protest, she doesn't relent. It is exhausting." He paused. "But enough about me. I would much rather discuss Lord William's bet that he placed in the book here."

"What bet?" Harred asked.

Caleb glanced between them. "You two don't know, do you?" he asked with a frown. "Lord William placed a bet that he would marry Lady Octavia in a fortnight."

Harred shook his head. His brother was an idiot. Had he learned nothing? He was gambling with money that he did not have... again. And he would lose this bet. Fredrick would never allow William anywhere near his sister.

With a clenched jaw, Fredrick said, "Lord William is not going to marry my sister; I can promise you that."

"That is a relief," Caleb remarked. "Octavia is far too good for the likes of him. I was worried that I was going to have to talk some sense into her."

"No, it is William that needs to have some sense knocked into him," Harred stated. "It seems my words are falling on deaf ears when it comes to him."

Fredrick gripped his teacup so tightly that Harred was afraid he was going to break the cup. "I would be happy to speak to him," he growled.

Harred didn't think that conversation would go well, considering his brother did not take anyone's advice to heart. "That won't be necessary," he assured his friend. "Besides, I wouldn't give the bet much heed. Gentlemen place ridiculous bets in that book all the time and most of the time they lose."

His words seemed to appease Fredrick. "Just remind Lord William that he is not welcome at my townhouse, for any reason," his friend said.

"I will." Harred pushed his teacup away from him. "I should depart. I have far too much work that I must see to before I depart for the House of Lords."

"But I just got here," Caleb attempted.

Harred rose. "Perhaps another time," he suggested. But he knew that it was an empty promise. He didn't have time to waste, and sitting idly at White's was a luxury Harred couldn't afford. His utmost priority was to ensure he didn't fail.

Caleb didn't look convinced. "You work too hard," he said. "Life isn't about working until the day you die. You must enjoy it."

"I'm afraid that is not possible, at least not yet. Once my estate is thriving, I will be able to take some time for myself."

"Don't put off happiness that you can have today," Caleb advised. "You don't know what tomorrow will bring."

Happiness? What an elusive thing. No, he didn't have the time or energy to seek out happiness. He was just trying to get through each and every day, and he was barely doing that.

"Good day, gentlemen," Harred said before he started to walk away. He knew that Caleb was just trying to help, but he didn't need anyone's help. He was doing just fine on his own. But he couldn't even fathom his own lie.

Octavia sat at the writing desk in the drawing room as she dipped the tip of her quill into the concoction that she'd made. She had wanted to see if she could write a letter using invisible ink and she had been successful. At least, she thought she was. She would need Fredrick to hold up the paper to a flame to see if it worked.

The sound of her companion's snoring filled the small room and she wished that she could rest so easily. How Mrs.

Harper could sleep sitting up in a chair was beyond her, but she seemed to be asleep more times than not.

After she placed the quill down, she blew on the paper to dry the ink. She felt silly blowing on a page that appeared blank but she was hopeful her experiment had worked.

Fredrick stepped into the room. "Good afternoon," he greeted.

Octavia placed her finger to her lips. "Shhh," she urged. "Mrs. Harper is sleeping."

Her brother looked unimpressed, but he did lower his voice. "What has kept you occupied today?"

Rising, Octavia walked over to her brother and extended him the paper. "I wrote you a note."

He accepted the paper and turned it over. "There is nothing here."

"Or is there?" Octavia smirked. "I used invisible ink to write the letter."

Fredrick gave her a look of disbelief. "How did you know how to do that?"

Octavia shrugged. "I asked our cook and she told me the ingredients that I would need. It was rather simple."

"Dare I ask how Mrs. Harris knew how to make invisible ink?"

"I didn't ask, and she didn't divulge the information," Octavia replied. "Now you just need to hold it up to a flame to confirm I did it correctly."

Fredrick folded the paper and slipped it into the pocket of his jacket. "I will do so later, but you need to go get ready."

"Ready for what?"

"Lord Kendal is coming to take you on a carriage ride through Hyde Park," he revealed. "Is that what you are going to wear?"

Octavia glanced down at her pale pink gown. "What is wrong with what I am wearing?" she asked.

Fredrick's eyes perused the length of her. "I suppose that will do."

"You suppose?" Octavia asked. "Do you even know anything about fashion? Mother insisted that I had new dresses commissioned for my Season. This gown is the height of fashion."

"I will admit that I do not know enough about ladies' fashions to have an opinion, but I do know you will need a hat."

Octavia reached up and smoothed back her dark hair. "You are right, but I do not understand why you care so much."

Fredrick placed a hand to his chest and feigned outrage. "I am your brother and I greatly care about all aspects of your life."

She eyed him curiously. Her brother was definitely up to something but she wasn't sure what it was. Was he trying to play matchmaker, she wondered. He had never been one to do so before, so why now?

Fredrick continued. "Lord Kendal has agreed to act the part of a devoted husband to you, for Mother's sake."

"He did?" she asked. The thought both excited and terrified her. Why was that? It was just a ruse, nothing more.

"That is why he is taking you on a carriage ride so you two can become better acquainted with one another," Fredrick said.

Octavia was truly grateful for Lord Kendal's assistance but why had he agreed to it in the first place? "What does Lord Kendal get out of this arrangement?" she asked. "Surely he isn't doing this out of the kindness of his heart."

"Actually, he is," Fredrick said. "He sympathized with our plight and he agreed to help- willingly. So you don't need to worry."

"But he intends to take me on a carriage ride through Hyde Park," Octavia pressed. "What will people think?"

Fredrick lifted his brow. "I hadn't taken you for someone who cared what others thought."

"Usually I am not, but it is a concern, is it not?" she asked.

"You are overthinking this, my dear sister."

"Or you are *under*thinking this, my dear brother," she countered.

Taking a step forward, Fredrick placed his hand on her sleeve. "Just go on the carriage ride and humor me. Everything will work out; you will see," he said. "Remember that you are doing this for Mother."

Octavia lowered her gaze as she shared, "She did ask about my husband this morning."

"What did you say?"

"I told her that he was away on business but he would visit her soon enough," Octavia replied. "Mother perked up after that and asked me all kinds of questions about him. I tried to be as vague as possible, but it was difficult."

"Be strong," Fredrick encouraged.

"I don't think I can be," Octavia admitted. "With every passing day, every conversation, I am watching Mother slowly wither away right in front of me."

Fredrick opened his arms and she stepped into them. As she rested her head against his chest, she allowed herself to cry. It was tiring to pretend to be strong. She was breaking on the inside, but she didn't want anyone else to know how much she was suffering.

A knock came at the front door and it echoed throughout the main level.

"Lord Kendal has arrived," Fredrick announced.

Octavia stepped out of his arms and swiped at her cheeks. She hoped she didn't look as if she had been crying. She couldn't bear the thought of anyone pitying her.

Fredrick reached into his jacket pocket and removed a handkerchief. Without saying a word, he extended it towards her.

Carson stepped into the room and said, "Lord Kendal would like a moment of your time. Shall I show him in?"

"Give us a moment," Fredrick ordered before turning back to face her. "Do not fear. You do not appear as if you have been crying."

"That is a relief," she murmured.

Fredrick's eyes held compassion as he assured her, "It is all right to cry and let your emotions out. No one will fault you for that."

"Can we not discuss something else?" she asked. She didn't want her brother to think she was a weak, simpering miss. She could handle hard things. So why did her heart ache at that thought?

It was a moment later when Lord Kendal stepped into the room. He was dressed in buff trousers, a blue jacket and his dark hair was swept forward.

When his eyes landed on her, he stopped and bowed. "Lady Octavia," he greeted.

She dropped into a curtsy. "Lord Kendal," she responded. "I just learned that we are to go on a carriage ride through Hyde Park."

"Yes, and I am looking forward to it," Lord Kendal said.

"Are you?" she asked boldly.

Lord Kendal looked surprised by her question. "I am," he replied. "Are you not?"

Octavia wasn't quite sure how she felt about the carriage ride. If she had to be honest with herself, she felt a sense of excitement at the prospect of spending time with Lord Kendal. He was a man that she wanted to know better. He had a way about him that made her feel safe.

Knowing he was still waiting for a response, she said, "I suppose I am."

Lord Kendal didn't look convinced by her words but he offered his arm anyways. "Shall we depart, then?" he asked. "My curricle is out front."

She approached him and placed her hand on his arm. "Thank you, my lord."

They didn't speak as they departed from the townhouse. As he went to assist her into the curricle, the sound of a peacock wailing could be heard in the distance.

Lord Kendal turned his head towards the gardens. "I must assume that is Freddy."

"Most likely," Octavia replied. "He is a rather vocal peacock."

"I feel as if I should thank him for running my brother out of the gardens, thus keeping him far away from you."

Octavia grinned. "You wish to thank a peacock?" she asked in an amused voice. "That is the most ridiculous thing I have ever heard."

The tip of Freddy's feathers could be seen as he walked along the gate, no doubt strutting around to impress the female peacocks.

Lord Kendal turned back to face her. "Why did you get a peacock as a pet?"

"I just wanted something exotic, something different than what most ladies have as a pet," Octavia explained.

"Well, you definitely succeeded at that," Lord Kendal said.

"I did, but I didn't realize how ornery male peacocks are. And Freddy…" Her voice trailed off. "He is a terror on two legs."

"If he is such a terror, why do you keep him around?" Lord Kendal asked.

Octavia was taken aback. That was a fair question, but she didn't have the answer to it. Why did she keep Freddy, despite the bird clearly tormenting her whenever she stepped foot in the gardens? It wasn't just for the feathers that the servants collected for her.

She met his gaze and admitted, "I don't rightly know why I keep Freddy."

"I have a theory," Lord Kendal said. "You may claim that

you don't like him. Hate him, even. But I do think it is a good thing that you have kept him. It proves to me that you don't give up on anyone when it is difficult, especially an ornery peacock." He hesitated. "Am I wrong?"

"You aren't wrong, but I feel as if you are giving me far too much credit," she said. "I always try to find the best in people, but Freddy is different. He is just a peacock."

"Yet he protected you when you were being harassed by my brother."

Octavia shook her head, causing the curls that framed her face to sway back and forth. "No, Freddy was just protecting the gardens from intruders. It had nothing to do with me."

Lord Kendal held his hand up to assist her into the curricle. "We shall have to agree to disagree on this, but I think there was more to it than that."

After she stepped into the curricle, Lord Kendal came around the other side and sat on the bench next to her. He reached for the reins and merged the curricle into traffic.

A silence descended over them but it wasn't uncomfortable or awkward. It was pleasant. She didn't feel a need to speak up and fill the silence with useless words.

Octavia snuck a peek at Lord Kendal as he drove the team. There was no doubt that he was a very handsome man, but he was so much more than that. He made her laugh, he made her think, and most of all, he had a kindness about him that made her trust him.

But that didn't mean she had any interest in him. No. Of course not. She couldn't bring her emotions into this. Lord Kendal was merely a newfound friend. Nothing more.

Chapter Six

Harred tightened the reins in his hand as he drove the team towards Hyde Park. The silence had gone on long enough and he decided it was time to become more acquainted with Lady Octavia. This was a task that he found he didn't mind. One might even say that he was pleased by the prospect. But now he had to get her to start talking.

When he had arrived at her townhouse, he had noticed her red-lined eyes and it was evident that she had been crying. He had to assume that she was upset about her mother, but was he presumptuous enough to ask her? And if she did admit to it, would she confide in him? He hoped she would.

After his parents had died, he had never felt more alone, despite having friends that had reached out to him. But he didn't want to discuss his great loss. He couldn't. So he kept it to himself and the burdens were still weighing him down.

He didn't want Lady Octavia to feel alone. Frankly, he didn't want her to feel one ounce of sadness. She deserved to be happy, and he loved nothing more than seeing her smile. For when she did, it lit up her entire face and her eyes reflected a happiness that he had once known.

Harred cleared his throat. This was it. He hoped she

wouldn't chide him on his impertinence. "I couldn't help but notice that you had been crying earlier," he said. "I do hope everything is all right."

Lady Octavia visibly stiffened. "A gentleman would not comment on a woman's discomfort."

"I would normally agree, but I wanted you to know that you are not alone in your grief," Harred said. "You have your family and your friends that want to help you."

"I do not wish to discuss this, especially with someone that I have only just become acquainted with," Lady Octavia remarked curtly.

Harred understood her resistance but he couldn't leave things as they were. He had to let her know that he understood. It was important to him.

In a voice that was far calmer than he felt, he shared, "My parents died not too long ago in a carriage accident."

Lady Octavia sucked in a breath. "I am sorry to hear that."

"I do not talk about it often since the grief is so raw, but I don't want you to make the same mistake as me. Do not withdraw and hold it in, thinking you have to be brave all the time. Truly being brave means that you have the courage to be vulnerable. It means you can admit that you don't have everything figured out. To ask for help when you need it."

He gave her a weak smile as he continued. "I do not mean to lecture you. I just couldn't stand the thought of you trying to go about dealing with your grief on your own."

Shifting on the bench, Lady Octavia remarked, "You are so insistent on helping me, but yet you don't ask for help when *you* need it. Why is that?"

"It is far easier to offer advice than to take it," Harred admitted sheepishly.

Lady Octavia watched him for a long moment, her expression giving nothing away. "I do not like feeling vulnerable with anyone. It makes me feel weak."

"I can relate."

"My first instinct is to pretend that all is well. It has been the only way I have been able to cope for this long."

Harred glanced at her. "Has that worked well for you?"

"No, it has been terrible, and not at all effective, but it is safe. Familiar." Lady Octavia sighed. "I know that my mother will pass soon but I am dreading that day."

"As well you should. It is not a day that you will likely forget."

Lady Octavia's lips quirked. "Aren't you supposed to tell me that it will get easier with time?"

"No, because I have no intention of lying to you," Harred replied. "Time slowed down for me when I was informed that my parents had been killed. The only thing I remember was the ticking of the long clock that timed my misery."

"You are not very helpful," Lady Octavia said.

"Every day, I struggle with my grief, not knowing if it will eventually consume me," Harred remarked. "The only thing that keeps me going is the thought that I must live up to being the man I am supposed to be. I can't let people down. People's livelihoods are dependent on me."

"What about letting yourself down?" Lady Octavia asked. "How can you take care of others if you are unable to see after yourself?"

"I manage the best that I can."

Lady Octavia grew quiet. "That is the way that I feel. I want to be happy, but the guilt always rears its ugly head at the most inopportune times. How can I be happy when my mother is dying, despite her insistence that I go out and enjoy the Season?"

Harred's gaze shifted forward as the team entered Rotten Row and joined the line of carriages. "I can see why you are so reluctant, but should you not honor your mother's final wish?"

"I am trying to, but it is not easy," Lady Octavia replied.

"What a pair we make," he said lightly.

Lady Octavia started fidgeting with her hands in her lap. "Besides being proficient at giving advice, I know little else about you."

"Well, you have already seen my exemplary horseback riding abilities," he joked.

She laughed, just as he hoped she would. "That was hardly your fault that you fell off your horse."

"You are right. It is not every day a young woman jumps a hedge right in front of me," Harred said. "But I am glad that you did. It gave me the opportunity to get to know you."

She ducked her head, but before she did, he saw a faint blush on her cheeks. Perhaps his words had affected her more than she was letting on.

Harred glanced up at the sky and said, "The weather is rather nice for this time of year." Drats. Had he truly resorted to speaking about the weather? Had they nothing else to talk about?

Lady Octavia brought her gaze up and asked, "Do you have any hobbies, my lord?"

"I do not have time for hobbies, I'm afraid."

"What do you do for fun?"

"I work."

"But what else?"

He shrugged. "What else matters?"

She eyed him curiously. "Surely you jest," she said. "You cannot possibly work all the time."

"If I am not working, I am at the House of Lords," he shared. "I have been given a great responsibility and I cannot fail."

"Why do you think you will fail?" she asked.

Perhaps it would be better if they discussed the weather, he thought. But he decided it was only fair that he answered her question. She had answered his, after all. "My father was an important man and he did great things for England. I am nothing like him."

"Why do you believe that?"

With a frown on his lips, Harred admitted, "I am barely keeping everything together. My brother is of no use and I have no idea how to properly run an estate. It is doing well, but for how long?"

"I see. So you are a naysayer."

"I wouldn't say 'naysayer' but more pragmatic," Harred said. "I have to be. The burden lies solely on my shoulders."

"I cannot imagine the stress that comes with running an estate, but expecting the worst can't be the best way to deal with it."

Harred adjusted the reins in his hand. "It is the only way I know how."

"Have you asked for help?"

He huffed at the mere thought. "I have a man of business, a solicitor, a steward and a myriad of servants that see to the estate thriving. I can't let them know that I have no idea what I am doing. What would they think of me?"

"Who cares what they think?"

"I do, greatly," he replied. "I can't let them think they are being led by an idiot."

Lady Octavia arched an eyebrow. "You, my lord, are no idiot. And I have seen plenty of idiots in my day. Your brother being one of them."

He laughed. And it felt good to do so. "William and I are two vastly different people. Sometimes, it is unbelievable to me that we were raised in the same household."

"You rose up to the challenges, despite what you have gone through. That says a lot about you," Lady Octavia said. "After all, I wouldn't pretend to marry just any man." She smiled, and it had a mischievous look to it.

Harred's eyes dropped to her lips and he had to force himself to look away. "I must admit that I am glad that

Fredrick came to me and asked me to do him this favor. It has given me an opportunity to learn more about you."

"I feel the same way about you."

At her admission, Harred felt his heart soar. But he couldn't help but wonder why he had such a reaction to her words. It wasn't as if he had any intention of pursuing her. He was just doing his friend a favor.

"I suppose this is the part where I ask if you have any hobbies," he said.

Lady Octavia blew out a puff of air. "I am proficient in all things that a lady is expected to be. My mother made sure of that."

"I did not doubt that."

"As of late, I have spent entirely too much of my time knitting reticules," she shared. "Would you care for one? They are an excellent place to stash a biscuit during the opera."

"Am I to assume you have snuck in biscuits to the opera?"

"Many times," she replied. "How can you watch the opera without a biscuit or two? It is unfathomable to me."

"I have never eaten a biscuit during the opera and now I am wondering what I have been missing all of these years."

Lady Octavia became animated as she started using her hands to emphasize her point. "I enjoy going to the opera but Roswell told me that he won't take me anymore. He claims I talk entirely too much during the performance."

"Do you?"

"Yes and no," she replied. "Yes, I talk too much but that is only because I find myself growing bored. Although, I do start off by making a conscious effort to pay attention. I just fail in that regard generally around the second act."

Harred found himself riveted by this conversation. He suspected that Octavia didn't even understand how delightful she was. "Then why do you go to the opera?" he questioned.

"What else am I supposed to do?" she asked. "Practice my embroidery with my aged companion?"

"Well, when given the choice, I can see why you pick the opera." Harred glanced down at the blue and gold-trimmed reticule that hung around her right wrist. "By chance, do you have a biscuit in your reticule now?"

Lady Octavia held up the reticule for his inspection. "I do not, but I will be sure to bring one on our next carriage ride."

The sound of pounding horse hooves drew his attention. He turned his head and saw his brother racing towards them with a thunderous expression on his face.

"What now?" Harred muttered to himself.

William reined in his horse next to the curricle and shouted, "This is the ultimate betrayal! How could you, Brother?"

Harred glanced around and saw that his brother was drawing some unwanted attention from the riders in the other carriages along Rotten Row. "Do keep your voice down," he urged.

"You knew I had every intention of pursuing Lady Octavia and you decided to go after her yourself," William growled. "Have you no shame?"

Harred held his brother's gaze, knowing he had done nothing wrong. He wasn't about to let William dictate his actions. "Leave us," he ordered. "We can discuss this later in the privacy of our townhouse."

"My own brother stabbed me in the back," William declared, his voice growing more irritated with each passing word. "It is a good thing I anticipated this and I planned accordingly."

Harred furrowed his brow. "What does that even mean?" he asked. "What did you plan?" He resisted pointing out the fact that his brother never planned anything. So why did he start now?

"You will see," William said before he kicked his horse into a run.

As Harred watched his brother race past the other

carriages, he felt the familiar urge to apologize for William's behavior.

Lady Octavia must have sensed this because she said, "Don't you dare apologize for him. You did nothing wrong."

"But William managed to ruin our carriage ride."

"It isn't ruined," she asserted. "I have rather enjoyed myself until now and I choose not to let Lord William's behavior disrupt our outing."

Harred was utterly taken aback. Lady Octavia was not bothered by William's outburst and even took it in stride. How could he not care for her? She was unlike any young woman he had known before. She let her uniqueness shine and now he was unable to look away.

Octavia knew that Lord William's outburst had dampened their outing but she refused to let him ruin it entirely. Lord William had some audacity. Not once had he asked her what she wanted. He only told her what *he* wanted. She had made it abundantly clear that she had no intention of taking him on as a suitor.

If Lord William persisted in pursuing her, she was fearful that Fredrick would call him out. But what could she say that would deter the pesky lord? He was so absorbed in his own desires that he was paying no heed to what she had already told him.

She glanced over at Lord Kendal. He hadn't said much since they had left Hyde Park and traveled back to her townhouse. She wished they could go back to the easy conversation that had flowed between them before Lord William had so rudely interrupted them.

Knowing their time was short, Octavia said, "Pardon my language, but your brother is a jackanapes."

Lord Kendal chuckled and some of the tension left his expression. "Yes, he is," he agreed. "But my brother has only gotten worse since our parents died."

"I am most fortunate to have two attentive, *very* protective brothers," Octavia said.

"You are," he responded. "And they are two of the best men that I know."

The curricle came to a stop in front of her townhouse and a footman exited through the main door to collect the reins.

Lord Kendal stepped down from the curricle and came around the other side to assist her onto the pavement. "Thank you," he said.

"For what?" she asked.

"You have managed to brighten my mood just by being yourself," he replied. "Whereas interacting with William tends to put me into a foul mood."

"I can see why. He is rather unpleasant."

"That he is," Lord Kendal readily agreed.

Carson held the door open and stood to the side to allow them entry.

Once they were in the entry hall, Lord Kendal dropped his arm and smiled. "I had an enjoyable time. Thank you."

Octavia found that she wasn't quite ready to say goodbye to him. But what could she say that would keep him here longer?

Fredrick's voice came from the top of the stairs. "Perfect timing," he declared. "Mother is asking for you..." he hesitated, "and your husband."

With a nervous glance at Lord Kendal, Octavia said, "I do not think we are ready for that. We hardly know one another. What if she sees through us?"

Lord Kendal placed a hand on her sleeve. "We can do this," he encouraged. "We will just have to work together."

Octavia didn't know why his words were so comforting,

but they were. And, most importantly, she believed them. "All right. If you are sure?"

"I am," Lord Kendal replied, removing his hand.

Fredrick waved them towards the stairs. "Come along, then," he encouraged. "You don't want to keep Mother waiting for too long."

Lord Kendal offered his arm and she accepted it. "I do not want you to worry. When I was younger, I would put on skits for my parents and they told me that I was quite believable," he shared.

Octavia smiled. "How old were you?"

"Six or so," he replied.

"Have you considered that they told you only what you wanted to hear because they were supporting you?"

Lord Kendal shook his head. "I would like to believe that I had a career in the theater if I wasn't a gentleman."

"Truly?" she asked.

He chuckled. "No. I was awful. I am much too pragmatic to play pretend, but that didn't stop me from trying."

"Was your story an attempt to encourage me or cause me to worry more?"

"It was to distract you," Lord Kendal replied. "And it worked."

She turned her head and saw that Fredrick was standing by their mother's bedchamber door. How had she been so distracted that she had failed to see what was right in front of her?

Coming to a stop in the corridor, Octavia turned to face Lord Kendal. "Before we go in, you must understand that my mother is not in her right mind. Furthermore, she is weak and gets tired very easily."

Lord Kendal's eyes held compassion. "You need not worry about me. Just remember that we need to act the part of devoted newlyweds," he said. "We must look at one another as if we are in love."

"That won't be a problem. I have perfected the art of flirt-ing." Octavia batted her eyes at him to emphasize her point.

In an amused voice, he said, "That was awful."

Fredrick interjected, "I must agree with Harred. If you do that again, Mother will surely see through your ruse."

"Then how am I supposed to look at you?" she asked, looking up at Lord Kendal.

Lord Kendal stared down into her eyes, holding her there like he could just with his gaze, mesmerizing her. A slow smile transformed his face and she found that he was keeping her captive, under his spell.

As she held his gaze, she felt the barriers that she had so carefully crafted around her heart begin to crumble. She wanted to look away- she *needed* to look away- but she found herself unwilling to do so. No one had ever looked at her how Lord Kendal was now. It made her feel special, as if she could do anything with him by her side.

"That is how you look at someone if you want them to believe you have fallen for them," Lord Kendal said in a hoarse tone.

Octavia felt a stab of disappointment at his words. Which was an odd reaction, she thought. She knew that Lord Kendal held no real attachment to her. But he had been so convinc-ing. For the briefest moment, she thought he might care for her.

Lord Kendal shifted his gaze towards Fredrick and she immediately missed the loss of contact. What was wrong with her? She was acting like a love-craved debutante.

"I think we are ready," Lord Kendal said.

Fredrick nodded his understanding and knocked on the door. It was promptly opened by her mother's lady's maid.

"Do come in," Nancy encouraged, opening the door wide. "Your mother has been expecting you. All of you."

Octavia noticed that Fredrick was standing back and she asked, "Aren't you coming?"

"I think it will be best if I remain in the corridor," Fredrick replied. "We do not wish to overwhelm Mother."

She wasn't quite sure what to think about that, but she didn't have time to dwell on it. After she stepped into her mother's bedchamber, she was aware that Lord Kendal had followed her in and was standing rather close to her. So close, in fact, that she could smell his shaving soap.

Her mother looked pale and so very thin as she rested in the middle of her expansive mattress. She moved to sit up but the effort appeared to be too great for her.

"Mother, do not tax yourself," Octavia ordered as she rushed over to the bed.

Her mother placed her head back down onto her pillow. "I am so glad that you came, and that you brought your husband," she said in a weak voice.

Lord Kendal moved to stand next to her by the bed. "Lady Cuttyngham," he greeted with a slight bow. "My name is Harred and it is a pleasure to meet you."

"I am sorry it has to be under these circumstances," her mother said. "I'm afraid today is not a good day for me. I feel tired, so tired."

"Would you like us to come back?" Octavia asked.

Her mother held her hand out. "Not at all," she replied. "Sit with me for a moment and tell me about your wedding. Was it grand?"

Lord Kendal repositioned two chairs by the side of the bed and indicated that Octavia should sit down.

Octavia sat on the proffered chair and reached for her mother's hand. She could hear in her mother's voice how eager she was to know the details about a wedding that never happened. What could she say that would appease her mother, but didn't reveal too much?

"The wedding was beautiful, but we missed you dearly," she attempted.

Her mother turned her attention towards Lord Kendal. "Was my Octavia a lovely bride?"

Lord Kendal bobbed his head. "Octavia was the most beautiful of brides," he replied.

The gentle way he said her name caused her heart to stir. It sounded so natural, so perfect, as if they always called each other by their given names.

"That makes me so happy to hear," her mother said. "Did you have a portrait made for the occasion?"

"Not yet, but we will soon," Octavia responded.

Her mother glanced between them with a line along her brow. "Why are you not on your wedding tour?" she asked. "Scotland is beautiful this time of year. Or so I have been told."

"That is where you and Father went on your wedding tour," Octavia reminded her. "You stayed at our family's hunting lodge in Dumfries. In fact, Roswell is staying there now with his new wife, Anette."

A smile came to her mother's lips. "I just adore Anette. Does she still climb trees with Roswell?"

"I do believe that she outgrew that," Octavia said.

Her mother closed her eyes for a moment before she addressed Lord Kendal. "Do you know Roswell?"

"I do, and he is a fine man," Lord Kendal said.

A reflective look came into her mother's eyes. "He fought in the war, you know."

"No, Mother, that is Fredrick," Octavia corrected gently. "He just returned from the Continent in time for Roswell's wedding."

"Roswell is married?" her mother asked, her voice rising in disbelief. "Who did he marry?"

"Anette Bolingbroke," Octavia replied.

"Ah, yes, I do adore Anette," her mother said. "She used to climb trees with Roswell. I could never get them to come inside. I wonder if she still climbs trees. Will you ask her?"

Octavia felt tears well up at the back of her eyes and she tried to will them away. Crying in front of her mother would do no good.

Lord Kendal stepped forward and placed a comforting hand on her shoulder, giving her the strength to continue on.

"You have a lovely bedchamber, my lady," Lord Kendal remarked.

Her mother's eyes roamed over the room. "It is far too dark in here, but the doctor believes that is for the best."

"I would be happy to open the drapes for you," Lord Kendal said.

"Would you?" her mother asked.

Lord Kendal removed his hand from Octavia's shoulder and walked over to the window. He opened the drapes and the light flooded into the room. "That is much better," he acknowledged.

Her mother's face softened. "I always did prefer the light."

A knock came at the door before it was opened, revealing Doctor Wallis. He gave a barely discernible frown at the window before he addressed her mother. "Lady Cuttyngham," he greeted. "How are you feeling?"

"I am well," her mother responded. "Have you met my daughter, Lady Octavia, and her husband…" Her voice trailed off. "Dear heavens, I forgot his name. How embarrassing."

"Not in the least," Lord Kendal said. "My name is Harred, and I will gladly repeat it as many times as you require."

Doctor Wallis's gaze swiftly shifted towards Octavia, and the confusion in his eyes was unmistakable. She cast him a pleading look, silently hoping he wouldn't expose the ruse they had concocted.

After a brief moment, Doctor Wallis tipped his head at Lord Kendal. "It is a pleasure to meet you." He smiled at Octavia. "My lady."

Octavia released the breath she had been holding, feeling reassured that the doctor was indeed willing to play along.

Her mother glanced at the satchel that was over the doctor's shoulder. "Are you here to apply the leeches?"

"I am," the doctor confirmed.

Turning her attention towards Octavia, her mother asked, "Will you visit me tomorrow?" She glanced up at Lord Kendal. "Both of you?"

Lord Kendal smiled down upon her. "We would be happy to." He held his hand out to Octavia. "Shall we, my dear?"

Octavia slipped her hand into Lord Kendal's and allowed him to assist her in rising. "Thank you," she murmured.

He took her hand and tucked it into the crook of his arm. It was so effortless that it just felt natural to be so close to him.

They didn't speak until they arrived in the corridor and saw that it was empty. Where had Fredrick gone to, she wondered.

Lord Kendal dropped his arm and took a step back, creating more than enough distance between them to be proper. "I say that went rather well," he said.

"That it did," she agreed. "I should warn you that my mother might ask the same questions tomorrow as she did today."

"That won't be an issue."

Hoping her words properly conveyed her gratitude, she said, "Thank you for what you did in there. You made my mother very happy, even if it was just for a moment."

Lord Kendal's eyes crinkled around the edges. "Then I accomplished what I set out to do."

Fredrick's voice came from down the corridor. "That didn't take too long," he acknowledged.

Octavia tore her gaze away from Lord Kendal as she revealed, "Doctor Wallis arrived."

"Ah, no doubt to apply the dreaded bloodsuckers."

Fredrick shuddered. "Those are terrible little creatures that are a form of torture."

Lord Kendal shifted in his stance and said, "If you will excuse me, I must be going. I have work that I must see to."

She was about to offer to walk him to the main door, but Fredrick spoke first. "I shall see you to the door," he said, indicating that Lord Kendal should go first.

With a glance at Octavia, Lord Kendal stated, "I shall return tomorrow so we can visit your mother once more."

"Thank you," she murmured.

As she watched Lord Kendal walk down the corridor with her brother, she knew in her heart that very few gentlemen would have done what he did. And what he did, playing the part of a devoted husband to her, meant everything to her.

Chapter Seven

The morning hour was late as Harred sat at his desk in the study. He was reviewing the ledger that his man of business had given him.

He leaned forward in his seat and rubbed his eyes. He had been at this for far too long and hadn't gotten much done. Perhaps he should take a break and eat breakfast. It might do him some good because his thoughts were constantly straying to Lady Octavia. Which was becoming a problem. He had no intention of pursuing her so why was he biding his time until he could call upon her again?

No good would come out of dwelling on Lady Octavia. She was his friend's sister and he had no intention of taking a wife, especially at this time. He barely had any time to himself and his brother was causing havoc wherever he went. Why would he wish to bring a wife into this house of madness?

Yet just the thought of her made him smile.

Botheration.

He needed to banish her from his thoughts and be done with it.

The sound of the main door slamming drew his attention and it was promptly followed by William shouting, "Harred!"

"What now?" he muttered to himself. This was a question that he found himself asking far too often.

He rose and came around the desk. His brother had disappeared after he'd confronted him in Hyde Park and failed to return home last night. Not that it mattered much to him, assuming he hadn't blown through more of his money.

Harred stepped into the entry hall and saw a short, petite brown-haired young woman standing next to William. Her eyes were downcast, but he could tell that the poor thing was nervous by the way she was fidgeting with her hands.

"Who is this?" Harred demanded.

William went and slipped his arm around the young woman's waist. "This is Ruth," he revealed. "She is my wife."

Harred was stunned. Nothing could have surprised him more than what William had just announced. As he stared at his brother in disbelief, he asked, "Surely you can't be serious?"

"I am," William said with a smug smile. "We were married by special license yesterday and we intend to stay here only long enough until we can find our own place. A bigger place than this one."

"William…" His words stilled. He didn't want to have this conversation in front of Ruth. "Can I speak to you privately?"

His brother scowled as he dropped his arm. "It won't change anything. What's done is done and you need to accept the fact that I have a wife now."

Knowing he was being rude to Ruth, Harred went to acknowledge her. "Forgive my brother for his lack of manners. My name is Harred." He bowed.

Ruth's voice was barely above a whisper. "I know who you are, my lord." She went to drop into a curtsy but William stopped her. "You don't need to curtsy to Harred. He is family now."

"Yes, of course," Ruth murmured.

William turned his head towards the butler and ordered, "Take my wife's things up to one of the empty bedchambers and find a maid to tend to her until we can find a proper lady's maid."

Mitchell stepped forward. "I shall see to it, my lord."

Placing his hand on Ruth's sleeve, William asked, "Are you hungry?"

"I am a little famished," Ruth admitted.

"Then a tray shall be sent to your bedchamber and you can eat in there," William said. "I will join you once I am done speaking with Harred."

Ruth offered him a weak smile. "Thank you," she acknowledged.

William turned his gaze towards Harred, and the usual look of contempt was in his eyes. "I suppose we must get this over with."

Not bothering to justify his words with a response, Harred headed towards his study. He stopped at the door and waited for his brother to enter before closing the door.

William dropped down onto the settee. "Isn't Ruth wonderful?"

"I wouldn't know," Harred replied. "I don't know anything about her."

"She is rich," his brother stated. "Far richer than you, I must say. Her father is Sir Percy Hall."

Harred lifted his brow. "The Merchant King."

William chuckled. "Yes, that is what people call him and Ruth is his only daughter. Her dowry was forty thousand pounds. When Sir Percy first approached me about this union, I figured he was using his money to secure his daughter a title and I didn't even give it any heed. But then it hit me. Why shouldn't I marry Ruth and live the life I was supposed to?"

Harred knew what the answer was, but he asked it anyways. "Do you even care for Ruth?"

William shrugged. "I will grow to care for her," he said. "She is a timid little thing, but I do believe with time that she will open up."

Harred ran a hand through his hair, wondering how William was so calm about this. "Did she even want to marry you?"

With a blank stare, William replied, "I don't know. I didn't ask her."

"You didn't ask her?" he repeated back. What was wrong with his brother? Was he so self-absorbed that he didn't even seek out Ruth's thoughts before the wedding?

"It wasn't like I forced her to marry me," William defended. "Her father procured the special license and she stood up with me at the chapel. She could have said no if she didn't want to go through with it."

Harred couldn't believe the audacity of his brother. He had done some stupid things over the years, but this was the worst one yet. He'd married a young woman- that he didn't know- just to have access to her dowry.

William abruptly rose and walked over to the drink cart. "You don't have a right to judge me. Did you forget that you stabbed me in the back yesterday?"

"I hardly stabbed you in the back," he replied. "I just took Lady Octavia on a carriage ride through Hyde Park."

"You knew I was interested in her, but you pursued her anyways." William picked up the decanter and poured himself a drink. "I think you are jealous of me."

Harred looked heavenward. Not this again. "Why, pray tell, would you think that?"

"I am rich and I didn't have to do a single thing to earn the money," William said as he retrieved the glass. "Whereas you have to work your fingers to the bone to ensure your estate is profitable."

"I am not jealous of you, but I do feel bad for Ruth. Does she know you just married her for her dowry?"

William scoffed. "Of course she knows!" he shouted. "Why else would I marry the daughter of a merchant? Someone who is so clearly below us."

Harred couldn't quite believe William had said something so high-handed. "Need I remind you that is your wife you are talking about?"

"Don't try to take the moral high road, Brother," William mocked. "We both know that Father would be rolling over in his grave with my choice of bride, but this was *my* choice. Not yours. Not his. Mine. And you have no right to say otherwise."

"Have you considered that the *ton* might not be so eager to accept her into their ranks?" Harred asked.

"Then we won't attend their stupid balls and soirees. It doesn't matter much to me anyways." William tossed back his drink and slammed the glass onto the tray. "Is this interrogation over or may I go see to my wife?"

"This is hardly an interrogation, but I am worried about you," Harred said. "You can hardly take care of yourself. How are you going to take care of a wife?"

"How dare you stand there and lecture me when you don't even have a wife!" William exclaimed. "At least one of us is doing our duty."

"You cannot be serious?" Harred asked. "My entire life is about doing my duty while I watch you do whatever the blazes you want to do."

William looked unaffected by his words. "Do you want me to apologize for being born after you? I am just the spare, the afterthought. You are the heir and inherited all that Father had. I was just given a paltry sum for my inheritance."

"It was more than generous and you could have lived on it for the remainder of your days had you been somewhat frugal. But you chose to spend it all on gambling and your mistresses," Harred contended.

"What else was I supposed to do with my life?" William asked. "I had no desire to be a vicar, barrister, or any of the other acceptable professions for a second son of a marquess. I had no real options afforded to me."

"I offered you a job—"

Wiliam huffed. "That was an insulting offer and you know it. You think you know what is best for me, but you don't. I am my own man."

Harred was at a loss for words. His brother had done something that would forever alter the course of his life. He couldn't undo what he had done, no matter if he came to regret it later. Which he would. His brother had always been impulsive.

"Don't look at me like that," William growled. "I know you think I made a mistake but I knew what I was doing the whole time."

"You married a young woman that you hardly know. You don't know her likes, or dislikes. How do you even know you two will be happy together?"

William looked amused by his question. "You are over-thinking this. Ruth is my wife. That doesn't mean we need to live happily ever after. We just have to have mutual toleration for one another."

"Is that all that you want?"

The humor left William's expression as he replied, "Talk to me after you take a wife. Besides, I never had the luxury of marrying for love anyways."

"You are wrong," he contended. "Our parents would have wanted more for you than just a marriage of convenience."

William grew tense at the mention of their parents. "It doesn't matter what they want anymore because they are dead. But I am still here and I made my choice. Accept it or don't. I truly don't care."

Before Harred could say his next words, William walked over to the door while he said, "If my wife asks for me, I will be at White's."

"I thought you were joining her for breakfast in her bedchamber?" he asked. Surely his brother wouldn't be so callous as to leave his wife alone after she only just arrived at the townhouse?

William opened the door and declared, "I am in no mood to entertain my wife right now. I need to get drunk and forget this blasted conversation ever happened."

After William departed from the study, Harred sat back in his seat and stared up at the ceiling. What in the blazes was he going to do with his brother? William had done something intolerably stupid and he had no intention of doing right by his wife.

Poor Ruth. Did she know what she had gotten herself into by marrying William? She may have married into this world, but that didn't mean she would be accepted by the *ton*- or her own husband.

As if his thoughts had conjured up Ruth, she stepped into the room and in a hesitant voice asked, "Do you know where Lord William is?"

Harred rose and he dreaded saying his next words. "He went to White's for a drink." Or two. Most likely, he would be gone for hours, but he didn't want to reveal too much.

"Oh," Ruth murmured as her eyes darted towards the drink cart. No doubt she was wondering why William couldn't have had a drink at his own home, but that was something Harred couldn't answer. "I shall wait for him in my bedchamber then."

Opening his arms wide, he encouraged, "This is your home for now. You are welcome to explore it. Perhaps you may find some solace in our library."

Ruth clasped her hands in front of her. "Thank you, my lord. I do enjoy reading."

"It is Harred," he corrected lightly. "We are family now and we don't make use of titles."

She gave him the same weak smile as she had before. "I do not wish to take up too much of your time. Thank you."

Harred watched as she ducked her head and practically fled from the study. Ruth seemed so unsure of herself, and he wished there was something that he could do for her. But that was not his place.

The long clock chimed, alerting him to the time. He had waited long enough. It was time to go call on Lady Octavia. And, quite frankly, he needed a reprieve.

Octavia watched safely from the window as Freddy strutted around in the gardens as he tried to impress the female peacocks that were giving him little heed. Poor Freddy, she thought. There were some days that she felt just like he did. She wanted to be noticed, but everyone was busy with their own lives.

She turned her attention back to her mother and watched her sleep. How she wished that this wasn't her life. How was it fair that her mother was dying when she was so young? If only she had the power to return her mother's health and her zest for life.

Her mother may have raised her with an intense desire for her to be a proper lady, but she always taught with love. And Octavia felt her love. She never had to seek it out because her mother gave it freely.

A knock came at the door.

Octavia rose from her chair and walked over to the door. She opened it up and saw Lord Kendal on the other side of the threshold.

He smiled. "Good morning," he greeted. "I hope I did not come too early to visit with your mother."

Just seeing his smile seemed to brighten her mood. "I'm

afraid she is asleep but she should be awake shortly." She opened the door wide. "Do come in."

He murmured his thanks and stepped into the bedchamber. His eyes strayed towards her mother and she could see the compassion in the depths of them. It was evident that he wasn't just pretending to care and that made her much more grateful to have him as a friend.

Friend? Is that what he was to her? She hoped so. She would consider herself lucky to have a friend such as him.

Octavia returned to her seat and shared, "My father went down to breakfast and I offered to sit with my mother. I didn't want her to be alone when she awoke."

"That was kind of you," he acknowledged.

"It was far better than practicing my needlework in the drawing room."

Lord Kendal positioned a chair next to hers and sat down. "I thought you were going to knit me a reticule so I could carry biscuits around."

Octavia laughed. "Could you imagine the attention you would garner if you started wearing a reticule around your wrist?"

"I care little about that, just as long as I have biscuits with me," he joked.

The sound of Freddy wailing in the gardens drifted into the bedchamber and she glanced out the window. "Freddy is not having any luck with the females today," she revealed. "He has been rattling his feathers all morning."

"I never thought I would hear you sympathize with Freddy, considering he chases you whenever you step foot into the gardens."

Octavia eyed him curiously. "Do you ever feel that despite your best efforts you are still overlooked?"

Her words seemed to have a somber effect on Lord Kendal. "Every day," he admitted. "My father was progressive and fought for his position in the House of Lords. But I feel like all my efforts aren't enough. No one gives me any heed and I am striving hard for my one bill to make it to the floor."

"That must be frustrating. I'm sorry."

"I just need to keep my head down and work hard, hoping one day that I can make a difference in people's lives."

Octavia placed a hand on his sleeve. "You have made a difference in my mother's life by being here. Do not discount what you have done."

Lord Kendal glanced down at her hand, and she quickly removed it. How brazen of her to touch him in such a familiar fashion.

"I just feel as if I am chasing after my father's legacy and I am failing," Lord Kendal admitted. "I am always failing at something."

Octavia could hear the anguish in Lord Kendal's voice and she knew he felt his words deeply. She didn't want him to feel as if she minimized his concerns, but rather that he was heard, and understood.

"Cast your father's legacy aside and focus on your own," she encouraged. "Everyone has their own path, and no one's is the same."

"You make it sound so simple," Lord Kendal said. "But my father did great things and I can't sit back and hang on his coattails."

"Then don't. But don't judge your success by your father's accomplishments. That isn't fair to you."

Lord Kendal shifted his gaze towards her mother. "I wish I could turn off the thoughts in my head that tell me I am going to fail. They are relentless."

"I have similar thoughts," Octavia admitted. "I worry that I will let my family down and that I will be a drain on their finances for the remainder of my days."

"How do you cope with those?"

Octavia shifted in her seat to face him. "I challenge the thoughts and realign my understanding of what failure truly is," she said. "If I let my family down, they will still love me. I just need to do the best that I can and hope it is enough."

Lord Kendal considered her words before saying, "I don't know how you do it."

"Do what?" she asked.

"Your words always seem to resonate with me, deeper than anyone else's, and I find myself wanting to be a better man because of you," he replied.

Octavia's lips twitched. "I am glad that someone is finally listening to me. It is exhausting being right all the time."

With mirth in his eyes, Harred said, "What a terrible burden you carry around with you."

"It is," Octavia teased. "Dare I ask how your brother is faring?"

That was apparently the wrong thing to say because Lord Kendal let out a groan. "William decided to go get himself married."

"Married?" Octavia repeated in surprise. "To whom?"

"Sir Percy Hall's daughter, Ruth," he replied. "William married her only for her dowry and abandoned her at the townhouse while he went to White's."

"Poor Lady William," Octavia murmured.

Lord Kendal leaned forward in his seat. "I'm afraid I can't do anything to help William. He has made his bed and now he must lie in it."

Octavia could see the frustration in Lord Kendal's expression and she hoped that he wouldn't be offended by her next words. "Let him fail," she replied.

"But I promised my father that I would see after William."

"Yes, but you have done everything for your brother, and it is time that he goes it alone," Octavia said.

Lord Kendal winced. "He will fail, and what then?"

"You pick him back up, and he tries again," Octavia replied. "Have you not considered that your brother is the way he is because you have always tried to save him?"

He grew silent and she feared that she had spoken too plainly.

As she went to apologize, her mother's eyes opened and she turned towards them. "Hello, Octavia," she greeted. "Is this your husband?"

Octavia's heart dropped. Her mother's memory seemed to be slipping more with each passing day. "It is," she said.

Lord Kendal rose from his seat and bowed. "My name is Harred, my lady," he greeted. "It is a pleasure to be meeting you."

"Are you in the Army?" she asked him.

"I am not," Lord Kendal replied.

Her mother smiled. "My Fredrick is in the Army but he hasn't returned home yet. He is fighting those dastardly Frenchmen."

Octavia interjected, "Fredrick has returned home, Mother. Would you care to see him?"

"What joyous news," her mother replied. "I shall send Edith to bring him to me."

"Edith was your mother's lady's maid. Nancy is your lady's maid," Octavia explained.

Her mother pursed her lips. "That doesn't sound right to me." She slipped her hand under the covers and retrieved a piece of dry sweetmeat. "Would anyone care for a treat?"

"No, thank you," Lord Kendal replied.

After her mother plopped the treat into her mouth, the door opened and her father stepped into the room. He tipped his head at Lord Kendal. "It is good to see you, Harred."

"My lord," Lord Kendal responded.

Her father approached the bed and said, "You two may go. I will sit with Fanny until I depart for the House of Lords."

Octavia smiled at her mother before saying, "I shall return then, and perhaps we can read another book together."

"I would like that," her mother responded.

Lord Kendal held his hand out to her. "Allow me, Octavia," he said.

She slipped her hand into his and he assisted her in rising. "Thank you, Harred." She had never called a gentleman by his given name before, but it just felt right in this case.

They didn't speak as he led her out of the bedchamber and into the corridor. Once her mother's door was closed behind them, Lord Kendal dropped his arm.

"Your poor mother," he murmured. "I can't imagine how difficult it is for you to see her like that. How do you do it?"

"How do I do what?" she asked, unsure of what he was asking.

He took a step closer to her. "How do you repeat the same thing over and over again but do it in a way that it seems like it is the first time you've said it?"

She sighed. "It has taken a lot of practice, but I do not want to do anything that would frustrate my mother. I know she is trying her best."

"You are an impressive young woman," he said. "I hope you know that."

"I daresay that you are being far too complimentary because I am doing what any good daughter would do," she responded.

Lord Kendal held her gaze before asking, "Will you sit next to me during the musical performance this evening at Lady Sarah Crowley's soiree?"

She could feel her heart take flight at his words. He wanted to spend more time with her, and she felt giddy at the prospect. In a calm, collected voice, she replied, "I would be honored to."

"Wonderful," he replied. "I shall see you there tonight, say eight o'clock."

Octavia didn't know why she couldn't look away but she found she didn't want to. It was as if he had a hold on her and she wondered what he saw in her gaze. Could he see more than anyone else saw? Perhaps he saw things that she couldn't even see herself.

Lord Kendal's voice was low as he said, "If you are not opposed, I would prefer if you continued to call me Harred in private."

"Then it is only fair that you call me by my given name."

"I would like that very much," Lord Kendal responded.

Her brother's voice came from further down the corridor. "Harred," he said, loudly. Much louder than was necessary. "Thank you for visiting with our mother today."

Harred took a step back, creating more distance between them. "It was my pleasure."

"Well, we do not want to keep you from your other tasks," Fredrick said. "Do we, Octavia?"

With a shake of her head, she replied, "We do not."

"I shall take my leave, but I will see you both at Lady Sarah's soiree this evening," Harred said before he walked down the corridor.

Fredrick crossed his arms over his chest as he gave her an inquisitive look. "I thought we decided we weren't going to Lady Sarah's soiree."

"I changed my mind," Octavia shared.

"You are not one to change your mind, especially about soirees," he reasoned.

Octavia patted her brother's sleeve. "Do not use your 'spy skills' to analyze me. It is very unbecoming of you."

"That is not what I am doing. I am merely asking you a question, and it has not failed my notice that you are attempting to avoid answering it."

"That is not true. You asked a question and I answered it," Octavia said. "You are just not happy with my response."

"Because I feel as if you are keeping something from me."

Octavia decided it was best if she changed subjects and hoped he wouldn't press her on it. She glanced at the door and said, "Mother was asking about you."

Fredrick uncrossed his arms and dropped them to his sides. "Fine. Do not tell me the truth, but just know that I am onto you."

"Yes, Brother," she said as she brushed past him.

It was true that she hadn't planned on going to the soiree this evening, but Harred had disrupted her plans. And she found that she had no objections.

Chapter Eight

Harred didn't think that anyone could ruin his mood after spending time with Octavia earlier that day but he was wrong. William managed to do just that.

He sat across from his brother in the darkened coach and couldn't help but notice how William was glowering at him. It didn't affect him much. He was used to William's fits of temper when he didn't get his way.

William had no desire to attend the soiree this evening, but his wife had asked him if they could go. Rather than turn her down, William agreed to go but was intent on showing his discontent about it. It was rather childish of him, but Harred expected no less from his brother. William seemed to believe that life revolved around him, and everyone else was not nearly as important.

Harred hoped that his brother would at least attempt to play the part of a devoted husband. Surely he could do that for one evening, for his wife's sake?

The coach came to a stop in front of Lady Sarah's townhouse and it dipped to the side as the footman exited his perch. The door was promptly opened and Harred waited as

William and his wife exited the coach before he stepped onto the pavement.

William took Ruth's hand and placed it into the crook of his arm. Without saying a word, he escorted his wife to the front of the line, bypassing the other patrons that had been waiting patiently to go inside.

He wondered if his brother would ever change.

Harred took his place at the back of the line and slowly made his way inside. The entry hall exuded grandeur, with its opulent dark blue-papered walls and rich wood paneling. An intricately painted mural adorned the ceiling, and the polished marble floors added to the overall sense of magnificence of this townhouse.

It wasn't long before he arrived at the parlor and he saw chairs set up in front of the pianoforte. His eyes roamed the room but he saw no sign of Octavia. Drats. He had arrived too early. He could have spent more time at home, reviewing the accounts, instead of standing around in a crowded hall, waiting for her to arrive.

The room suddenly went quiet. Too quiet. He turned to see what had caused everyone to stop speaking and he saw William and Ruth walking further into the parlor.

To Ruth's credit, she held her head high and kept her face expressionless. She may have looked the part of a lady with her elegant blue gown and diamond-encrusted headpiece positioned in her stylish coiffure, but she had to know that it would take much more than her marrying William for her to ever be accepted into the *ton*'s good graces. And it didn't help that William's reputation was one of ill-repute.

William, on the other hand, didn't appear to be bothered at all by the *ton*'s reaction to them. He led Ruth over to a table and retrieved a flute of champagne for himself. He didn't even bother to offer one to his wife.

"What a gentleman," Harred muttered under his breath.

Several of the women had retrieved their fans and begun

speaking in hushed tones to their companions, all the while continuing to openly fix their gazes on William and his wife.

Harred didn't feel bad for William, but his heart lurched for Ruth. She didn't deserve such a poor reception. But what could he do? It wasn't as if he could demand the *ton* accept Ruth. Members of high Society looked down on people that were different than them, and Ruth was a daughter of a merchant. A rich merchant, but a merchant, nonetheless.

As he debated about what he should do, Octavia stepped into the parlor on her brother's arm. She was dressed in an alluring jonquil gown that hugged her figure perfectly and her hair was piled high atop her head. She looked radiant, but he had expected nothing different from her. But her beauty was not just skin deep; it penetrated deep into her soul.

Octavia's astute eyes scanned the room until they stopped on Ruth. She said something to her brother before they walked straight over to Ruth, causing a stir amongst the other guests. It was evident that they thought the daughter of a marquess shouldn't speak to someone so beneath her.

He couldn't hear what was being said, but he watched as Octavia spoke to Ruth as if they were well acquainted. And Ruth seemed to visibly relax as she spoke to Octavia. A smile even graced her lips a time or two.

Harred heard a few disapproving huffs from the people in the parlor but eventually they went about their own business.

Octavia dropped into a curtsy before she walked away. Ruth then turned towards William, but he appeared disinterested in whatever it was she had said to him.

With a shake of his head, Harred disapproved of his brother's behavior towards Ruth. His poor wife was trying, and he wasn't doing anything to help her. If anything, his aloofness to his new bride was causing more of a scandal.

But, once again, his brother only seemed to care about himself.

Regardless, he was not here to watch over his brother and

Ruth, but he came to spend time with Octavia. He watched as Fredrick led his sister to the back of the parlor and they came to a stop next to a pillar.

It only took Harred a moment before he found himself walking towards Octavia. Frankly, he cared little about this soiree. He had used it as an excuse to be able to spend more time with Octavia.

As he approached her, he looked for any sign that she was pleased to see him, but she gave nothing away. Which was odd. She usually was very expressive with her emotions.

He stopped a short distance away and bowed. "Lady Octavia," he greeted.

Octavia dropped into a curtsy. "My lord," she greeted.

Harred wished that they could forego the formalities but he couldn't risk being too familiar with Octavia. The *ton* would start speculating what that meant and he didn't want to open her up to any gossip.

After he acknowledged Fredrick, Harred turned his attention back to Octavia. "Thank you for what you did for Ruth."

Her face softened. "I felt bad for Lady William and I knew I needed to do something for her. Besides, she seems sweet."

"Quite frankly, I don't know her well enough to make a determination but I can contest that she doesn't deserve the *ton*'s ill-treatment of her."

"No, she does not," Octavia readily agreed.

Fredrick spoke up. "I never thought I would see the day that your brother got married."

"I'm afraid he did it for all the wrong reasons," Harred shared. "William just wanted to be rich and not have to work for it."

With a shake of his head, Fredrick remarked, "That is awful. When will your brother understand that nothing is worth having in this life if you don't have to work hard for it?"

"I'm afraid he missed that lesson when he regularly skipped his classes at university," Harred joked.

"What a shame," Octavia said. "I wish I had the opportunity to go to university. That is something that I would have never taken for granted."

Fredrick looked put out. "A woman at university? Could you imagine?" he teased.

"Do be serious, Brother," Octavia argued. "Why can't women be educated? What is everyone so afraid of?"

"A woman's place is within the home," Fredrick said. "Do not underestimate your importance there."

Octavia blew out a puff of air. "But I can do more than just run a household."

Fredrick placed a hand on his sister's sleeve. "I know that to be true, but change does not happen overnight. Be patient."

"I do not like being patient," Octavia admitted. "It is not one of my strengths."

"Say it isn't so," Fredrick joked as he removed his hand.

Octavia laughed, and the sound was like music to Harred's ears. But he wanted to be the one to make her laugh.

Harred spoke up, drawing back Octavia's attention. "I think it is noble that you want more from your life than what is expected of you."

She looked at him with approval in her eyes. "Thank you, my lord," she said. "That is kind of you to say."

A loud, booming voice announced that the musical performance was about to begin.

Harred offered his arm and asked, "Shall we take our seats, my lady?"

Octavia accepted his arm and he led her towards the chairs. Once they were both situated, Harred leaned in and asked, "Do you play the pianoforte?"

"Every respectable young woman can play the pianoforte," came her reply.

"Dare I hope that you will play a piece for me one of these days?"

Her lips quirked upwards. "I would like that, but do not

expect too much. I said that I can play the pianoforte. I never said that I excelled in it."

"I will gladly take you as you are," Harred said as he returned her smile.

Her eyes dropped to his lips for a moment before her smile dimmed. "You are far too complimentary of me. You should see some of my paintings. They are awful."

"I am sure they can't be that bad," Harred attempted.

"No, they truly are," Octavia said. "I am not talented like my friend, Lady Lizette Westcott. Her paintings are exquisite."

"But they aren't yours." Harred paused before saying, "I know I am bold in my speech, but I would greatly appreciate one of your paintings to hang on my walls."

Octavia shook her head. "I do not find you bold, but I could never do such a thing to you. No doubt you have fine works of art in your home, and my paintings would pale in comparison to them."

"I disagree. Art is an expression of our inner thoughts, feelings and experiences, making every one of your paintings special," Harred said.

"I see that you are not easily convinced that my paintings are nothing special. Perhaps you should come to call and see them yourself."

Harred nodded. "I shall come tomorrow, assuming that is acceptable to you."

"I have no objections, but I would not get your hopes up," Octavia said.

Fredrick sat down next to his sister. "I do apologize for my delay. I had to speak to someone for a moment."

"Is everything all right?" Octavia asked.

"Yes," Fredrick replied firmly.

Octavia looked as if she had more to say on the subject, but she didn't press her brother. Instead, she said, "Lord Kendal has asked for one of my paintings."

Fredrick gave him an amused look. "You are in for a treat, but I should warn you that my sister is no Michelangelo."

She swatted at her brother's sleeve. "You are one to talk. I have seen your paintings, as well."

"I never claimed to be talented at painting," Fredrick said. "It is the one thing I am not good at."

"One thing?" Octavia repeated. "I can think of many things you are not good at."

The room went silent as a young lady approached the pianoforte. As she began to play, the music filled the air and Harred found himself relaxing against his seat.

He noticed that Octavia had opened her reticule and retrieved a biscuit. She extended it towards him. "Biscuit?" she whispered.

"Thank you," he replied as he accepted it.

Fredrick gave his sister a disapproving look. "Why did you bring biscuits to the soiree?" he asked. "There is a refreshment table in the corner."

"But I wanted a biscuit," Octavia replied before retrieving another one and taking a bite of it.

Harred resisted the urge to laugh. He didn't know why he found Octavia's antics to be so amusing. He just did.

Octavia held up two paintings for her mother's inspection. "Which one do you like best?" she asked.

Her mother, who was sitting up in her bed, replied, "They are both nice, dear."

"But which one is better?" she pressed.

A smile came to her mother's lips. "May I ask why it matters so much to you?"

Lowering the paintings, Octavia explained, "Harred has

requested one of my paintings and I want to ensure that I give him my best piece."

"I am sure that Harred will love whichever painting you decide to give to him," her mother remarked.

Octavia blew out a puff of air. Her mother was being of no use to her. "This is your fault, you know," she joked. "You should have insisted I spend more time on painting so I was proficient at it."

With a laugh, her mother responded, "You were far more interested in jumping hedges on your horses than painting."

A thought came to her. "Perhaps I will purchase a painting from Lady Lizette."

"But won't Harred be disappointed since it won't be from you?" her mother asked.

Octavia sat down and rested the paintings against the edges of the chair. "Maybe I am just overthinking this."

"I believe you are. Your husband will cherish any painting you give him," her mother reasoned.

She reached down and picked up one of the paintings. "I will give him this one since it is a painting of our country estate."

"That one is lovely."

Octavia shook her head. "I daresay you are far too complimentary of me."

"That is a job of any good mother." Her mother closed her eyes for a moment before asking, "Will you help me write a letter to Fredrick this afternoon? I do worry about him being on the Continent."

In a gentle voice, Octavia reminded her mother, "Fredrick is home from the war so there is no need to write him a letter."

Her mother's eyes grew wide. "When did he return?"

"He arrived a short time ago," Octavia replied.

"And he didn't think to visit?" her mother asked, her voice rising.

Octavia placed the painting down and leaned forward in her seat. "Fredrick has visited you many times. Daily, in fact," she said.

Her mother raised a hand to her forehead. "Why can't I remember that?"

"It is all right," Octavia encouraged. "If it helps, I will ensure Fredrick visits you today. I know he always looks forward to it."

"I would like that very much," her mother responded.

A knock came at the door before it was opened by her mother's lady's maid. "Good morning," Nancy greeted, holding a tray in her hands. "I have come with your breakfast."

"You can take that right back down to the kitchen," her mother stated. "I have no desire to eat such a bland offering."

Nancy didn't look upset by her mistress's refusal. "Why don't you look at what the cook has prepared for you before you turn it away?" she asked as she placed the tray on the bed.

Her mother stuck up her nose at the food. "I would prefer to eat pudding."

"For breakfast?" Nancy asked. "You know the doctor would never allow that. He suggested you eat some toast and eggs."

"I am quite sure that I do not like eggs," her mother responded.

Nancy picked up the teacup from the tray. "Perhaps you would care for a cup of tea," she suggested, extending it towards her.

Her mother made no effort to take the teacup as she complained, "I would prefer chocolate."

As she returned the teacup to the tray, Nancy said, "You need to eat, my lady. You are already too thin."

"Then find me food that I will eat," her mother promptly said.

Octavia felt some sympathy for her mother. Why couldn't

she eat whatever she wanted? Hadn't she deserved that right? But the doctor believed a bland diet would help her memory. She wasn't convinced of that.

Nancy picked up the tray and moved it to the table next to the bed. "I will speak to the doctor and see what we can do."

Her mother reached under her covers and retrieved a piece of dry sweetmeat. When her lady's maid wasn't looking, she plopped it into her mouth and winked at Octavia.

Octavia resisted the urge to giggle. Her mother loved her treats and she was glad that she was eating something.

The door opened and her father stepped into the room. He glanced at the untouched plate of food with disapproval before shifting his gaze to his wife. "Fanny, you need to eat to keep your strength up," he said.

"Then tell the cook to make me pudding," her mother retorted. "I will eat pudding all day, every day."

"You could get sick if you ate so much pudding," her father mused.

Her mother tilted her chin. "I used to eat pudding for breakfast, but no one seems to believe me."

With a sigh, her father said, "You never ate pudding for breakfast. In fact, you would eat one egg, one piece of buttered toast and a cup of tea. It was always the same."

"That doesn't sound right," her mother responded.

Her father turned his attention towards Octavia. "Lord Kendal is waiting for you in the drawing room," he shared.

At the mention of Harred's name, she felt herself smile. "I shouldn't keep him waiting," she said, rising.

"Do bring Harred by for a visit soon," her mother remarked. "It has been far too long since I have seen him."

"You saw him yesterday, Mother." Octavia picked up one of the paintings and held it up for her father's inspection. "What do you think of this painting?"

He shrugged. "It is nice, I suppose."

Octavia stepped closer to her father and kissed him on the

cheek. "Thank you," she said. "I know I can always trust you for an honest response."

After she departed from her mother's bedchamber, Octavia could feel the doubts bubbling up inside of her. Did she dare give Harred a painting of hers? What if he didn't really want one but was only being polite?

She descended the stairs and headed into the drawing room. Harred was staring out the window with his hands clasped behind his back, and it gave her a moment to silently observe him. Why did he affect her so much? Her heart always seemed to beat faster when she saw him.

"Harred," she greeted.

He turned and a slow smile spread across his face. "Octavia," he responded. "I do hope I did not call too early."

"You did not."

His eyes dropped to the painting in her hand. "Dare I hope that painting is for me?"

"It is, but I do not want you to get your hopes up. I am no great talent," she replied.

Harred walked closer to her but stopped a short distance away. "May I see it?"

She took a deep breath before she held up the painting for his inspection. As his eyes studied it, she rushed out, "I hope you aren't too disappointed—"

"I love it," he said, speaking over her. "I do believe you are selling yourself short, my lady. The painting is exquisite."

Now she knew he was just trying to flatter her. No one had ever said her paintings were "exquisite." But as she started to contradict him, he spoke first.

"I shall place this in my study," he said as he accepted the painting. "That way I can look at it whenever I want."

Octavia thought it was best if she told him what she had painted. "This is my country home- Alwick Hall- and the surrounding gardens."

"You have a beautiful country home," Harred said. "It looks peaceful."

"It is," she readily agreed. "It was the most idyllic place to be raised when not in London. There were plenty of places to explore and I spent most of my time in the woodlands, which are depicted in the far left corner."

Harred brought his gaze up to meet hers. "Thank you," he said in a gentle voice. "I shall treasure this always."

Octavia could hear the sincerity in his voice and she was touched. Why was it that he seemed to break through her senses, allowing her to be vulnerable around him? Frankly, she hated being vulnerable around anyone. So why was Harred different?

Fredrick's voice came from the doorway. "Harred," he said in a booming voice that echoed more loudly than the small room required. "What a pleasant surprise. What brings you by at this early hour?"

Harred broke her gaze and turned towards Fredrick. "I have come to see if Lady Octavia would care to go on a carriage ride with me."

Octavia went to respond but Fredrick interjected, "That sounds rather enjoyable. I do believe I will join you."

"Wonderful," Harred said, albeit his words tight. "That is assuming Octavia doesn't have any objections."

Fredrick leaned his shoulder against the wall and asked, "Do you have any objections, Octavia?"

She had many objections, but she didn't dare admit that to her brother- or anyone else for that matter. "I have none," she said.

Harred placed the painting down onto a table. "I will retrieve this after our ride. I don't want it damaged."

With a curious glance at the painting, Fredrick asked, "Isn't that one of Octavia's paintings?"

"It is," Harred confirmed. "She was gracious enough to give it to me."

Fredrick arched an eyebrow at her, but he didn't say anything. For which she was most grateful. She didn't want to explain why she'd agreed to give Harred a painting, partly because she didn't know why she had in the first place.

Harred stepped forward and offered his arm. "Shall we, my lady?"

Octavia placed her hand on his and allowed him to lead her out of the townhouse and onto the pavement. After they were both situated on the phaeton, Fredrick sat down next to her, forcing her to sit in the middle of them.

She didn't dare complain about how cramped she was, but surely everyone was uncomfortable, as well. Why had Fredrick insisted on coming on this outing? A phaeton was designed for two riders, not three.

Harred reached for the reins and urged the team forward. As they merged into the street, the left back wheel hit a rut, causing it to fall off. The phaeton tipped to the side as the rear left axle dragged on the ground and Octavia felt herself being ejected from the vehicle.

Chapter Nine

Harred was thrown from the phaeton and landed with a thud on the pavement. He rolled onto his back and stared up at the sky as he caught his breath. What had just happened? He was all too aware that wheels could break but he had never heard of a wheel coming completely off the rear frame.

He groaned as he sat up and reached for his head. When he pulled his hand back, he saw blood on his fingertips. He must have hurt himself worse than he had thought.

Octavia!

What had become of her?

Harred turned his head and saw Octavia sitting up on the pavement with Fredrick by her side. It appeared as if they were fortunate, and no one was seriously injured.

As he went to rise, the main door of Fredrick's townhouse opened and his butler ran out, followed by five footmen.

The butler crouched down by Fredrick and Octavia and started conversing with them. The footmen went to secure the team of horses that had come to a stop in the center of the street. They then worked together to move the phaeton to the side of the pavement.

Harred had a terrible headache and everything seemed to hurt. He slowly made his way over to Fredrick and Octavia.

"How are you?" he asked Octavia.

Octavia remained in her seated position. Her face was pale, which greatly concerned him, and a slight grimace appeared on her lips. "It hurts every time I blink," she informed him. "But nothing appears to be broken."

Fredrick's eyes flashed with fury. "What in the blazes happened, Kendal?" he half-asked, half-demanded.

"The wheel came off," Harred said as he saw the large wheel resting on the pavement a short distance away.

"Wheels just don't come off," Fredrick declared. "Not unless your grooms are completely and utterly incompetent."

Harred shook his head, and he regretted doing so almost immediately. "I will speak to my grooms, but I can't imagine that they made such a terrible mistake."

Fredrick rose and dusted off his trousers. Then he reached down and offered his hand to Octavia. "Come, let us look at the phaeton. Perhaps it will give us some clues as to what just happened."

Harred followed his friend over to the back of the phaeton and studied the frame. "Nothing appears out of place, other than the wheel being gone."

A footman approached him and said in a hushed voice, "My lord, something is amiss with the reins."

"Show me," Harred ordered.

The footman took a step back and reached for the reins. He held them up for Harred's inspection and revealed, "Someone cut them and one good jerk would have broken them completely."

Fredrick stepped over to stand next to him and studied the reins. "This was no accident. Someone didn't want us to walk away from this carriage."

"But who would do such a thing?" Harred asked. "I have no enemies or anyone that wants to see me dead."

"Clearly, someone does," Fredrick said. "If the roads had been any busier, we could have been trampled by another carriage. Or you could have snapped the reins and lost control of the team. Which would have been catastrophic when the wheel came off."

Octavia's voice came from behind them. "We are drawing some unwanted attention," she remarked. "Perhaps we could continue this conversation in the privacy of our townhouse."

Harred glanced around and saw that Octavia was right. People were standing around, gawking at them and their predicament.

Without saying a word, Fredrick offered his arm and led his sister back towards their townhouse. Harred followed behind them and it wasn't long before they were standing in the drawing room.

Octavia dropped down onto the settee and rotated her right wrist in a slow motion. "It isn't broken, but it is rather sore," she revealed.

"How did you let this happen?" Fredrick growled, advancing towards Harred. "My sister could have been killed."

Harred understood Fredrick's anger, but it was misplaced. He would never have placed Octavia intentionally in harm's way. "It wasn't as if I planned for this to happen," he tried to explain. "I didn't even know that someone wanted me dead until now."

"You should have known," Fredrick pressed.

"Pray tell, how would I know?" Harred asked.

Octavia rose from the settee and stepped between them. "I think it would do us all some good if we sat down and had a cup of tea."

"Tea won't solve this problem," Fredrick said, his eyes narrowing on Harred. "We need to find out who is trying to kill Harred before either one of us gets hurt again."

Placing a hand on her brother's chest, Octavia advised, "It

might be best if you stop glaring at Lord Kendal and try to have a productive conversation."

Fredrick frowned as he took a step back. "My apologies, but I do not like the thought of you being in harm's way," he told his sister. "You could have died."

"But I didn't," Octavia responded. "And playing the blame game will help no one in this situation. We should be trying to help Lord Kendal, not threatening him."

"I haven't threatened him yet," Fredrick said.

"Good, let's skip that step, shall we?" Octavia asked. "Take a seat and I will pour you a cup of tea."

Fredrick did as his sister requested and let out a groan as he sat down onto the settee.

Octavia turned her attention towards Harred. "My lord, will you not take a seat as well?" she asked.

Harred knew there was no way that he could refuse Octavia's request without appearing rude. He dropped down on the proffered chair without complaint.

Once they were all situated in their seats, Octavia leaned forward and poured three cups of tea. She handed them both one before collecting her cup.

Harred looked down at his cup and had no interest in taking a sip. But he didn't dare refuse Octavia's offering. By the look on Fredrick's face, he felt the same way.

Octavia took a long sip before lowering her cup to her lap. "Now, let's have a right proper discussion. Shall we?" she asked.

Leaning forward, Fredrick placed his full teacup onto the tray, earning a look of disapproval from his sister. "Who wants you dead, Kendal?"

"I cannot truly think of one person."

Fredrick considered him for a moment before asking, "Who would benefit the most from your death?"

There was only one person who would benefit from his death, but he didn't dare believe that William would be capable of murder. His brother wouldn't have tried to kill him.

"You have an idea, don't you?" Fredrick pressed.

Harred tightened his hold on his teacup. "It would be my brother, William, but he wouldn't have done such a thing. He couldn't have," he said. "My brother may be jealous of me, but he claims that he is richer than me now that he is married."

"But you have the title, and everything that is entailed," Octavia pointed out.

"No, you have it all wrong," Harred defended. "My brother has never tried to hurt me before. I do believe murder would be a drastic step for him."

Octavia gave him a questioning look. "Haven't you been fighting with Lord William as of late?"

"Yes, but nothing that is out of the ordinary," Harred replied. "William only seems to care about himself. It has been that way since we were children."

Fredrick abruptly rose. "I need to speak to Lord William."

"Why?" Harred asked. "I am telling you that William would not have done such a thing. Yes, William is a pain, and is self-absorbed, but he is no murderer."

"Let me be the judge of that," Fredrick responded. "I will just ask him a few questions."

Rising, Harred suggested, "Perhaps it would be best if we contacted the constable."

"No," Octavia and Fredrick said in unison.

Harred lifted his brow, surprised by their blunt responses. "Whyever not?" he asked. "If someone is trying to kill me, shouldn't we contact the one person that can help us?"

"Constables are useless," Fredrick said.

"Have you worked with a constable before?" Harred asked.

With a shake of his head, Fredrick replied, "No, but if we need to hire an investigator, it will be a Bow Street Runner.

Not a constable. They just get in the way of a real investigation."

Harred didn't want to fight with Fredrick, but he didn't understand why he held such animosity for constables. He had never had the need of one before, so he had no opinion of them.

Octavia placed her teacup down and rose to stand by Fredrick. "Shall I inform Carson that we need the use of one of our coaches?"

"Yes, but you are not coming with us," Fredrick informed her.

"I beg your pardon?" Octavia asked.

Fredrick shot her a stern look. "I do not think I could have spoken any plainer. It is not safe for you to be around Harred until we have this resolved."

Octavia placed a hand on her hip. "I do not think so, Brother," she said. "I am a part of this, whether you like it or not."

"No, Octavia!" Fredrick exclaimed with a swipe of his hand. "I forbid it. I do not want you in harm's way."

Turning towards Harred, Octavia smiled sweetly at him. Too sweetly. "Will you kindly tell my brother that he does not control me or my actions and that I will do as I please?"

Harred put his hand up. "I do not wish to get involved." He paused. "But if I did, I must side with your brother. I do not want to see you hurt."

Octavia's smile dimmed. "I am going to tell Carson that we need a coach and then I am going to sit in that coach. I challenge either of you to try to stop me."

With her head held high, she spun on her heel and departed from the room.

Fredrick's eyes remained on the doorway that Octavia had stepped through. "My sister is a stubborn thing," he said. "I would be furious if I wasn't so blasted proud of her."

"She is going to come with us, regardless," Harred

remarked. "It might be best if we just accept that fact and move on."

"If it comes down to saving you or Octavia, I will save my sister every time," Fredrick informed him.

"I would expect no less from you."

Fredrick's eyes held a fierce determination. "Very well, let's get this over with," he said. "If your brother is involved, I can't promise I won't challenge him to a duel for what he has done."

"William is many things, but I do not think he is a murderer," Harred stated.

Octavia stepped back into the room and announced, "The coach is being brought around to the front. Have you two resigned yourself to the fact that I will be joining you?"

Fredrick approached his sister and said, "You are infuriating, my dear sister."

"Thank you," Octavia replied.

"That wasn't a compliment," Fredrick responded.

Octavia grinned. "I took it as one," she said.

As they made their way towards the coach, Harred retreated to his own thoughts. Someone had gone to great lengths to ensure he was killed. Who could have done such a thing? It couldn't have been his brother. So why was the doubt creeping in?

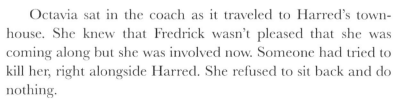

Octavia sat in the coach as it traveled to Harred's townhouse. She knew that Fredrick wasn't pleased that she was coming along but she was involved now. Someone had tried to kill her, right alongside Harred. She refused to sit back and do nothing.

Lord William had a dishonorable reputation but would he

try to murder his own brother? Harred didn't think so, but she had her doubts.

The coach came to a stop in front of a whitewashed townhouse and Harred moved to exit the coach. Once he was on the pavement, he reached back in to assist Octavia.

"Thank you," she murmured as she withdrew her hand.

Fredrick came to stand next to her. "I wish you would remain in the coach. It might not be safe for you in there."

"I do believe I have proven that I can handle myself under difficult circumstances," Octavia said as she stared back at him, challenging him to deny it.

Fredrick pursed his lips before saying, "Just remain by me and do not let your anger get the best of you."

Harred spoke up. "Again, I do not think my brother could do something such as this."

"We shall see," Fredrick muttered.

They walked towards the main door and it was promptly opened by the butler.

Stepping inside, Harred asked, "Where is my brother?"

The butler closed the door behind him and shared, "He left a short time ago, but he has yet to return."

Harred did not look pleased by that information. "I need to speak to the grooms that are responsible for tending to my carriages."

"That would be Steven and James. I will go inform them at once." The butler eyed him with concern. "You have blood on your forehead. Would you like for me to send for a doctor?"

"That won't be necessary," Harred said. "Just send Steven and James into my study when they arrive."

"Yes, my lord," the butler said before he walked off.

Harred turned to face Octavia. "I apologize. I should have asked for some tea to be brought up for you or at least a biscuit. I know how fond you are of those."

"I have had enough tea and biscuits, but thank you, my lord," she replied in a gracious tone.

A smirk came to Fredrick's lips. "I didn't think it was possible for you to ever have enough biscuits," he joked.

"It is a rare thing, but it is possible," Octavia said.

Harred gestured towards a corridor and suggested, "Why don't we wait in my study for the grooms? It will be far more comfortable than just standing around in the entry hall."

Octavia had to admit that she wouldn't mind sitting down. Her body was still aching from the fall she'd had earlier. "That is a wonderful idea," she said.

As she followed Harred to the study, she couldn't help but notice the tenseness that exuded off of him and her brother.

She had just stepped into the study when she saw Lady William sitting on the settee and she had a book in her hand.

Lady William looked up when they entered the room and let out a slight gasp. "My lord," she said as she rose. "I do hope it is all right that I am in your study. You said I could go anywhere and…"

Harred put his hand up, stilling her words. "You are welcome to be in my study. This is your home now."

Lady William's shoulders relaxed and she looked visibly relieved. "Thank you, my lord," she said as she closed the book in her hand. "You are most generous."

"I believe I asked you to call me Harred," he chided lightly. "Family doesn't make use of titles."

"Yes, of course," Lady William rushed out. "I'm sorry. I am not used to being so informal or having a new brother, for that matter."

Octavia felt bad for Lady William since she seemed to feel so unsure of herself. "Hello, Lady William," she greeted. "You remember my brother, do you not?"

Lady William dropped into a curtsy. "Yes, I do remember Lord Chatsworth. You both were so kind to come speak to me at the soiree."

"It was our pleasure," Fredrick chimed in.

With a glance at the bookshelves along the side wall, Lady William said, "Harred has an impressive number of books in here. I do believe I could get lost in here rather often." She paused as she seemed to collect her thoughts. "But I will avoid reading any books on religion or politics. I know those aren't appropriate topics for women to learn about."

To Octavia's pleasant surprise, Harred said, "I think it is important that women learn about those topics. For how else will we avoid making the same mistakes as we did in the past? An educated woman is a powerful woman, indeed."

"I hadn't realized you felt that way," Octavia responded.

Harred nodded. "My mother was rather progressive in her views and I grew up with lively debates in my home. It is one of the things that I miss most about my parents being gone."

Fredrick stepped forward and addressed Lady William. "Do you know where your husband is, my lady?" he asked gently. But there was a firmness to his words.

With a barely discernible frown, she replied, "I do not know. He hasn't spoken to me since we left the soiree last night. I heard that he left the townhouse earlier, but I have no indication as to where he went."

Octavia could hear the heartache in Lady William's voice. She had only just married Lord William, but it appeared as if he had tossed his new wife aside in pursuit of other entertainments.

Lady William walked over to the bookshelf and slipped the book back into place. "I shouldn't be in here anyways. William instructed me to stay in the drawing room in case I have callers." She winced. "Not that anyone will call upon me, considering I am just a merchant's daughter."

Feeling compassion well up inside of her, Octavia asked, "Would you like me to accompany you to the drawing room for a visit?"

Lady William perked up. "Yes, I would greatly appreciate that. Thank you," she gushed.

"Very well," Octavia said. "Shall we?"

With a newfound skip in her step, Lady William crossed the room and departed from the study. It would appear that she was rather eager for this visit.

As Octavia turned to leave, her brother placed his hand on her arm and acknowledged, "That is most kind of you, Sister."

In a hushed voice, Octavia said, "I had to do something. I can recognize a kindred soul that is just trying to find her place within Society."

Fredrick removed his hand. "Regardless, you did a good thing."

"Do not praise me for doing what my conscience dictates," she said. "I would like to think that most people would have done what I did."

Harred interjected, "Sadly, I believe very few people amongst the *ton* would have, but you have made Ruth very happy with your thoughtful act."

Octavia smiled at Harred. "Thank you, my lord."

"What? Where is my 'thank you'?" Fredrick teased. "I do believe I said something similar."

"Yes, but Harred said it so much better than you," Octavia said lightly.

And with that retort, she departed from the room and headed towards the drawing room. She stepped into the room and saw that it was cluttered with furniture of all sizes.

Lady William was sitting on a settee in the center of the room and she gave her an understanding look. "It is a bit crowded in here," she explained. "William told me that his mother collected antique furniture and had yet to decorate before her death."

"So they left the drawing room like this?" Octavia asked in disbelief.

"Apparently so," Lady William said. "It might have been too hard for them to remove the furniture."

Octavia carefully navigated her way through the furniture towards the settee. "It is almost a maze in here. Perhaps you should redecorate now that you are the lady of the house."

Lady William's eyes grew wide, as if that thought hadn't occurred to her. "I wouldn't dare. Besides, I won't be the lady of the house for too long. William is insistent that we find our own place."

"Is he looking for a place?"

"I know not, but he says he doesn't want to live under the same roof as his brother," Lady William said, wincing. "I'm sorry, I shouldn't have said that."

Octavia raised her eyebrows in a look that she hoped conveyed her compassion for Lady William's plight. "You do not have to apologize for anything. I will not betray your confidences."

Lady William gave her a timid smile. "I don't want to give William a reason to be mad at me, especially since we see each other so little as it is."

"I'm sorry," Octavia said, unsure of what else to say.

"It is all right," Lady William replied with a wave of her hand. "We are just newly married and I am not naive enough to think he married me for anything but my dowry."

Octavia pressed her lips together, afraid of saying something that might hurt Lady William's delicate constitution. It was evident that she was hurting, but what advice could she offer her? They were hardly in the same situation, and she didn't want her words to sound ingenuine.

Lady William gestured towards the tea service. "Would you care for a cup of tea?" she asked.

"I would," Octavia replied.

Her hostess leaned forward and picked up the teapot. As she went to pour, her hand started shaking and she placed the teapot down. "I do apologize but I'm afraid my emotions are getting the best of me."

"You did nothing wrong," Octavia encouraged.

With a glance at the door, Lady William asked, "How do you suppose I can convince my husband to be..." she hesitated, "intimate?"

"I'm afraid I cannot speak on that."

Lady William let out a despondent sigh. "I know I shouldn't say anything, but I don't know who to talk to about this. My husband and I haven't even kissed each other, and he hardly touches me. I can't help but wonder what I am doing wrong."

"I don't believe you are doing anything wrong."

"Clearly, I am doing something wrong because I suspect my husband is with another woman right now." Lady William clamped her hands over her mouth. "I shouldn't have said such a thing."

Octavia's heart dropped for Lady William. She was trying so hard to win her husband's favor but Lord William was being a jackanapes.

Reaching for the teapot, Octavia poured two cups of tea before handing one to Lady William. In a soothing voice, she attempted, "Just give it some time. You and Lord William are just getting to know one another, and it should get better with time."

"But what if it doesn't?" Lady William asked softly. "Did my father doom me to a loveless marriage?"

"Your father pressed you into this marriage?"

"I'm afraid so," Lady William admitted. "He told me that this would elevate my status in high Society, but I do not believe it worked. You saw how everyone shunned me at the soiree. I will always be an outcast to them."

"Do not give up just yet," Octavia encouraged. "The *ton* can be manipulated, just like anything else."

After she took a sip of her tea, Lady William said, "In my

boarding school, I was teased relentlessly by the other young women because my father was just a merchant. It didn't matter to them how rich we were. And now, those same young women have made their debuts right alongside me. I will never be free of them and their condescending words."

"Words are just words until you start to believe them. Don't give them the power to hurt you," Octavia stated.

"I appreciate what you are attempting to do, but until I can win over my husband, what chance do I have with the *ton*?" Lady William asked.

Octavia had a thought. "I can help you win over the *ton*."

"How?"

"What if you and Lord William hosted a ball?" she asked. "It could be in celebration of your recent wedding."

Lady William looked doubtful. "What if no one wishes to attend?"

"People will come; they always do," Octavia replied. "Members of high Society love nothing more than a reason to dress up and drink excessively."

"I will need to ask William about his thoughts. I do not wish to upset him," Lady William said. "But it would be fun to host a ball. It would be my first as a married woman."

Octavia bobbed her head. "Furthermore, I shall start introducing you to some of my friends. Their association will go a long way in helping you become accepted by high Society."

"Thank you," Ruth gushed. "I could always use more friends."

"Couldn't we all?" Octavia asked.

The long clock in the corner chimed, alerting Octavia of the time. Spending time with Lady William was far preferable to working on her embroidery with her companion.

Chapter Ten

Harred sat at his desk as he watched Fredrick pace back and forth in his study. They were waiting for the grooms to arrive so he could question them about the carriage. He doubted they would provide any new insight, but it was a place to start.

He understood why Fredrick was upset, and he didn't blame him. Octavia could have been seriously hurt or worse, killed. That thought terrified him.

A knock came at the door and Fredrick stopped pacing.

"Enter," Harred ordered.

The door opened and his two grooms stepped into the room. They both were of similar height but Steven was much more stout than James.

James held his cap in his hand as he said, "Mr. Mitchell said you wanted to speak to us, my lord."

"I do," Harred confirmed. "Will you close the door?"

As James went to do his bidding, Harred rose from his desk and came around the side. "Did you inspect the phaeton this morning?"

Steven bobbed his head. "I did, my lord."

"Did you notice anything unusual about it?" Harred pressed.

"No, I did not," Steven replied as he shifted in his stance. "Was there a problem with it?"

Fredrick huffed. "You could say that."

Steven looked genuinely confused. "I'm afraid I don't understand. Did I do something wrong?"

Harred decided it would be best if he just told Steven what happened. "The wheel came off while I was departing from Lord Chatsworth's townhouse."

"The wheel?" Steven repeated. "I don't know how that could have happened. I ensured the bearings were fastened before we hitched the horses to the phaeton."

"Then how can you explain the wheel coming off?" Harred asked.

Steven shrugged. "I can't, my lord," he replied. "The only thing I can think of is that someone loosened the bearings after you departed from here."

That is what Harred had suspected but who would have done such a thing? Would William even know how to tamper with a carriage?

Fredrick spoke up. "Who has access to the reins for the teams?" he asked the grooms.

"All the grooms," James replied. "They are secured by a hook on the wall when they aren't in use. However, they are inspected when we harness the horses."

Harred didn't think they would get any further information out of the grooms. He didn't have any reason to suspect they had something to do with the tampering of the carriage. "You will need to go collect the phaeton from Lord Chatsworth's townhouse. It is being stored at his stables for the time being," he shared.

"Very good, my lord," Steven said. "Will there be anything else?"

Harred did have one more question, and it was delicate in nature. "Has my brother visited the stables lately?" he inquired.

James exchanged a look with Steven before saying, "Lord William did come down to the stables this morning, but it was to request his horse to be saddled. I thought nothing of it at the time, but he did linger around the carriages."

"But it isn't uncommon for Lord William to come to the stables," Steven attempted. "He always brings his horse a treat before he rides him."

Harred leaned back against the edge of his desk. "Thank you," he said. "That will be all."

After the grooms departed from the study, Fredrick walked over to the settee and sat down. "Should we go to White's and look for your brother?"

"I doubt he is at White's," Harred replied. "He tends to prefer to go to more disreputable places, places that I don't really care to visit."

"Your brother is a scoundrel," Fredrick said.

"I won't dispute that. I wish I could say that I was surprised by the callous way that William is treating his new wife, but I can't."

Fredrick glanced at the opened door. "Will you be all right staying here?" he asked. "I only ask because until we know for certain that Lord William is behind this, you are in danger."

"I will be fine. My staff is loyal to me."

As he said his words, William stepped into the room with the usual annoyed look on his face. "You asked to see me, your lordship," he grumbled with an exaggerated bow.

With a frown, Harred asked, "Where were you?"

"Why should that concern you?" William demanded. "I don't answer to you." He shifted his gaze to Lord Chatsworth and tipped his head. "Lord Chatsworth."

Fredrick rose from his seat. "I wanted to wish you congratulations on your wedding. You have a lovely wife." His words were pleasant enough but there was a sternness to them.

"She is tolerable, I suppose," William responded.

Harred crossed his arms over his chest as he studied his

LAURA BEERS

brother. William's hair was slightly disheveled, which was in
stark contrast to how it normally was. His brother always took
great care with his appearance so why had he stopped?

"I need to know where you were," Harred pressed.

William met his gaze and narrowed his eyes. "Why should
I tell you?" he mocked. "You may try to lord yourself over me,
but not for long. My solicitor is looking for a place for Ruth
and me to reside in for the rest of the Season."

"I am not trying to lord myself over you, but it is important that I know where you were," Harred said.

"Pray tell, why is that?" William asked.

Fredrick did little to hide his disdain for William as he
shared, "Because our carriage was tampered with and we
were fortunate to escape the accident with minor injuries."

Realization dawned on William's face and his mouth
dropped open. "And you think I might have something to do
with it?" he asked. "Surely, you cannot be that daft."

"We don't know what to think at this point, but if it wasn't
you, then who else could it be?" Fredrick asked.

With a swipe of his hand, William said, "I resent the
implication, especially since I had nothing to do with it."

Harred noticed that William was growing increasingly
angry, but he still hadn't answered the question as to where he
had been for the last few hours.

"It is simple," Harred started. "Just tell us where you were
these past few hours and we can move on."

"I won't do it," William said. "My business is my own, and
I don't need to explain myself to you."

"William, be reasonable—" Harred attempted.

William cut him off. "You want me to be reasonable? Yet
you are accusing me of getting my hands dirty and tampering
with a carriage. Why in the blazes would I do that?" he asked.
"Is it not more likely that this was a terrible accident?"

"No, it wasn't," Harred replied. "Not only were the bearings loosened on the wheel, causing it to fall off, but the reins

134

had been tampered with. Someone didn't mean for us to walk away from the attack."

Walking over to the drink cart, William picked up the decanter and poured himself a generous helping of brandy. "I can't help you, Brother," he said. "But look elsewhere. I had nothing to do with this."

Harred had a fairly good idea as to where his brother was so he decided to confront him about it. "Were you with another woman?"

William's face blanched, but he quickly recovered. "Would it matter if I was?"

"Good gads, you just got married," Harred replied. "How could you treat your wife with such disrespect?"

Picking up his drink, William said, "Ruth knows that this is a marriage of convenience and nothing more. I do not owe her an explanation."

Harred shot Fredrick a look of disbelief. He was at a loss for words. His brother hadn't changed one bit now that he had a wife. If his brother was so callous in his treatment of Ruth, he was beginning to wonder what else he was capable of. Furthermore, William didn't seem too bothered that someone had just tried to kill him, alongside Fredrick and Octavia.

William took a sip of his drink before saying, "If this inter-rogation is over, I have things I need to see to before I go back out tonight."

"What of your wife?" Harred asked.

With a baffled look, William responded, "What about her?" He walked over to the door and stopped. "Do not meddle in my affairs."

After his brother had departed from the study, Harred turned his attention towards Fredrick. "I don't know what is wrong with William. I hardly recognize him anymore."

"I think it might be time for me to make some inquiries as to William's whereabouts," Fredrick said. "But there is a chance that he had someone else tamper with the carriage."

"I would like to think William had nothing to do with this, but I am not sure anymore."

Some of the tension left Fredrick's face. "We will get to the bottom of this," he assured Harred. "But I think it would be best if I collected Octavia and returned home."

"I will accompany you to the drawing room," Harred said.

As they walked towards the drawing room, Harred could hear Octavia's laughter drift out into the entry hall. Her laughter was like a quest that he wanted to spend his whole life exploring. It just made everything seem better.

Harred stepped into the drawing room and he saw Octavia and Ruth were engaged in conversation.

The smile on Ruth's lips dropped when she saw Harred. "Oh, I do hope we didn't disturb you by our conversation."

"Not at all," Harred assured her.

Fredrick placed his hand on a wood chest and asked, "Dare I ask why you have all this furniture in the drawing room?"

"My mother collected antique furniture and she would store it in here until she found a place for it," Harred explained.

"Do you have no other place to store these items?" Fredrick asked.

Octavia rose. "I think it is sweet," she said. "But Lady William will need a proper drawing room if she intends to entertain callers."

Ruth rushed to say, "No one is going to visit me."

"I plan on doing so, and I will bring my friends with me," Octavia said.

Fredrick chuckled. "That almost sounded like a threat."

Octavia rolled her eyes. "My friends are a delight and I have no doubt that they will adore Lady William."

Ruth gave Octavia a grateful look. "Thank you, my lady,"

she said. "I would greatly appreciate that. It will help with the humdrum."

While Octavia walked towards her brother, Harred wasn't quite ready to say goodbye so he asked, "Will you save me a dance at Lady Compton's ball this evening?"

Octavia smiled at him, and he felt her light fill his soul. "I would like that very much," she replied. "I am glad that I did not scare you off after our last dance."

"I don't know why you were worried since you danced superbly," Harred said.

"Did you hear that, Fredrick?" Octavia asked with a mischievous gleam in her eyes. "Lord Kendal said that I danced superbly."

Fredrick looked amused. "I should note that Harred only just hit his head. He is probably confused and just spouting nonsense."

Ruth giggled but brought her gloved hand to cover her mouth. "Excuse me," she murmured.

"There is nothing to excuse," Octavia said as she accepted Fredrick's proffered arm. "I will be seeing you shortly."

Harred followed them out of the drawing room and to the main door. Mitchell opened the door and stood to the side.

Fredrick met Harred's gaze and advised, "Be careful. Don't take any unnecessary risks right now and do try to avoid your brother."

"I intend to," Harred replied.

As he watched Fredrick escort Octavia to the coach, he wished that he had thought of a reason for her to remain with him. But at least he had secured a dance for this evening. He resisted the urge to groan at the thought of attending yet another ball.

But could he truly wait until this evening to see Octavia again? Not likely.

Octavia held the guitar in her hands as she played a song for her mother. It was a song that her mother used to sing to them every night before bed. How she cherished that simple time. She wished they could go back to that time when her mother was healthy and full of life. It was so hard to watch her wither away right in front of her.

As she sang the song, she felt tears prick in the back of her eyes and she blinked them back. It would do no good to display her emotions and it could very well upset her mother. What was worse was that the light that had been so prevalent in her mother's eyes was starting to dim.

She finished singing and removed her hands from the strings of the guitar.

Her mother smiled as she leaned her back against the wall. "That was nice, dear. What song was that?"

Her heart dropped at her mother's innocent words. "It was a song that you used to sing to us before bed," Octavia replied.

The smile left her mother's face. "I'm afraid I don't remember that. Did I sing it often?"

Octavia lowered the guitar to the floor and rested it against the chair. "You would, but now I get to sing it to you."

"You have the most beautiful voice," her mother praised.

She knew that wasn't true but she decided it would be best not to argue with her mother. "Thank you," she replied.

Her mother glanced at the door and asked, "Where is Harred?"

As if on cue, the door opened and Harred stepped into the room. "Hello, Lady Cuttyngham," he greeted. "It is good to see you looking so well."

Her mother shook her head. "I look awful but thank you for your kind words."

Octavia rose and asked, "What are you doing here?" Not that she was complaining. She was pleased that he was here, but she was just surprised.

"That is no way to greet your husband," her mother chided lightly.

Harred approached Octavia and kissed her cheek before he whispered directly into her ear. "I thought you might need me here."

She reveled in his nearness and realized how much his presence comforted her. Why was that? Hadn't she been doing just fine on her own? But she already knew that answer. She was barely holding on and she needed Harred's strength to sustain her.

Leaning back, Harred said, "I must admit that I was listening at the door. I arrived when you were singing and I didn't wish to disturb you."

Octavia felt a blush come to her cheeks. How mortifying. She never sang in front of people, other than family.

Harred met her gaze and the lines crinkled at the edges of his eyes. "I do not think I have heard such a lovely song before."

"You flatter me but we both know that isn't true," Octavia said as she ducked her head. "My voice is nothing special."

In a soft voice, Harred replied, "It is special because it is yours."

Octavia brought her gaze up and the way he was looking at her caused her to pause. His eyes held a tenderness that she had yet to see before and it was directed at her. But was it just an act? It had to be. He was just playing the role of a devoted husband. So why was a part of her disappointed by that thought?

Her mother's voice broke through the silence. "How did Harred offer for you, dear?"

She reluctantly dropped Harred's gaze and turned

towards her mother. "He got down on one knee and did a proper proposal. It was sweet and simple."

"It was much more romantic than that," Harred remarked.

"Was it?" Octavia asked. "I'm afraid I can hardly remember it anymore."

Harred reached for her hand and a thrill of excitement coursed through her at his touch. "I told you that I would love you forever and asked for you to marry me. If I recall correctly, you were rather taken by surprise by my offer."

"That is true, because we hardly knew one another," Octavia said.

"Yes, but I knew that you were the one for me the moment I met you," Harred continued. "I rather love the way you look at me, as if you're seeing me for the first time. It makes my heart beat only for you."

Octavia was stunned into silence. Which didn't happen very often. She couldn't seem to find the words to express what she was feeling. Although, quite frankly, she wasn't sure what she should feel after what Harred had just shared.

Her mother clasped her hands together. "What a wonderful proposal," she gushed. "You should write those words down so you won't forget them."

"I won't," Octavia said. Which was the truth. How would she feel if Harred had meant what he had said? Would she welcome his advances?

Harred dropped her hand but remained close. "Your mother is right. We should write down the memorable moments in our lives so as not to forget them."

"I have forgotten far too many things," her mother admitted, her voice growing sad. "I don't even remember your father offering for me or our wedding."

With a smile, Octavia revealed, "You and Father's love story is one that I aspire to. I have never met two people that have loved each other as much as you have."

"What of your own love story?" her mother asked. "I can see the love that you two have for one another in your eyes."

"Yes, well, there is that," Octavia attempted.

Harred gestured towards the guitar and suggested, "Perhaps we should sing some more songs for your mother."

"We?" Octavia asked.

"I was a tenor in the boys' church choir at Eton," Harred shared. "I rather enjoy singing, assuming I have the right partner."

Octavia picked up the guitar. "Is there a particular song that you have in mind?" she asked.

"Are you familiar with the ballad 'Love in a Village'?" Harred asked.

She shook her head. "No, but I can play 'God Save the King.'"

Harred chuckled as he reached for the guitar. "Allow me, then," he said. "I might be out of practice but I should be able to make it work."

As Octavia released the guitar, she asked, "You play the guitar and you can sing?"

"I am a man of many talents, my dear," he said with a wink.

Harred strummed a few chords before he brought his head back up. "Now, I can't promise perfection, but I only aim to entertain."

Octavia sat down and stared up at Harred as he began to sing a ballad. She had heard gentlemen sing before, but never for her own benefit. His voice was perfect, just as she thought it would be. For a man that claimed to be "out of practice," he captivated her, utterly and completely.

Harred stopped singing and lowered the guitar to his side. "I hope I didn't assault your ears just now."

Her mother clapped. "That was wonderful, Harred. You are a man of many talents, I see."

Octavia rose. "That was rather impressive. Now I will be

mindful not to sing around you again since I know what you are capable of."

"I hope that isn't true, because I could never get tired of hearing you sing," Harred said.

A knock came at the door before it was opened, revealing Fredrick.

Her mother gasped, just as she had earlier this morning when she had seen her son. "Fredrick!" she exclaimed. "You have returned."

As he walked further into the room, Fredrick replied, "I have. I came to see you, Mother." It was the same thing he always said to their mother now.

"Come closer," her mother insisted. "Let me have a look at you."

Fredrick approached their mother and kissed her cheek. "How are you faring?"

"I'm much better now that you are here," she replied.

"The doctor is in the hallway since it is time for your bloodletting," Fredrick revealed.

Her mother reached for Fredrick's hand. "Will you stay with me?" she asked in a hopeful tone. "I hate bloodletting."

"I would be happy to," Fredrick replied as he went to sit down.

Octavia wasn't quite ready to say goodbye to Harred so she asked, "Would you care to have a tour of the gardens?"

"I would enjoy that greatly but are you not worried that Freddy will torment you?" Harred asked. "I have heard the stories."

"Yes, but I am hopeful Freddy will leave me alone when I am with you," Octavia said.

Harred offered his arm. "I will gladly be your protector from a ferocious peacock," he responded with a teasing lilt in his voice.

While they walked to the door, Fredrick's voice broke

through the silence. "I will be down shortly to join you on the tour."

"Wonderful," Octavia said, unsure of how she felt about that. She always welcomed spending time with Fredrick, but she was rather eager to speak to Harred alone. It didn't happen very often, and she cherished those moments.

Once they walked down the corridor, Harred acknowledged, "Your poor mother. I do believe she is trying her best to remember."

"I believe so, as well," Octavia responded. "I just wish I could snap my fingers and bring my old mother back to life."

"If only life worked that way."

With a curious glance, she asked, "How did you handle losing both parents at once?"

"Not well," he admitted. "It is a daily struggle and I don't always come out the victor. I just wish I could have told them how much they meant to me before the carriage accident."

"I am sure they knew," she attempted.

Harred didn't look convinced, despite her best effort. "I am not sure if that is true or not," he said. "Even then, I was so busy trying to live up to my father's expectations of me."

"What did he expect of you?"

"Perfection," Harred quickly replied.

Octavia cocked her head. "Was that his expectation for you or your expectation for yourself?" she asked.

Harred shrugged his shoulders. "Does it matter?" he asked. "My father was a force to be reckoned with and I am…" His voice trailed off. "I am nothing like him."

"That can't be true," Octavia said. "I find you to be exemplary."

He grinned, but it didn't reach his eyes. "I see that I have you fooled."

Octavia acknowledged the footman that held the door open with a tip of her head before they stepped out onto the veranda. Once they were outside, she stopped and turned to face Harred. "Why is it that you do not see yourself for who you truly are?"

"And who is that?" Harred asked, the grin slipping from his face.

"You may not be your father, but there was already one of him. You are your own person, and you can make a difference in your own way," Octavia said.

Harred's shoulders drooped, burdened by the weight of his troubles, as if the accumulated load had become too much for him to carry. "I am responsible for so many livelihoods and I'm afraid to let them down."

"Then don't," she encouraged.

"It isn't that simple," he said.

She nodded. "I may not know everything about you, but I know you are capable of great things. You just have to convince yourself of that."

Harred's gaze left hers and she could see the doubt in his eyes. It was the same doubt that she recognized in herself.

Taking a step closer to him, Octavia waited until he looked at her again before urging, "Stop it."

His brow furrowed in response. "Stop what?" he asked.

"Stop doubting yourself," she replied. "If you don't believe in yourself, who will?"

"Octavia..." he started.

She spoke over him. "Surely you know I believe in you."

Harred grew silent for a long moment, his expression unreadable. "Why do you believe in me?" he asked, his words hesitant.

"I don't know why, but I just do," Octavia replied.

He stared at her with an incredulous look on his face, as if he could scarcely believe her words. "I have not had anyone who believed in me since my parents died," he admitted. "My heart has been laden and twisted with suffering and loneliness."

"You are no longer alone," Octavia said. "I am here, and are we not friends?"

Harred grew visibly tense. "Yes, we are friends," he responded. His words were spoken plainly enough but they seemed to lack any real conviction.

The sound of a squawk came from the gardens and Octavia spun her head towards the direction of the noise.

"Freddy is here," she whispered. "Don't move."

"How would that help?" Harred asked.

"Shhh. He might hear you," she insisted.

In the distance, she could see Freddy walking down a path, his back feathers dragging along the ground.

Octavia pointed towards Freddy. "I don't think he sees us yet. It might be best if we backed out of here, slowly, so as not to disturb him."

"I can protect you from a peacock," Harred stated in a voice that was slightly higher than hers.

After Harred uttered his words, Freddy turned his head and his black, beady eyes met her gaze. They stared at one another for a long moment, neither one daring to move, before Freddy's feathers shot up in the air and he let out a loud, booming noise.

"Run!" Octavia shouted.

Octavia and Harred ran towards the opened door that a footman had rushed ahead to open. Once they were inside, she let out a sigh.

"It is too late now," she said, tossing up her hands in defeat. "I have lost the ability to walk in the gardens. I must accept that fact and move on."

Harred looked thoughtful. "Let me go speak to Freddy."

She grabbed his arm and declared, "No, it is too dangerous. Stay where you are and live."

"Aren't you being slightly overdramatic?" Harred asked. "Freddy is just a peacock. Nothing more."

Octavia dropped his arm and took a step back. "Fine. If

you don't believe me, go ahead. But it is your funeral," she said. "If you die, I will place peacock feathers over your coffin in lieu of flowers."

Harred chuckled. "I will not die," he assured her. "I will prove to you once and for all that Freddy is not evil." He turned towards the footman and ordered, "Open the door."

The footman hesitated. "Are you sure, my lord?"

"I am," Harred's confident reply came.

With a nervous glance at Octavia, the footman opened the door and stood back.

Harred had just stepped outside when a deafening noise could be heard as Freddy rattled his feathers.

It was but a moment later that Harred stepped back into the safety of the townhouse and the footman rushed to close the door.

Harred appeared shaken by his encounter with the peacock. "I do believe that Freddy wishes to be alone right now."

"You are probably right," Octavia said as she attempted to keep the smile off her face. It would do her no good to gloat right now.

"Perhaps I should depart so I can prepare for the ball this evening," Harred said as he tugged down on the ends of his waistcoat. "I am looking forward to our dance."

"As am I," she replied. Why had she just admitted that? Why hadn't she played coy like her mother had taught her? "Allow me to walk you to the door."

They didn't speak as they headed towards the entry hall and Octavia felt the silence had gone on long enough. So she blurted the first thing that came to her mind. "My sister-in-law has a dog named Mr. Fluffy."

"Mr. Fluffy, you say?" Harred asked. "What an interesting name."

"He is residing with Anette's mother until they return from their wedding tour," Octavia revealed. Why couldn't she have just kept her mouth shut? Why would Harred care about a puppy?

Coming to a stop in front of the main door, Harred bowed. "Until tonight, my lady."

Octavia dropped into a curtsy.

After Harred departed through the door, Fredrick's voice came from the top of the stairs. "You told Harred about Mr. Fluffy?"

"I did," she replied. "I just thought he should know."

Fredrick smirked, but he tried to hide it behind his hand. "Fair enough. Who am I to question your attempt at polite conversation?"

Not wanting to continue this line of questioning, Octavia headed up the stairs. "If you will excuse me, I do believe a nap will do me good."

"Happy napping, dear sister," Fredrick teased as she passed by him.

Chapter Eleven

Dressed in his finery, Harred had just started to descend the stairs as his brother opened the main door to leave.

"Where are you going?" Harred demanded.

"Out," came William's curt reply.

"Out, where?"

William kept his hand on the door as he turned to face Harred, an exasperated look on his features. "Does it matter?" he asked. "Last I checked, I do not answer to you."

Harred stepped down from the last step onto the marble floor. "No, but you do answer to your wife. Or have you forgotten you went and got yourself one?"

"I haven't forgotten," William snapped. "Ruth's father is the bane of my existence. He won't release her dowry until I agree to certain stipulations."

Harred knitted his brow. Surely his brother couldn't have been this foolish. "You didn't discuss this before you were married?"

"I didn't think it was necessary," William replied. "I married the chit. I should get her dowry. But Sir Percy is being difficult. He wants provisions in place to protect his daughter."

"Dare I ask what those provisions are?"

William dropped his hand from the door. "The usual, I suppose. If I die within two years of our wedding, a portion of the dowry is to be returned to her."

"That is fair, and not the least bit uncommon."

"Yes, but that isn't the worst of it," William admitted. "Sir Percy wants to put the dowry in a trust and I must come to him to ask for permission to withdraw from it. Can you imagine? How dare he even propose such a thing!"

Harred crossed his arms over his chest. "Considering your reputation for gambling, I do not fault Sir Percy for that."

William scoffed. "I should have known you would take his side," he grumbled.

"I'm not siding with anyone," Harred said. "All of these negotiations should have been done before you married Ruth. That way there would have been no surprises when it came time to collect her dowry."

Tossing his hands up in the air, William asked, "Do you truly wish to rub it in? Don't you think I have suffered enough?"

"What, pray tell, have you suffered?"

"I married someone far beneath me and now I am dealing with the consequences of it," William declared, his voice rising.

Harred glanced over his shoulder before he lowered his voice. "Do keep quiet. What if Ruth overhears you say such a thing?"

"Perhaps she would convince her father to release her dowry to me. It is the least she could do since I married her and elevated her status in high Society."

"You are an idiot," Harred muttered.

"On that note, I am leaving for the evening," William said as he turned to leave.

Harred was done with his brother's disreputable behavior. If William didn't have enough sense to be a decent husband, then he would force him to do so. "You are not going anywhere," he asserted.

William narrowed his eyes. "I beg your pardon?"

Advancing towards him, Harred replied, "Until you receive Ruth's dowry, you are still dependent on me and I expect you to take care of your wife. If you don't, I will not give you one farthing."

"What would you have me do?" William asked. "Should I pretend to care about Ruth when I know nothing about her?"

"Have you even made an effort to get to know her?"

"Why should I?" William demanded. "By marrying her, I was supposed to be rich. Now I'm in the same position I was in before but with a wife in tow."

"That was by your own doing. You have always acted too impulsively for your own good. If you had only thought through the repercussion of your actions—"

William cut him off. "I do not need a lecture from you. Not now! Not ever!"

Harred was not about to be dismissed by his brother. He drew himself up to his full height and his next words brokered no argument. "If you want to remain in my townhouse for another day, you will go upstairs and invite your wife to the ball this evening."

"Yes, because the soiree was such a rousing success," William mocked.

"Ruth needs to be out in Society, and often. Furthermore, her devoted husband needs to be by her side," Harred said. "You made your choice by marrying her. It is time you at least attempt to do the honorable thing."

William glared at him. "Father would never have threatened to remove me from our family home."

"I am not Father, am I?" Harred asked in a stern voice. "I am doing things my own way from now on."

Harred held William's irate gaze, knowing his brother was trying to see if he was bluffing. But he wasn't. Octavia was right. He had tried too long and hard to be like his father. It was time that he acted more like himself and carved his own path.

William must have sensed his determination because he dropped his gaze. "Fine, you win. I will see if Ruth is even interested in attending a ball this evening."

"That is the right thing to do."

"Is it?" William asked as he brushed past him.

Harred turned on his heel and watched as his brother ascended the stairs. He didn't feel bad for William, not one bit. His brother had rushed into a marriage to prove a point, but now he was dealing with the consequences that came from his actions.

Mitchell stepped out of a side room and informed him, "Your coach is readied and is out front, my lord."

"Thank you," Harred acknowledged.

As he stepped out of the townhouse, he saw Steven was standing next to the coach with a tool in his hand.

"These wheels are going nowhere, my lord," Steven announced. "I triple-checked the bearings and they are as tight as I can get them."

"Very good," Harred responded as he stepped into the coach.

It was only a short distance to Lady Compton's townhouse, but it was enough time for him to dwell on what he intended to do with his brother. William may have made terrible choices, but Harred wanted to believe that deep down he was a good person. Perhaps William just needed a shove in the right direction.

The coach came to a stop in front of Lady Compton's townhouse and Harred exited the conveyance. He followed the line of guests into the entry hall and he waited politely in the receiving line to greet the hostess.

As he approached the white-haired Lady Compton, her eyes seemed to assess him. "Lord Kendal," she greeted. "What a pleasant surprise to see you this evening. I haven't seen you since…" Her voice trailed off.

"My parents' funeral," he said, finishing her thought.

"I do hope you are doing well," Lady Compton responded. The sincerity in her voice was undeniable and he found himself touched by her concern.

Harred offered her a weak smile. "Every day it gets a little easier."

"Your mother was one of my dearest friends. If you ever need anything, please do not hesitate to call upon me," Lady Compton offered.

"Thank you, my lady," he said before he moved down the line.

Once he stepped into the ballroom, his eyes roamed over the hall, looking for any sign of Octavia. She was the only reason why he was here this evening. He wanted her in his arms, even if it was just for a moment.

When he didn't see her, he made his way towards the rear of the ballroom and stepped out onto the veranda. He looked up at the night sky and marveled at the brilliance of the stars.

Octavia's voice came from behind him. "They are beautiful, are they not?"

Harred nodded, knowing the stars paled in comparison to her beauty. But he didn't dare say such a thing. It was far too bold and Octavia had given him no indication she would welcome his advances.

"Where is Fredrick?" Harred asked as he turned around to face her.

"Do not worry, your virtue is safe with me," Octavia joked. "Fredrick is just on the other side of the French doors. He is speaking with Lord Rushcliffe."

Harred chuckled. "I did not mean to imply such a thing."

Octavia's eyes twinkled with merriment. "I know," she replied. "I was just teasing you. It is becoming by far my favorite thing to do."

"I'm flattered."

"You should be," she said with a smile. "I only tease the people that I care about."

Harred felt his heart pounding deep within his chest, and he was fearful that Octavia could hear it. "You care about me?" he asked, softly. Hopefully.

Her smile dimmed as she asked a question of her own. "We are friends, are we not?"

Friends.

That was not the answer he was hoping for.

As he tried to appear unaffected by her words, he replied, "Yes, I consider you a dear friend." He considered her so much more. He *wanted* her to be so much more.

The sound of the orchestra warming up drew his attention and he knew that the time for their dance had come.

He offered his arm and asked, "Shall we dance the next set, my lady?"

"That sounds like a splendid idea, my lord," she replied as she placed her hand on his.

Harred started leading her towards the townhouse when he heard a grinding sound coming from above him. He looked up just as he saw something falling towards them at a rapid pace. He shoved Octavia to the side, causing her to fall back on the ground, and he dove out of the way. A large stone decorative planter shattered right where they had been standing only a moment ago.

His eyes immediately sought out Octavia. He was pleased to see that she had risen and was dusting off her ballgown.

When their eyes met, she said in a teasing voice, "Really, Harred, if you didn't want to dance with me, you should have just said so."

Harred couldn't quite believe that Octavia was making a joke at a time like this but he appreciated her sense of humor even more.

Fredrick rushed out of the ballroom and his eyes grew

wide when they landed on the broken planter. "What in the blazes happened?" he demanded.

Rising, Harred replied, "I daresay that it is fairly obvious. A planter nearly killed us."

Looking towards the direction of the balcony above them, Fredrick said, "I do not think this was an accident, given the circumstances from yesterday."

"Neither do I," Harred replied.

Fredrick waved his hand towards his sister. "We need to depart before anyone else comes to investigate the noise," he said. "The music from the orchestra muffled the noise, but I don't want to take any chances."

Octavia remained rooted in her spot. "But Harred and I were going to dance the next set."

In a firm, unwavering voice, Fredrick pointed out, "The bottom of your dress is ripped. I would imagine that happened when Harred pushed you out of the way. We can't let anyone see your gown in this state or it could cause a scandal."

"Oh, I hadn't realized," Octavia murmured as she inspected her gown.

Fredrick approached his sister and said, "We shall depart out the back gate."

Harred watched their retreating figures before he headed into the ballroom. He spotted his brother by the refreshment table and Ruth was looking decisively unsure of herself as she remained close to her husband.

When their gazes met, William raised his glass up but his eyes held a coldness to them that Harred hadn't seen before.

Could his brother have been behind the broken planter? He didn't want to suspect William, but he couldn't overlook what was right in front of him. Besides, who else had anything to gain if he died?

Octavia enjoyed the wind on her face as she raced her horse through the fields of Hyde Park. She didn't ever want to slow down. For once she did, she knew that Fredrick would chide her for riding her horse too fast. But that didn't deter her. It never had before, so why start now?

The Serpentine River appeared in front of her and she reined in her horse. She loved how the fog hung low on the water during the early morning hour. It reminded her of the lake by their country estate where she'd spent hours reading in the chair that had been placed by the water, specifically for her.

Fredrick's horse came to a stop next to her. "Are you mad?"

"Last I checked, I was not," Octavia replied cheekily. "Why do you ask?"

Not looking the least bit amused, her brother continued. "You are going to break your neck if you keep riding like that."

"I know how to ride my horse," Octavia said as she ran her hand down her mare's neck. "I have been riding Rosie since I was in braids."

"That doesn't mean Rosie wouldn't ever get spooked and toss you off," Fredrick advised.

Octavia leaned closer to her horse and said, "You would never do that to me, would you? You are a good horse."

"It is like talking to a wall when I speak to you."

"Yet you keep doing it, expecting a different result. Who is the mad one now?" Octavia joked.

Fredrick gave her an exasperated look. "You are impossible."

Adjusting the reins in her hand, Octavia found herself curious about something. It had been bothering her since the last time they had gone to Gunter's. "Are you happy to be home?"

"I am," came his quick reply. It was too quick. Now she suspected that Fredrick was hiding something.

"You don't seem happy," she remarked.

Fredrick smiled, but it looked more like a grimace. "Do I not look happy?"

"On the outside, yes, but your eyes are telling me a different story," Octavia said. "I know it must be hard to leave your comrades—"

"Leave it, Octavia," Fredrick ordered.

"But I feel—"

He cut her off again. "You don't get to feel anything about what *I* have gone through. What *I* have seen. It is enough to ruin any sane man."

"I am here if you want to talk about it."

"I don't."

Octavia knew she should drop it but she had one more thing she wanted to say. "You may think you are alone, but you aren't."

Fredrick clenched his jaw. "I know you are trying to help, but there is no helping me. And I refuse to burden you with what I was forced to do as a soldier. That wouldn't be fair of me."

She opened her mouth to respond, but Fredrick spoke first. "We should be heading back," he said.

Octavia wasn't quite ready to leave. "What if we talk about something else?" she asked. "Could we stay for a few more moments?"

Her brother looked as if he were going to refuse her, but to her surprise, he replied, "Very well. What else would you care to discuss?"

She decided to ask the first question that came to her mind. "What if I got a miniature horse as a pet?"

"A miniature horse?"

Octavia nodded. "Yes, I saw one at the fair and they are absolutely adorable. And we would be in good company because I was told that the Prince Regent has been gifted many over the years."

With a shake of his head, Fredrick asked, "Why not a dog? Or a cat?"

"A cat is for a spinster," Octavia replied. "At least that is what my dear friend Esther told me. But I am not opposed to a dog and a miniature horse."

Before Fredrick could respond to her, Octavia saw two familiar riders in the distance and she put her hand up in greeting to acknowledge Lord and Lady Rushcliffe.

Enid reined in her horse a short distance away and smiled. "Good morning," she said. "What a pleasant surprise to see you both here."

"It is, considering I needed to speak to Fredrick anyways," Lord Rushcliffe stated as he came to a stop next to his wife.

Fredrick tipped his head. "Rushcliffe," he said. "You may speak plainly, if you would like. Octavia is familiar with the situation."

Lord Rushcliffe didn't hesitate as he shared, "I made some inquiries and I discovered that Lord William left a gambling hall a few hours before the carriage was tampered with."

"Did you happen to learn where he went after the gambling hall?" Fredrick pressed.

"According to my sources, he claimed he was going home, but no one can confirm his whereabouts," Lord Rushcliffe replied.

Octavia spoke up. "So it is entirely probable that Lord William had something to do with the carriage accident."

"Yes, but we do not know for certain," Lord Rushcliffe responded. "Furthermore, Lord Kendal seems to be respected amongst his peers and he hasn't made any enemies in the House of Lords."

Fredrick considered Lord Rushcliffe's words before saying,

"That is my understanding as well, making it more likely that Lord William is behind this."

Enid met Octavia's gaze. "It is far too early to be discussing such unpleasant things," she said.

"Perhaps you can call on me later and we can discuss the weather," Octavia joked.

With a laugh, Enid responded, "I would be happy to call upon you, but I do not wish to discuss the weather."

"I shall be looking forward to it," Octavia said.

Lord Rushcliffe turned to address his wife. "We should hurry if we want to be there when Marigold wakes up."

"Yes, quite right," Enid agreed. "It is my favorite part of the day."

"Mine, too," Lord Rushcliffe confirmed.

As Lord and Lady Rushcliffe continued on the path, Fredrick turned his attention towards Octavia and he had a solemn look on his face. "I think it would be best if you stayed away from Harred for the time being."

"Absolutely not!" Octavia exclaimed as she squared her shoulders. "I do not abandon my friends, especially when they need my help the most."

"Be reasonable," Fredrick attempted. "What could you do to help him?"

"I don't know, but staying away from him cannot possibly be the answer."

Fredrick ran a hand through his hair, making it terribly disheveled. "You are infuriating. Why can't you just agree with me for once and we can avoid this fight?"

"I will when you say something that I want to agree with," Octavia responded. "Besides, there is no one else I would rather fight with."

"Regardless, someone has attempted to hurt Harred twice now. What happens if that person doesn't stop with just Harred?" Fredrick asked.

"Then I shall carry a pistol in my reticule like Anette

does," Octavia said. "I am a good shot when I practice on the targets."

Fredrick gave her a knowing look. "Do you honestly think you could shoot someone?" he asked. "You are far too tender-hearted for that."

"Given the right circumstances, I think I could, especially if that person was hurting someone that I loved."

The moment the last word slipped out, Octavia wished that she could take it back. Why had she said such a thing?

Fredrick studied her. "You don't love Harred, do you?"

"Of course not!" Octavia declared as her cheeks grew flushed. "I care for him, as a friend would, but I do not love him. We hardly know one another. It was just an expression."

She ducked her head, attempting to evade Fredrick's searching gaze. She didn't love Harred. She couldn't. But she did hold him in high regard. Which was a far cry from being in love. Her emotions were just muddled. That was all it was.

Thankfully, Fredrick didn't press her and looked up at the sky. "We should return home before our breakfast gets cold."

"I will race you back," Octavia said before she kicked her horse into a run.

She was relieved to be done with that ridiculous conversation. All she wanted to do was just pretend it had never happened. If she was lucky, Fredrick wouldn't bring it up again.

They raced their horses until they arrived at the south entrance. It wasn't long before they were walking alongside each other down the street towards their townhouse.

The silence seemed to stretch on for far too long so Octavia asked, "Do you intend to visit Mother before breakfast?"

"I haven't decided," Fredrick admitted. "I grow tired of having the same conversation with her every day."

"But she is our mother."

"That she is, but it is still tiresome to pretend that all is well."

Octavia grew silent. "I know that feeling. I just wish I could fix this, but I know I can't. Which makes it that much harder."

Fredrick's eyes held compassion. "We will be just fine when Mother passes."

"Will we?" Octavia asked. "I don't think Father can live without his wife and I don't want to go a day without seeing Mother."

"You will always have me and Roswell," Fredrick said. "And Freddy."

Octavia knew that her brother was attempting to lighten the mood by bringing up Freddy, but she found it difficult to summon even a hint of a smile. She could feel the tears well up in her eyes and she blinked them back. It would do her no good to cry, especially in public. That could cause a scandal, and that was the last thing she wanted.

With remarkable composure, far more than she felt inside, she confessed, "I am most grateful for that, but I am not ready to say goodbye."

"Neither am I, and with any luck, Mother will be around for longer than the doctor predicts," Fredrick said.

"I hope so."

"Chin up, dear sister," Fredrick encouraged. "Remember that today is a good day to be happy."

Octavia sighed. "Mother has told me that she wants me to be happy, no matter what happens to her."

"Then be happy, for Mother's sake," Fredrick said. "And stay away from Harred, for my sake."

She laughed. "I will honor Mother's request but not yours."

"It was worth a try," Fredrick said with a smirk.

Chapter Twelve

The late morning sun streamed through the windows, casting a warm, golden glow across Harred's desk as he diligently reviewed the accounts. He had been working since the early hours of the morning and he was desperately in need of a break.

Mitchell had brought in his breakfast tray but it sat untouched on his desk. Perhaps he just needed to eat his breakfast before he continued his work.

His eyes strayed to Octavia's painting that hung on the wall near his desk. It was the most prized painting that he owned because it would always remind him of Octavia.

A knock came at the door.

"Enter," he ordered.

The door opened and Ruth stepped into the room with a plate of treats in her hand. "Good morning, Harred," she greeted.

"Good morning," he repeated.

She approached the desk and gave him a timid smile. "I made some Shrewsbury cakes and I was wondering if you would like one."

"You made them?" he questioned.

Ruth nodded. "I enjoy cooking, much to my father's chagrin. I love nothing more than creating new recipes with our cook. I would spend hours toiling in the kitchen every day."

Knowing it would be rude to refuse her offering, he rose from his seat. "Then I must try one, especially since you made it yourself."

She extended him the plate and said, "I hope you enjoy it."

As he took a bite of the Shrewsbury cake, he immediately noticed how dry and flaky it was. He chewed it slowly, hoping his face didn't show his displeasure. It tasted bland but he didn't dare tell her how awful they were.

He swallowed the dry cake and he found himself coughing.

Ruth put down the plate and walked over to the drink cart. "Would you care for something to drink?" she asked as she picked up the decanter.

"No need," he managed to say. He reached for his teacup on the tray and took a sip of the lukewarm tea.

Ruth glanced at the uneaten portion of his cake and asked, "Was something wrong with it?"

"No," he lied.

With a look that implied she didn't believe him, she walked over to the plate and picked up a Shrewsbury cake. She took a bite and made a face. "These are awful," she said as she looked at the treat in disbelief. "I can't imagine what went wrong. They are supposed to be soft and moist."

"It is all right," he encouraged.

Her shoulders slumped slightly. "Can I not do anything right?" she asked. "Cooking is the one thing I thought I excelled at, but I was wrong."

"Things like this happen," he responded.

Tears came into her eyes. "I'm sorry," she said. "I am

trying, but no matter what I do I will never be good enough for William. Will I?"

It was obvious that this was about more than her failed attempt at making Shrewsbury cakes. He came around his desk. "You are doing nothing wrong. William is rather complicated, but I do believe he will come around."

As the words left his mouth, he didn't quite know if that was true or not. He hoped it was true, but William always seemed to find a way to disappoint him and others.

Ruth looked up at him and swiped at the tears that were rolling down her face. "I am sorry, my lord. I should not be discussing this with you."

"You don't need to keep apologizing," he remarked. "We are family, and we support one another."

"Perhaps it would be best if I returned home to my father until William has a change of heart towards me," she said in a soft voice. "I don't feel as if I belong here."

Harred wanted to kick some sense into his brother. William was doing a terrible job at being a husband, but he suspected his brother didn't care.

"You do belong here," Harred insisted. "Let me speak to my brother and I will see if I can work this out."

Ruth chewed on her lower lip before saying, "No matter what I do, William will always consider me beneath him. I heard him say as much."

"You heard that?" he asked in dismay.

"William hasn't been exactly discreet in his opinions of me," Ruth shared, her gaze turning downcast. "I heard you two discussing my dowry before the ball last night and William's words were rather hurtful."

"Don't despair," he encouraged. "William will soften."

Bringing her gaze back up, Ruth's eyes were red-lined. "What if he doesn't?" she asked. "Can I endure a lifetime of a husband that hates me?"

Harred could continue to lie to her or give her false hope, but she deserved better than that. She was being honest with him so it was only fair that he treated her with the same kindness.

"You are too good for my brother," he said.

She let out a disbelieving huff. "I am only a daughter of a merchant," she challenged. "I wasn't born into this world of nobility."

"That doesn't matter. Worth is not defined by someone's title. You mustn't start seeing yourself through the eyes of those who don't value you. You must know your own worth, even if they don't." He paused. "I hope that helped and I didn't just preach to you."

Ruth sighed. "What is wrong with me?" she asked. "I was given everything, but I feel as if I have nothing."

Mitchell knocked on the door before he stepped into the room. "Lady Octavia and Lord Chatsworth have arrived and I showed them to the drawing room," he announced.

"Very good," Harred said. "Is Lord William home?"

Mitchell remained stoic as he replied, "He is not. He failed to return home last night."

Harred resisted the urge to express his thoughts on the matter. Instead, he ordered, "Inform me at once when he arrives home."

"Yes, my lord," Mitchell responded before departing from the room.

Ruth looked up at him with eyes that betrayed her emotions. "Tell me the truth. Is William with another woman right now?"

Harred could only imagine how much strength it took for Ruth to ask that question. "I don't know where he is," he replied. And that was the truth. He didn't know what his brother was capable of anymore. He truly felt terrible for Ruth. She was an innocent in all of this and Wiliam was mistreating her horribly.

"Well, I did not mean to take up too much of your time.

You have guests you need to see to," Ruth said in a quivering voice. "I need to accept what I cannot change."

"You must join me in receiving Lord Chatsworth and Lady Octavia," he encouraged. "I know they will welcome your presence."

"Thank you," Ruth murmured before she started walking to the door.

They didn't speak as they walked the short distance to the drawing room. What else could be said between them? Harred didn't have the power to fix this; only his brother did. Which didn't give him much hope.

Harred followed Ruth into the drawing room and saw that Octavia was standing by her brother near the window. She was a vision of grace and elegance, dressed in a captivating pale blue gown that accentuated her figure. Her dark hair was piled high atop her head, and a coral necklace hung around her neck.

Ruth spoke up, drawing everyone's attention. "May I get anyone a cup of tea?" she asked in a steady voice.

Octavia waved her hand in front of her. "No, thank you, and my brother doesn't want one either."

Fredrick's lips twitched at his sister's words. "Now you are refusing a cup of tea for me?"

"Did you want one?" Octavia asked.

"No, but that is hardly the point," Fredrick replied. "I can speak for myself."

Octavia grinned. "My apologies, Brother. I did not mean to take away your voice, especially since it is such a lovely, gruff voice."

Harred chuckled.

"Do not encourage her," Fredrick said, shifting his gaze to Harred. "Octavia is becoming more hoydenish with every passing day. Soon, she will start getting ideas and thinking…" He shuddered. "I cannot bear the thought of that."

"It is far too late for that," Octavia stated.

Ruth interjected, "I think it is praiseworthy for a woman to know her own mind. By doing so, she has more influence than she could ever imagine."

The moment the words left her mouth, Ruth lowered her gaze and said, "I apologize. I had no right to say such a thing."

"You have every right," Octavia declared. "You must never apologize for having an opinion on a matter."

Fredrick chimed in. "I may joke with my sister, but I do value her mind. What a boring existence if we can't express what we are truly feeling."

Ruth appeared genuinely surprised by Fredrick's response, as if she hadn't considered a gentleman could think that way. "Thank you," she murmured. "You two are very kind."

Harred clasped his hands together. "Now that you are here, and we established that neither of you wish for tea, shall we sit down and converse?"

"Before we do, I need to speak to you," Fredrick informed him. "Privately, if you don't mind."

"We can speak in my study," Harred replied.

Octavia approached the settee and said, "If you two don't mind, I will stay with Ruth. We have much to discuss. Don't we?"

Ruth smiled, looking at ease. "Yes, we do."

As Harred followed Fredrick out of the drawing room, his friend asked, "How are you dealing with the events from last night?"

"Not well," Harred admitted. "I know someone is going to great lengths to kill me, but I just don't believe my brother is capable of such a thing."

They stepped into the study and Fredrick closed the door before saying, "I was able to confirm that William visited a gambling hall before the carriage accident, but he had left with plenty of time to tamper with the phaeton."

Harred dropped down onto the settee. "Would my brother

be so cold-hearted to do such a thing?" he asked. "I know we have never been close, but I didn't think he would wish to see me dead."

"Just be cautious," Fredrick said.

"And wait for him to try to kill me again?" Harred asked. "I think it would be best if I hired a Bow Street Runner to investigate my brother."

Fredrick looked pleased by his admission. "I concur, which is why I have been in contact with someone who can help us."

"Dare I ask who that is?"

"Lord Rushcliffe," Fredrick said. "He used to work as a Bow Street Runner and he has agreed to take the case."

Harred's brow shot up. "Greydon used to be a Bow Street Runner?" he asked. The funny thing was that it didn't surprise him as much as he thought it would. Greydon had always had secrets, even when they attended Eton together.

"I wouldn't reveal that to just anyone so you must keep that in confidence," Fredrick said with a sternness to his voice. "I do not think you want to upset Greydon by revealing his secret."

"No, I most assuredly do not," Harred agreed. "I am grateful for his assistance. When can I speak to him?"

A deep, baritone voice came from the open window. "I am here now," Greydon said. "I was just waiting for a proper introduction."

Harred turned towards Greydon. "Why did you not come by the way of the main door?"

"The fewer people that know I am here, the better," Greydon replied as he crawled through the window. "Blasted windows. They keep getting smaller and smaller."

"I do not think windows are made for people of your size," Fredrick joked.

Once Greydon was in the study, he said, "Lord William is a scoundrel. I do not trust that man and I would encourage you to do the same. I doubt he has an honorable bone in his body."

"I said something similar," Fredrick stated.

Greydon walked over to the decanter and picked it up. He sniffed it before walking it over to the open window and dumping the contents onto the flowerbed outside.

"Was that truly necessary?" Harred asked.

"It was," Greydon replied. "It smelled fine, but arsenic is odorless and tasteless when mixed with something. It is better to be safe than sorry." He pulled out his pocket watch and studied the time for a long moment. Then he stuck his head out the window and stated, "Your brandy had arsenic in it."

Harred reared back, stunned. "Are you positive?"

"I am. The arsenic caused the plant to wilt since the roots soaked it up," Greydon explained as he placed the decanter down onto the desk.

"Would it have killed me?" Harred questioned.

Greydon shrugged. "That, I cannot answer. I don't know how much was administered. I can just confirm the presence of arsenic in the brandy."

Harred wasn't sure how to process this. Whoever was trying to kill him was determined, that much he knew. But was William truly trying to kill him? The evidence was pointing at his brother, making him question everything he knew about him.

"I will investigate Lord William further," Greydon said as he approached the window. "Try to avoid your brother as much as possible until we sort this out."

"I can do that," Harred responded.

After Greydon climbed through the window, he turned back around and said, "You might want to find the root of the reason why Lord William wants you dead."

Harred went to reply but Greydon walked off.

Fredrick's eyes held sympathy as he urged, "I know this is a lot to take in, but your brother is not to be trusted."

"I already knew that," Harred said. "But taking someone's life goes above and beyond that."

Harred retreated to his thoughts, wondering what he was going to do about William. He refused to sit back and do nothing. But his brother did have the means and the opportunity to kill him. This was a game that he hoped he would come out as the victor.

Octavia sat in the drawing room as she studied Lady William. It had been evident by her red-lined eyes that she had been crying, but she didn't dare ask why that was. At least not yet. She hoped to coax the information out of her.

"How have you been faring?" Octavia prodded.

Lady William smiled, but it was hardly convincing. "I am as well as can be expected," she replied vaguely.

"I am unsure of what you mean by that."

With a glance at the open door, Lady William revealed in a hushed voice, "My husband hates me."

Octavia tried to keep the displeasure off her face. "He said this to you?"

She shook her head. "No, but it is obvious," Lady William replied. "I hardly see him, and when I do, he ignores me. I wish I knew what I have done wrong."

"Perhaps you did nothing wrong," she suggested.

"Then why is he treating me so standoffishly?" Lady William asked with a solemn expression. "My father told me that I would eventually be embraced into Society since I married the son of a marquess and to be patient. But how will Society ever accept me if my own husband won't?"

"Your father was right. You must be patient," Octavia said. "You are only newly married. I am sure couples deal with this all the time." Did they? She had no idea.

Lady William reached for the teapot and poured herself a cup of tea. "I tried to make Shrewsbury cakes this morning and I failed," she admitted. "I have never made a bad batch before. I even offered one to Harred before I realized how terrible they were."

"That could happen to anyone," she attempted.

"Has it happened to you?" Lady William asked.

"No, but that is only because I have not cooked anything in my life," Octavia admitted. "I doubt my cook would even let me in the kitchen to attempt such a thing."

Lady William took a sip of tea before revealing, "My mother was poor growing up and she was insistent that we learn how to do things for ourselves. She thought it was a vital part of our education."

"I think that is a good thing. Our differences are what makes us unique."

"I was taught that the *ton* disapproves of anyone that is different," Lady William remarked. "My father was adamant that I must conform if I want to be accepted."

The worst part about this conversation is that Octavia knew that Lady William wasn't entirely wrong about the *ton*. They weren't exactly a forgiving lot and they loved nothing more than gossiping about other people's misfortunes. Fortunately for her, she had yet to make a misstep in Society and had been left alone for the most part. It also helped that her father was a marquess.

As Octavia tried to think of something to say that might give Lady William some ounce of comfort, the butler stepped into the room and announced, "Lady Rushcliffe has come to call, my lady."

Lady William looked around in surprise, as if she could scarcely believe it. "Lady Rushcliffe is here to see me?" she asked. "Did she say what she wanted?"

"I asked her to come," Octavia explained. "She is newly

married herself and I thought she might be able to offer you some advice."

"I do hope so." Lady William turned her attention to the butler. "Please send her in."

The butler spun on his heel to do her bidding.

A moment later, Lady Rushcliffe stepped into the room and smiled warmly at their hostess. "Thank you for agreeing to see me," she said.

Lady William quickly reached for the teapot. "Would you care for some tea, Lady Rushcliffe?" she asked, her words sounding rushed.

"That would be lovely," she replied. "But please, I must insist that you call me Enid. All my friends do."

While Lady William poured a cup of tea, she said, "Thank you, Enid. You must call me Ruth then, both of you. I do not care to stand on formalities either."

Enid came and sat across from them on the camelback settee. "This is a lovely home," she acknowledged as she looked around the extensively furnished drawing room. "It is full of charm."

"It is Lord Kendal's townhouse," Ruth said as she extended a teacup to Enid. "William wants to move out as soon as the negotiations end for my dowry."

"I see," Enid responded. "And what of the furniture? Is it yours?"

Ruth shook her head. "No, this all belonged to William's mother. She collected the pieces before she died and no one has had the heart to move it yet."

"I find that sweet," Enid said before taking a sip of her tea.

In a low voice, Ruth asked, "Did Lord Rushcliffe argue with your father in regards to your dowry?"

Enid choked on her tea. "Heavens, no," she replied. "I had no dowry. My father was just happy that I married Lord Rushcliffe."

"You didn't have a dowry?" Ruth asked. "How did you come to marry Lord Rushcliffe then?"

Lowering the teacup to her lap, Enid explained, "I was married once before Lord Rushcliffe. I ran off and married someone that I thought I loved, but he deceived me."

Realization dawned on Ruth's expression. "I read about this in the newssheets. Your husband died under interesting circumstances."

"He is dead, and that is all I wish to say about it," Enid said. Her voice emerged soft and firm, and there was more emotion in that quietness than Octavia would have thought possible.

"Of course," Ruth murmured. "My apologies. I didn't mean to pry."

"Think nothing of it," Enid responded.

There was a slight lull in the conversation so Octavia shared, "Ruth was married only a few days ago."

"How lovely!" Enid exclaimed. "How are you enjoying married life?"

Ruth looked unsure and she started fidgeting with her hands. "It is not what I thought it would be," she admitted. "William is cold and distant. How do you get your husband to want to spend time with you?"

Enid gave her a blank stare. "Lord William doesn't wish to spend time with you?" she asked. "Has he given a reason as to why that is?"

"No, he just mostly ignores me," Ruth shared.

With a look of concern, Enid said, "I must assume this is a marriage of convenience then."

Ruth bobbed her head but remained silent.

"Were you two even acquainted with one another at all before the marriage took place?" Enid asked.

"No, I didn't meet him until we stood in front of the vicar," Ruth admitted. "I had heard of William and his reputation prior to our nuptials, but I had hoped it was exaggerated to sell newssheets. I didn't think that he could be so cruel." Her voice cracked on the last word, as if she were holding back tears.

Enid leaned forward in her seat. "I don't normally speak of such things, at least not anymore, but my first marriage was not a happy one. I tried to change everything about myself to make him like me, but in the end, he took issue with me. Nothing I did would please him," she shared, her voice full of compassion. "You have to remember that this is not about you, it is about him. He is miserable. He is lonely."

"But I am married to him," Ruth remarked. "Do you think I could get a divorce?"

Octavia winced. "That would take an act of Parliament and I daresay that they wouldn't even listen to your case."

"So I am stuck, is that it?" Ruth asked.

The main door opened with a bang and it was followed by Lord William shouting, "Ruth! Where are you, Wife?" His words were slurred and angry.

Ruth hesitantly rose from her seat, looking deucedly uncomfortable.

Lord William staggered into the drawing room and he waggled his finger at Ruth. "You!" he exclaimed. "Do you know your father expects me to ask permission from *you* before he will give me a farthing of your dowry?"

"I… uh…" Ruth started.

He cut her off. "I am not going to come to you for anything," Lord William exclaimed. "That is my money, not yours!"

Ruth's eyes nervously darted between the ladies and her husband. "Could we discuss this later, please? I have company and—"

Lord William advanced towards his wife, but Octavia jumped up and blocked his path. "You have no right to speak to your wife in such a way," she chided.

He huffed. "No right?" he asked. "She is my wife and I will do with her as I please. Now, move!"

"William!" Harred shouted from the doorway. "What is the meaning of this? Have you lost your senses?"

"This does not concern you," Lord William mocked.

Harred walked further into the room and Fredrick was right behind him. Octavia felt great relief at seeing both of them. She wasn't quite sure what Lord William would have done if her brother and Harred hadn't interceded when they did.

"You made this my concern when you stepped out of line," Harred stated. "Come to my office and we will discuss this."

Lord William spun around to face his brother. "Why, so you can lecture me?" he asked. "I have no desire to speak to you."

Harred gestured towards the door. "Then leave," he ordered. "You are no longer welcome in my home."

"You are kicking me out?" Lord William asked.

"It is long overdue," Harred replied. "Your wife is welcome to stay until you have secured proper lodging or until she decides to return to her father."

Lord William moved to stand in front of his brother, his nostrils flaring. "You have no right to order me around like I am some peasant."

Harred held his gaze, showing no sign of hesitation. "I have every right and I am done trying to help you. I do believe I have coddled you for too long and it is time that you go about it on your own."

The tension in the room was palpable as Octavia watched Harred continue the standoff with his brother, neither one appearing to be willing to concede.

Ruth walked over to Lord William and placed a hand on his sleeve. "I will speak to my father about releasing my dowry if you go."

Lord William broke his brother's gaze and turned towards his wife. "That is most gracious of you," he drawled. "Come, we will go now."

Ruth didn't make an attempt to move. "I think it would be best if I remained here for the time being."

"Why?" Lord William asked.

"You are drunk and aren't acting rationally," Ruth explained. "Father will never agree to see you in this inebriated state."

Lord William reached for her arm. "No, but he will agree to meet with you."

Ruth yanked back her arm and stepped out of his reach. "No, William. I think not."

Lord William's mouth dropped open. "You think not?" he repeated back. "Who do you think you are? You are nothing but an upstart."

Octavia opened her mouth to defend her friend when Harred spoke first. "Leave now or you will be escorted out," he ordered. His tone brokered no argument. "Do not make this harder on yourself than it already is."

"Fine!" Lord William exclaimed, tossing up his hands. "I will go, but this is not over. I will return tomorrow and we will finish this conversation."

No one spoke as Lord William departed from the drawing room. His exit was followed by the main door being slammed shut.

With kindness in his voice, Harred addressed Ruth. "Are you all right?" he asked.

Ruth's eyes were moist. "I will be," she replied. "Thank you for what you did. I do hope that William calms down before he returns tomorrow."

Fredrick spoke up. "We should go, Octavia," he said.

Enid jumped up from her seat. "I should probably go as well." She approached Ruth and reached for her hand. "Thank you for a lovely visit. I shall call upon you again."

Octavia studied Harred for a moment, taking in the tell-tale signs of his tension. Yet, as she looked deeper into his gaze, she detected a new layer of sadness that had etched itself into his eyes. It was a silent sorrow, hidden beneath a façade of composure, and it became evident that turning away his brother was affecting him more than he was letting on.

Harred met her gaze, and she felt embarrassed that she had been caught staring at him.

"I shall call upon you later today, assuming you have no objections," he said. She felt a thrill of excitement course through her body at the prospect of seeing him again.

"I shall be looking forward to it," Octavia responded. And that was the truth. She didn't think she would ever tire of seeing Harred. She was growing far too dependent on him. But she wasn't afraid of that thought.

Chapter Thirteen

It had been hours since he had thrown his brother out of his townhouse, but Harred was still reeling with anger. How dare William treat his wife so distastefully, especially in front of her guests? What had he been thinking? But that was easy to answer. William was only thinking about himself, just as he always did. Harred had said it over and over, and it made it no less true.

How he wished his father was here, and not for the first time. He had made that blasted promise to watch over William, but he couldn't enable him anymore. It was time for his brother to see what he was capable of.

The coach came to a stop in front of the House of Lords and Harred went to open the door. As he stepped down onto the pavement, he saw Lord Rushcliffe approaching him with his usual solemn expression.

"Good afternoon, Greydon," Harred greeted.

Greydon came to a stop next to him and said, "I understand that you tossed your brother out of your townhouse earlier today."

"I did," he replied. "I must assume that your wife told you the circumstances around that decision."

"She did, and I applaud you for doing so," Greydon said.

"Please apologize to Lady Rushcliffe for me. William's behavior was entirely inappropriate and I am embarrassed she had to witness our family's spat."

"You mustn't apologize for your brother's actions," Greydon chided lightly. "You did nothing wrong."

"I'm afraid it is a habit at this point."

Greydon glanced over his shoulder before saying, "We do have a problem. Your bill to conserve the woodlands round about London is causing quite a stir."

"I know some people are opposed to it, but it is important that we preserve the woodlands for our future generations."

With a bob of his head, Greydon responded, "I do not dispute that. But some of the lords do have objections. They want to develop various parts of that land and build factories."

"That is the exact thing I wish to avoid," Harred stated. "London already has far too many factories and they create an enormous amount of waste."

Greydon crossed his arms over his chest. "If your bill passes, the interested parties are in a position to lose a lot of money."

"I do not care about the money. It is the right thing to do."

"The question that you should be asking yourself is if there is a chance that someone might be trying to kill you to ensure this bill never makes it to the floor."

Harred stared at Greydon in disbelief. "You believe someone would kill me over the bill?" he asked. "That is ludicrous. We are dealing with lords here."

"It is probable and should be considered," Greydon replied. "I know we liked your brother for it, but that was early on in the investigation. We just need to be open-minded about it."

"But the bill is so inconsequential," Harred stated. "Who

would kill someone over preserving woodlands, especially since they can build the factory somewhere else?"

"Greed is a powerful motivator, and you would be wise to remember that." Greydon removed his pocket watch from his waistcoat and read the time. "We have tarried long enough. The session is about to start."

They started walking towards the House of Lords as Greydon revealed, "In case you are wondering, your brother went straightaway to the brothel he usually frequents."

"How lovely," Harred muttered.

"I know you might not want to hear this, but I do believe Lord William is spiraling." Greydon paused. "Which makes me wonder why that is."

"I know why," Harred said. "William only thinks about himself."

Greydon looked thoughtful as he asked, "How did your brother react when your parents died in the carriage accident?"

Harred shrugged. "I do not know. After we were informed of their deaths, William headed to the gambling hall and drank away his woes. I don't think he has stopped drinking since that day."

"You haven't spoken to him about it?"

"I have tried, but we always end up arguing about it," Harred admitted. "It is a vicious cycle that I have grown tired of."

Greydon stepped up to open the large wood door that led to the entry hall of the House of Lords. "I would try again."

Harred understood what Greydon was attempting to do, but talking to William was like talking to a wall. Nothing got resolved and they both grew more frustrated with one another. His brother may be hurting, but so was he. The difference was that he wasn't masking his pain by drinking.

After they stepped into the House of Lords, Lord Drycott approached them with a cane in his hand. The bothersome lord had shiny, slicked-back hair. His round belly protruded out and his fine clothing did little to hide it.

Lord Drycott stopped in front of them and acknowledged them. "Lord Rushcliffe. Lord Kendal," he greeted in a curt voice.

Harred responded in kind. "Lord Drycott," he said.

"I thought you should know that I am making a motion to have your nonsensical bill dismissed from being discussed," Lord Drycott announced.

"My bill is not nonsensical. It has merit, and you know it," Harred responded. "The woodlands need to be preserved."

"You would stand in the way of progress?" Lord Drycott asked.

"I have no objections to progress, assuming we go about it the right way," Harred contested.

"And who determines what that 'right way' is?" Lord Drycott pressed. "Why should you have that right?"

Harred held Lord Drycott's gaze, not being cowed by the quarrelsome lord. "It is the right thing to do."

"My factory was slated to be built on the woodlands that you designated in the bill," Lord Drycott revealed. "I will not stand by and let you take that from me."

"I am taking nothing from you. The bill needs to be passed by a majority of peers or did you forget that fact?"

Lord Drycott raised his nose up at him. "Need I remind you that you are nothing in the House of Lords? Your father was important but you just pale in comparison. It is pathetic that you are even trying to be like the great man he was."

Harred wasn't about to be intimidated by Lord Drycott. "No matter what you say, I am going to push the bill through."

"Then you better not make a misstep because I will be there waiting to take everything from you," Lord Drycott growled.

Greydon stepped forward. "That almost sounded like a threat."

"My apologies," Lord Drycott said. "I must have said it wrong because it was most definitely a threat."

Harred cocked his eyebrow. "Why, pray tell, can't you build your factory somewhere else?"

"The section north of London is the perfect place for the factory since it has a village nearby that would sustain the workers," Lord Drycott explained. "You would deny all those people work? I thought your father was a champion of the poor. He would be so disappointed in you."

Harred was done fighting with Lord Drycott. They would never see eye to eye on this and he was tired of the insults that the infuriating lord was hurling his way.

"Good day, Lord Drycott," Harred said with a slight bow.

As he started walking away, Lord Drycott shouted, "You will see how little support you have in the House of Lords. You are nothing."

Greydon appeared at his side as they made their way to their seats. "I'm afraid that Lord Drycott isn't the only one that feels that way about your bill."

"He appears to be the most vocal about it," Harred said. "Do you think he would resort to murder to achieve his purposes?"

"Lord Drycott isn't the most scrupulous man so I cannot answer that question," Greydon replied. "I have worked a few cases that have led me to his factories and they can only be described as cesspits. He treats his workers terribly and cares little if they live or die in the horrid conditions."

Harred glanced over his shoulder and saw that Lord Drycott had remained rooted in his spot but was watching them. "Why haven't his factories been shut down then?"

"Because they employ hundreds, if not thousands, of people in the rookeries," Greydon replied. "If his factories were shut down, where would those people go?"

"That doesn't make it right."

"No, it most assuredly does not," Greydon agreed. "That is why I want to create a bill that will regulate the factories' conditions."

Harred sat down on the bench that faced the floor. "That has less of a chance to pass than my bill."

"I still have to try," Greydon responded firmly as he claimed the seat next to him.

"I will support it, but I am not sure how much that will help," Harred said. "As Lord Drycott so kindly pointed out, I do not have a lot of support in the House of Lords."

"You have more influence than you realize," Greydon remarked. "Don't let someone else's opinion of you define who you are."

Harred huffed. "I am not quite sure who I am, but Lady Octavia seems to believe in me." Why had he just admitted that?

Greydon looked pleased by his admission. "The influence of a good woman cannot be overstated." He shifted on the bench to face Harred. "I must assume that you are pursuing her."

"No, I am not," Harred replied. "We are just friends."

His friend chuckled. "I see. You are in denial."

With a slight wince, he boldly admitted, "I care for Lady Octavia but it is complicated."

"Uncomplicate it, then," Greydon responded. "Do not make the mistake of losing her. My wife adores Lady Octavia and I think she would be perfect for you."

"She has given me no indication that she favors me," Harred admitted. "What if I make a misstep?"

"You may make a lot of missteps, but isn't she worth the risk?"

Harred grew silent. He cared for Octavia, more so than he dared to admit to himself, but what if she didn't reciprocate his feelings? Would he lose her? That mere thought terrified him.

Greydon leaned closer to him and said, "I was once where you are now. I loved Enid, but I was scared of losing her."

"What did you do to overcome that?" Harred asked.

"I faced my fears, knowing nothing could be worse than not having Enid in my life, always," Greydon admitted. "And now that she is my wife, I have never known such happiness. To be loved unconditionally is a gift; one that I will never take for granted."

The room went silent as it was announced the session was about to begin.

Harred turned his attention towards the speaker and the image of Lady Octavia came to his mind. She was the one good thing in his life that had meaning. And he couldn't lose her. Though he had initially entered into this charade, pretending to be her husband, he now found himself no longer willing to merely pretend. His feelings for her had grown too real, too deep to deny any longer.

Octavia knocked on her mother's bedchamber door and it was promptly opened by her lady's maid.

"Good afternoon, my lady," Nancy greeted as she opened the door wide. "Do come in. Your mother is just resting."

She walked into the room and saw her mother was reclining in bed, looking peaceful as she slept. "Perhaps I should come back at another time," she said in a hushed voice.

"If you wouldn't mind, would you stay with your mother while I go retrieve fresh sheets?" Nancy asked. "The doctor has requested that she not be left alone right now."

"Of course," Octavia replied.

Nancy offered her a grateful smile before she departed from the room, closing the door behind her.

Her mother peeked out of one eye before asking, "Is she gone?"

"Nancy just left," Octavia replied. "Do you need something?"

Moving to sit up in bed, her mother replied, "No, but we need to call the constable. Nancy is stealing from me."

Octavia blinked. What a ludicrous notion. Nancy had been nothing but a faithful servant for all these years. "What do you think she stole?" she asked.

"My dry sweetmeats," her mother said in a serious tone. "The bag was under my covers this morning and now it is gone."

"Could you have eaten all the dry sweetmeats and just have forgotten?"

"I would not have forgotten such a thing," her mother replied in a firm tone.

Coming to stand next to the bed, Octavia asked, "Why do you suppose it was Nancy that took the treats?"

Her mother stared blankly at her. "Who else could it have been?"

Octavia would have found this conversation to be amusing if it wasn't for the fact that her mother was in earnest. She really believed that Nancy stole her treats.

"What if you just misplaced the dry sweetmeats?" Octavia asked. "May I help you look for the bag?"

A determined look came to her mother's expression. "I did not misplace anything. I know that Nancy is stealing from me."

"Will you just humor me and look for them again under the covers?" Octavia asked. "I just want to know for certain before I contact the constable."

"Very well," her mother replied as she slipped her hand under the sheets.

Octavia had no intention of calling the constable over dry sweetmeats gone missing but she didn't want to upset her mother.

Her mother removed her hand from under the covers and she was holding up a small cloth bag. "Nancy must have put them back when I was resting. That could be the only explanation," she stated.

"I am just glad that you found them," Octavia said as she sat down on the chair that was positioned next to the bed.

"I don't want Nancy to be my lady's maid anymore," her mother declared. "I want Sarah to come tend to me. Will you send her up?"

"Who is Sarah?"

Her mother frowned. "Sarah has been my lady's maid since my debut. She would never think of stealing from me."

"I don't know this Sarah, but Nancy has been your lady's maid for almost twenty years," she replied.

"No, that can't be right," her mother said, bringing her hand to her forehead. "I want you to dismiss Nancy and bring me Sarah."

"I'm sorry, Mother, but I can't do that."

Her mother dropped her hand and had a look of displeasure on her face. "I want Sarah!" she shouted.

Octavia stared at her mother in disbelief, knowing she was not one to raise her voice. She just had to remind herself that her mother wasn't acting like herself anymore.

A knock came at the door.

"Enter," Octavia ordered. She was grateful for the reprieve from the conversation that she was having with her mother. She wasn't quite sure what to say to make it better.

The door opened and Harred stepped into the room with two cloth bags in his hand. "Ladies," he greeted. "I have come bearing treats."

Octavia felt as if she needed to warn Harred that her mother wasn't in her right mind. She rose and approached him. After she went on her tiptoes to kiss his cheek, she whispered, "My mother thinks her lady's maid is stealing from her."

Understanding dawned on Harred's features and she felt relief that she wasn't alone in this anymore.

Harred turned his attention towards the bed and held up one of the bags. "I understand that you enjoy the dry sweetmeats from Gunter's," he said.

Her mother perked up. "I do," she responded.

He walked closer to the bed and extended her the cloth bag. "I heard your favorite is the cherry flavor. I hope I remembered correctly."

Her mother accepted the bag. "You did, and thank you," she replied. "These will replace the ones that Nancy stole from me."

Harred turned back to face Octavia and held up the second bag. "I chose the mango flavor for you," he said. "It is their newest flavor and it is all the rage."

Octavia smiled, hoping it conveyed her gratitude. "You are kind to think of me and my mother," she responded as he handed her the bag.

"You must know that you are never far from my mind," Harred said in a soft voice, causing her heart to take flight. How she wished his words were real.

Her mother rolled to her side and reached for the table that sat next to the bed. She pulled out the small drawer and deposited her dry sweetmeats inside. "Now I will know when Nancy is trying to steal my treats."

"I have an idea," Harred declared as he walked over to the writing table in the corner. "Why don't you write down every time that Nancy steals from you and we can document it for the constable?"

"That would do quite nicely," her mother stated.

Octavia wasn't entirely sure what Harred was up to but she trusted that he knew what he was doing.

As he walked the paper and quill over to the table, he continued. "Don't let Nancy know that you are on to her, though. Just smile and pretend that all is well, but we will know the truth."

"What if Nancy tries to read my list?" her mother asked.

Harred gave her a thoughtful look. "I will tell her not to read any of your private correspondences."

Her mother bobbed her head. "That is wise," she replied.

"Now this may take some time since the constable will expect a thorough list," Harred explained. "You will need to be patient. Can you do that?"

"I can, and will," her mother asserted.

Harred grinned. "Very well," he said. "Shall we start now?"

Her mother returned his smile, and it was the first time that it reached her eyes in a long time. "I think that is a fine idea."

A knock came at the door before it was opened, revealing Nancy.

The lady's maid approached the bed with a tray in her hand. "It is time to take your medicine," she said.

"Do I like the medicine?" her mother asked.

Nancy placed the tray down on the table. "Yes, but you prefer it with a cup of tea."

Harred caught Octavia's eyes and he said, "I should be going."

A line along her mother's brow appeared. "Where are you going?" she asked. "Do you not live here with Octavia?"

Without a hint of hesitation, Harred replied, "I just came from the House of Lords, but I need to review a bill that I proposed."

Her mother nodded in approval. "Do you know my father?" she asked. "He frequents the House of Lords as well."

Octavia interjected, "Your father passed away nearly fifteen years ago."

"That is impossible," her mother replied. "I just saw him yesterday when he came to visit. We talked about my upcoming Season and we made plans to visit the menagerie."

She didn't wish to fight with her mother so she decided it would be best to concede. "My apologies, Mother. I must have forgotten."

Harred reached for Octavia's hand and asked, "Will you walk me to the door, my dear?"

"I would be happy to," she replied.

After they walked into the corridor, Octavia expected Harred to release her hand but he made no effort to do so. Not that she minded. She rather liked being this close to him.

Harred glanced at her and said, "Your poor mother seems to be getting worse."

"She does, but that was ingenious on your part about having her make the list," Octavia acknowledged. "With any luck, she will stop accusing Nancy of stealing from her."

"My neighbor had dementia and he grew increasingly paranoid of his servants. My father would oftentimes find him wandering the pavement, shouting that his servants were trying to kill him," Harred shared. "My father proposed he made a list of every time one of his servants tried to kill him and it seemed to calm him for a period of time. He carried the list everywhere he went."

"Well, I do thank you for your kindness towards my mother."

"It is the least I can do," Harred said. "Our true character is revealed by how we treat the people that can offer us nothing in return."

As they descended the stairs, Octavia asked, "Have you heard from your brother yet?"

"Not yet, but I am sure he will return home soon. No

doubt he is licking his wounds and blaming me for his troubles."

"You did the right thing."

Harred sighed. "I hope so," he replied. "No matter what happens between us, we are still family. Although, he might be trying to kill me, so there is that."

Octavia saw the pain in his eyes and she knew that his decision had cost him more than he could have ever imagined. It hurt her to see him so conflicted about his brother.

As they stepped onto the marble floor of the entry hall, she turned to face him and asked, "What is going to happen with Ruth?"

"I don't rightly know," Harred admitted. "She is married to William and I can't keep her from him forever. Furthermore, Parliament will never grant them a divorce, especially since they used a special license to get married in the first place."

"I think it was incredibly brave of you to stand up for her," Octavia shared.

Harred's lips twitched. "You seemed to have it handled by yourself."

Fredrick's booming voice came from the doorway to the drawing room, causing them to jump apart. "Good afternoon, Harred," he greeted.

Octavia turned towards her brother with an uplifted brow. "Why are you yelling?"

"Am I?" Fredrick asked. "I suppose I was just ensuring that you heard me."

"I think all of Mayfair could hear you," Octavia replied.

Her brother walked over to Harred and said, "I could use a drink. Will you join me at White's?"

"But you don't drink," Octavia remarked.

With a smirk, her brother shared, "There is more to do at White's than just drinking. Sometimes I go for the rousing conversations."

"Then you must not be taking part in it," Octavia quipped.

Harred chuckled. "I do believe that she got you there."

Fredrick lowered his voice and directed his remarks to Harred. "Do not encourage her," he said. "She only becomes more and more insufferable."

Octavia made a show of rolling her eyes. "Perhaps it is you that is insufferable, Brother."

"Everyone else seems to like me," Fredrick remarked.

"Have you considered that they are nice to you only because you are a lord?" she asked with mirth in her eyes.

The butler stepped into the entry hall and announced, "The coach is out front, my lord."

"Thank you," Fredrick replied before turning towards Harred. "Shall we continue our conversation at White's?"

Octavia studied her brother for a moment. His words were cordial enough, but he was up to something. She was sure of it.

Chapter Fourteen

Harred had just sat down across from Fredrick in the coach when his friend demanded, "What are your intentions towards my sister?"

Harred had two options. He could lie and pretend he knew nothing about what his friend was talking about. Or he could tell Fredrick the truth, admitting that he was completely beguiled by his sister and he wanted to pursue her.

But was he ready to admit the depths of his feelings to Fredrick, much less to himself?

Fredrick crossed his arms over his chest and stared at him with the nonsensical look of his. "Well, what is it?"

As the coach merged into traffic, Harred thought it would be best if he was somewhat honest with Fredrick- but not too honest. He didn't want to give Fredrick a reason to challenge him to a duel.

In a voice that was far more steady than the emotions whirling inside of him, Harred said, "I find Octavia to be…" His voice stopped. What could he say that would deflect from his true emotions? Finally, he decided on it. "Intriguing."

"You find my sister to be intriguing?" Fredrick asked.

"Yes." That much was true. He had never met anyone

quite like Octavia and he doubted he ever would again.

Fredrick's expression grew thunderous. "Do you just intend to have a dalliance with her?"

"Good gads, no!" Harred exclaimed. "How could you even suggest such a thing? I would never disrespect your sister in such a horrendous way."

Some of the anger dissipated from Fredrick's expression at his words, but his friend did not seem fully satisfied. "If that is the case, then why were you holding her hand in the entry hall?"

Drats. What could he say to that? He had been entirely too familiar with Octavia but he hadn't wanted to let her go. He wanted to keep her by his side, always. But he didn't dare confess that to Fredrick. What would he think?

Fredrick's voice broke through his musings. "I would prefer the truth, if you don't mind. I don't really have time for your half-truths anymore. They are exhausting to listen to."

Harred knew it was time to confess the truth and be done with it. "I would like to pursue your sister," he admitted.

"And if I told you no?" Fredrick asked, eyeing him closely. "Would you still pursue her?"

He nodded. "I would, knowing it might stoke your ire. But I am utterly captivated by Octavia and I can't bear the thought of not at least trying to fight for her affection."

Fredrick grew silent, and his expression was unreadable. The only sound to time his misery was the turning of the wheels. Finally, he spoke up. "You do realize that Octavia is stubborn, vexing, and says whatever is on her mind."

"I am aware."

A smile slowly spread across Fredrick's face. "Good, because I do think you two would be good together."

Hesitantly, Harred ventured, "You have no objections?" He wasn't sure if this was a trick. After all, he had expected a much different reaction from his friend.

Fredrick chuckled. "I have many, but in this case, I will bite my tongue."

"Thank you," Harred said with relief in his voice. "Was I so obvious in my affections?"

"You could have tried a little harder, but I saw through your charade," Fredrick replied. "I will say that Octavia believes she doesn't need anyone, but I do believe she needs *you*."

"I do not presume she cares for me."

"That is for you to discover on your own," Fredrick said. "But if you hurt my sister, that will be the last mistake you will ever make."

The way his friend spoke his words, Harred knew that he had spoken true. Fredrick was many things, but he was not a liar.

The coach came to a stop in front of White's and a footman promptly opened the door. They both stepped out of the coach and entered the gentlemen's club.

Harred's eyes roamed over the main hall and he saw Mr. Caleb Bolingbroke was sitting at the table in the corner.

Fredrick gestured towards Caleb and said, "Follow me."

As they approached Caleb, Harred saw that his normally well-groomed hair was disheveled, and his fine clothes were wrinkled. The luster had faded from Caleb's eyes, and his countenance now expressed a weariness that Harred hadn't ever seen in his friend before.

Caleb looked up as they approached and acknowledged them, "Good afternoon." His words were cordial enough but there was no enthusiasm behind them.

Fredrick pulled out a chair and sat across from him. "Why do you look like you were just hit by a coach?"

"I don't look that bad," Caleb attempted.

"You do," Fredrick pressed.

Caleb took a sip of his drink before saying, "I had something that I had to see to in the rookeries and it went awry rather quickly."

Harred spoke up, hoping his words properly expressed his concern. "You shouldn't have gone to the rookeries. That is a lawless place."

"I know, but I had no choice," Caleb responded.

"Everyone has a choice," Harred said.

Something flickered through Caleb's eyes so quickly that there was no time for him to read it. Guilt? Pain?

"I don't." Caleb turned to Fredrick and said, "I have the information that Greydon requested about Lord Drycott."

Fredrick leaned forward in his seat. "What did you discover?" he asked in a hushed voice.

"Lord Drycott's finances are in dire straits. If he doesn't build this factory like he promised his investors, then he will lose everything," Caleb shared.

"How exactly did you discover this?" Harred asked.

Caleb shrugged. "Would you believe me if I said I asked his solicitor nicely?"

"No," Harred replied.

"Then it is best if you don't know," Caleb said. "Just trust me when I tell you that Lord Drycott's situation makes him dangerous. The factories that he owns now are no better than workhouses. People die, but no one questions their deaths. They are just taken out and buried."

Fredrick grew solemn, his brows knitted. "Do you know what kind of factory that Lord Drycott intends to build?"

"The plans that were submitted did not specify, but I would guess it is nothing more than just slave labor," Caleb replied.

"We have to do something to stop Lord Drycott," Harred said.

"You are doing just that by pushing through your bill," Caleb insisted. "Do not give up, and do not let Lord Drycott intimidate you to withdraw your bill."

"I have no intention of backing down," Harred responded.

Caleb bobbed his head in approval. "Good, but be cautious. Lord Drycott is not a man that you want to trifle with and it is entirely possible that he is behind the attempts on your life."

A server approached the table and asked, "Can I get anyone something to drink?"

"Nothing for me," Fredrick responded.

Harred pointed at Caleb's glass and said, "I will have what he is having."

After the server walked off to do his bidding, Caleb shoved back his chair and rose. "I should depart. I have work that I need to see to."

"Does this work include visiting the rookeries again?" Fredrick pried.

Caleb didn't appear to have any reservations as he replied, "I'm afraid that is the only place where I can get the answers that I seek."

Harred wasn't sure what Caleb was involved in, but it sounded dangerous. And he was concerned. The rookeries were not a place that any respectable gentleman should ever go to. But as he went to express his opinion, Caleb walked off without another word.

Fredrick's eyes followed Caleb's retreating figure. "Perhaps I should go after him."

"And do what?" Harred asked. "Caleb has no business being in the rookeries and neither do you."

"Caleb doesn't seem like himself right now," Fredrick mused. "He seems bogged down with worry."

The server approached and placed a drink in front of Harred. "Will there be anything else, my lord?"

"No, thank you," Harred replied as he reached for his glass.

Fredrick shifted towards him and said, "Your brother just walked in."

Harred's eyes shot towards the door and met his brother's piercing gaze. "What now?" he muttered under his breath.

William advanced towards them, skirting the other tables, all while keeping a hawk-like gaze on Harred. If his brother was here to try to intimidate him, it would not work. But he was worried that William might make a scene, making the situation even worse.

His brother came to a stop next to the table and asked, "May I sit down?"

Harred studied his brother, wondering what kind of game he was playing. "You may," he finally replied.

William pulled out a chair and sat down, acknowledging Fredrick with a tip of his head. "I need money," he said.

Harred should have known that was what his brother needed. "What happened to Ruth's dowry?"

"Sir Percy and I are still negotiating it, but I need money to establish my own household- one that doesn't include you lording over me," William replied. "Now that you've kicked me out of my house—"

Harred spoke over him. "You mean 'my house'?"

William scowled. "We both grew up there. I doubt that our parents would have thought you would kick your own brother out."

"That was because you were treating your wife so horrendously," Harred said. "When will you accept there are consequences to your actions?"

"I did not come here to fight with you. I just need your help, and I figure you owe me this much," William stated.

Harred was frustrated to no end. William would never accept fault for his actions, and he doubted he ever would. He couldn't keep doing the same thing and expect a different outcome.

He knew his brother would react poorly to his next words, but he had no choice in the matter. He had to stop this vicious cycle. "I am sorry, but I can't give you any money."

"Can't or won't?" William asked, his voice rising.

"As you have pointed out, repeatedly, you are now richer than me with Ruth's dowry. You need to work with Sir Percy to gain access to it."

"But he is being entirely unreasonable," William pouted. "He should be grateful that I took his daughter off his hands."

Harred gave his brother a stern look. "You shouldn't say such things about Ruth. She is a sweet young woman who is just trying to win your favor."

William abruptly rose and shoved in his chair. "I should have known you would side with Ruth," he grumbled.

"What is it with you and sides?" Harred asked. "Regardless, you have a wife now, whether you like it or not. You can't keep going on as you have been."

"You will come to regret this," William declared in a haughty voice.

"I don't think I will."

William narrowed his eyes. "You think you are so clever, but you aren't. You are no better than me. You just won't admit it to yourself."

As he was about to reply, William stormed off in a huff.

Harred took a sip of his drink before he addressed Fredrick. "I'm sorry about that," he said. "William is exhausting."

Fredrick chuckled. "That is a good way to describe it."

"Now I just have to figure out who is trying to kill me- my own brother or Lord Drycott," Harred said. "And I have to do so before they try again."

Placing a hand on Harred's shoulder, Fredrick said, "Don't despair. We are working on it."

Octavia had just descended the stairs when a knock

sounded at the door that echoed throughout the whole main level. Carson crossed the entry hall and opened the door, retrieving two bouquets of flowers.

As Carson walked across the hall to set them down onto the table, he said, "These were sent by Lord Kendal, my lady. Would you care to read the card?"

"I would," she replied as he extended the card towards her.

She opened the folded piece of paper and read the short message:

I hope these flowers bring a smile to your face, just as you always bring a smile to mine. I do hope you will join me for a tour of Vauxhall Gardens later this afternoon.

-Harred

Now, Octavia couldn't help but smile at the sweet gesture. Maybe, just maybe, he had developed true feelings for her- just as she had for him. Or was she trying to see something that wasn't there? She hoped not.

Fredrick's voice came from behind her. "Who are those flowers from?"

"Lord Kendal," she replied.

"Both of them?"

Octavia turned to face her brother and explained, "One is for me, and the other one is for Mother."

Fredrick nodded in approval. "That was nice of him to think of Mother."

"It was," she replied, knowing that was just one of the many things she admired about Harred. He was such a thoughtful man, which was a rarity amongst men.

"Would you like me to take the flowers up to Mother?" Fredrick asked.

"That would be lovely. I just left Mother and she was resting," Octavia revealed. "I do believe she would enjoy waking up to some fresh flowers in her room."

Fredrick picked up the vase and said, "I thought we could go riding after breakfast."

"I would greatly enjoy that," Octavia replied. "Mrs. Harper has been spending more time in her room as of late and I find myself to be utterly bored."

"You are always bored," Fredrick teased. "But I would have thought you would have enjoyed Mrs. Harper not bothering you to constantly work on your needlework."

"You make a good point. I shouldn't complain or else I fear Mrs. Harper will sense I need to practice my needlework more."

Fredrick looked fairly amused by her explanation. "How would Mrs. Harper sense that?"

"I think she has old lady senses, just as I have spy senses."

"You do not have 'spy senses,'" Fredrick stated.

Octavia smirked. "Don't I?" she asked.

"No, you don't."

"Or perhaps you are just intimidated by my abilities and are trying to discourage me from using them," Octavia joked.

Fredrick chuckled. "Sometimes I fear that you live in your own fictitious world and you hear only what you want to hear."

"It is the best world to be in," Octavia countered.

"I pity the man that you marry," Fredrick said with a shake of his head. "Whoever it is will have his work cut out for him."

Their conversation was interrupted by someone knocking on the main door. The butler went to answer the door and held it open wide, revealing Ruth.

"Ruth!" Octavia greeted. "What a pleasant surprise."

Ruth looked uncertain as she stepped into the entry hall with a basket in her hands. "I hope I didn't come too early. I don't wish to intrude, but I wanted to drop off some of my Shrewsbury cakes. I discovered what I did wrong to make them so dry last time and I corrected my error."

Octavia stepped forward and accepted the basket. "Thank you." She reached inside of the basket and removed one of the cakes. After she took a bite, she gushed, "These are delicious."

"May I have one?" Fredrick asked.

Octavia extended him the basket and it was only a moment later when he said, "I concur. These are quite scrumptious."

"Thank you." Ruth looked pleased with herself as she turned back towards the door. "If you will excuse me, I should be going now."

Octavia wasn't quite ready to say goodbye to her friend, especially since she had come this far to give them a basket full of treats. "You should stay and join us for breakfast," she suggested.

"Are you sure it isn't too much of an imposition?" Ruth asked hesitantly as she glanced at Fredrick as if she were gauging his reaction.

Fredrick bowed. "You must join us, Lady William."

"Thank you. I would greatly appreciate that." Ruth placed a hand to her stomach. "I haven't been eating much lately due to nerves and whatnot."

"Then you must eat," Octavia asserted.

Fredrick held the vase up and addressed the butler. "Will you see that these flowers are placed in my mother's room at once?"

Carson tipped his head. "Yes, my lord."

Octavia looped arms with Ruth. "Come, I shall escort you to our dining room. It isn't far but one could get lost very easily in this townhouse."

Ruth's eyes roamed over the entry hall. "Your townhouse is exquisite."

"It is," Octavia agreed. "My grandmother designed most of it herself, but my mother has made a few changes here and there."

As they walked towards the dining room, Ruth said, "It must be wonderful to decorate your own home."

"You will have the chance one day," Octavia encouraged.

Ruth made a face. "I think it would be best if I hired someone to design my home. I do not have an eye for such a thing." She lowered her voice. "You should see how well I paint. It is awful."

Octavia turned towards Ruth. "I do believe we have something in common."

"Truly?" Ruth asked.

Fredrick's voice came from behind them. "Octavia may excel at many things, well, maybe not *many* things. Perhaps I overexaggerate—"

Octavia spoke over him. "Your point being, Brother?" she asked in the same teasing voice her brother used.

"My point is that Octavia is not going to win any awards for her paintings," Fredrick said. "Unless the judges are blind."

"Thank you for that," Octavia stated. "You are no longer my favorite brother. It goes Roswell, Freddy, then you."

"Freddy is a peacock," Fredrick pointed out.

"Yes, but I like him more than you right now," Octavia said.

Fredrick grinned. "That will change after I take you on a ride through Hyde Park."

Octavia led Ruth into the dining hall and dropped her arm. "Take a seat and a footman will serve you."

Fredrick stepped forward and pulled out a chair for Ruth. "My lady, allow me to help you," he said.

Ruth offered him a tentative smile. "Thank you, my lord," she responded as she sat down.

Octavia claimed the seat next to Ruth and placed the basket down on the table. Then she leaned to the side as a footman placed a cup of chocolate in front of her.

"This is why I wake up every morning," Octavia joked as she reached for the cup.

"Not because of my pleasant conversation?" Fredrick asked.

Octavia took a sip before saying, "Pleasant? Hardly."

Fredrick picked up the napkin off the plate and placed it over his lap. "You used to be much nicer to me," he quipped.

Ruth let out a soft laugh but quickly brought her hand up to cover her mouth. "My apologies. I shouldn't find your conversation so humorous, but I do."

"It is all right," Octavia said. "We are quite hilarious, are we not, Brother?"

"I am, more so than you," Fredrick replied. "But that is because I inherited father's quick wit."

Octavia rolled her eyes. "I am far funnier than you. Everyone has told me so."

"Who is 'everyone'?" Fredrick inquired.

"Lucy at the flower shop, Sarah at the milliner shop, Melinda at Gunter's—"

Fredrick cut her off. "Are any of these real people?" he asked with suspicion in his voice.

"They are real people, but they may not recall telling me that I am funnier than you, so you shouldn't bother asking them," Octavia responded.

"You are a terrible liar," Fredrick teased. "You might just want to stick to knitting reticules."

A footman placed a plate of food in front of Octavia and she reached for a fork and knife. "We are being terribly rude to our guest," she said.

Ruth perked up in her seat. "I am just enjoying the

conversation. It has been rather lonely at William's townhouse."

"You mean 'your townhouse,'" Octavia corrected.

"Well, technically, it is Lord Kendal's townhouse but he is gracious enough to let me reside there until William finds a place for us to live," Ruth said.

"He is a kind man," Octavia stated.

Ruth nodded in agreement. "That he is. He has shown far more concern about my well-being than my own husband." Her eyes grew wide. "I do apologize. I shouldn't complain so."

"Will you stop apologizing?" Octavia asked. "There is no judgment here. Sometimes you must complain so you can move on."

"I am so grateful to have a friend such as you," Ruth said.

Octavia offered her a kind smile. "We ladies have to stick together if we want to take over the world one day."

Fredrick huffed. "Do you think before you speak?"

"I do, and my mind approves," Octavia replied. "Why can't women take over the world? We populate it."

Shifting in his seat to face Ruth, Fredrick said, "Now it is my turn to apologize. My sister might be inebriated at this early hour. For that is the only thing that would explain her behavior."

Ruth let out a snort of laughter and her hands flew up to cover her reddening cheeks. "I can't believe I just did that."

"Do not concern yourself," Fredrick said. "Octavia has been known to snort a time or two when she laughs really hard."

"It is true," Octavia agreed. "That is when I know a joke is truly amusing."

Ruth lowered her hands as she admitted, "The girls at my boarding school weren't as understanding as you two. They used to say that I sounded like a pig when I snorted."

"That is awful," Octavia said.

"They would take table scraps from our meals and pile

them onto my bed. They said if I acted like a pig then I should eat like a pig," Ruth revealed.

Octavia placed her fork down and reached for Ruth's hand. "What they did to you was cruel and wrong."

"My father just told me to grin and bear it since it was such a distinguished boarding school," Ruth said. "But sometimes, I didn't want to grin and bear it. I wanted to fight back, but I was afraid of being kicked out."

"That is over and done with now. You are stronger now because of it," Octavia encouraged as she released Ruth's hand.

"You are kind, but I do intend to start fighting back now," Ruth said.

"Good," Octavia praised. "Do you intend to engage in fisticuffs or words?"

Ruth looked thoughtful. "I thought words would be more appropriate."

"Well said." Fredrick pointed his fork at Octavia. "You could learn a lot from Lady William and her discretion."

"Then who would I learn from?" Ruth asked.

Octavia lifted her brow. "Out of curiosity, would you say that I am delightful? I only ask because that is the general consensus as of late."

"I would say that you are most definitely delightful," Ruth agreed.

With a smug smile at her brother, Octavia said, "Yet another person that has called me delightful."

Fredrick let out a dramatic sigh as he met Ruth's gaze. "I had such high hopes for you."

Octavia found that her heart felt lighter. She loved nothing more than bantering with her brother and it felt good to laugh.

Chapter Fifteen

The curricle came to a stop in front of Lady Octavia's townhouse and Harred climbed out and stepped onto the pavement, not bothering to wait for the footman to come around.

He had been counting down the moments until he could see Octavia. He shouldn't find her so intriguing, but he did. He loved spending time with her, and she was quickly filling the voids in his heart, making him wonder how he had ever been able to live without her in his life.

But did she feel any affection towards him? He suspected that she cared for him, or was he just being hopeful?

As he approached the main door, it opened and Fredrick stepped out. "Good afternoon," his friend greeted. "I understand that you are escorting Octavia to Vauxhall Gardens."

"I am," Harred replied.

"Good, then I shall join you," Fredrick said. "After all, it wouldn't be prudent if you didn't have a chaperone."

Harred mustered up a smile. "Wonderful," he muttered. He no more wanted Fredrick there than he wanted a thorn in his boot. How was he going to woo Octavia with her brother standing watch?

Fredrick descended the stairs and approached his curricle. "You may send your curricle home. One of my coaches is being brought around the front and we will ride in it to Vauxhall Gardens."

"May I ask why?" Harred asked.

"It is better to be safe than sorry," Fredrick responded, stepping back. "Shall we wait for Octavia in the drawing room?"

Harred tipped his head, not bothering to fight his friend on this. It was so inconsequential. "I think that sounds like a better idea than waiting on the pavement and drawing unwanted attention."

Fredrick brushed past him and disappeared inside the townhouse. Harred wished, and not for the first time, that he could spend time alone with Octavia. How were they going to have a frank conversation with Fredrick loitering about?

As Harred arrived in the drawing room, he saw Octavia was speaking to Fredrick. She was wearing a pale yellow gown and she had a straw hat slightly askew on her head. It seemed as if she only grew more beautiful the more he got to know her. For her beauty wasn't just skin deep. No, it was heart deep. Soul deep. Her type of beauty couldn't be bought or made but it was enhanced through being herself. Her true self. Not the person that Society wanted her to be.

Octavia shifted her gaze towards him and smiled, making his heart pound in his chest. Good gads, why did he have such a reaction to such a simple gesture? But he knew. He wanted to be the one that made her smile.

"Good afternoon, Harred," Octavia greeted.

He bowed as he tried to regain his composure. "Good afternoon, Octavia," he said.

Freddy let out a grunt as he walked past the window with his feathers on full display, drawing everyone's attention.

Octavia shook her head. "One day, I will reclaim the gardens as my own."

"That won't be anytime soon," Fredrick teased. "Freddy is the keeper of the gardens and he will only allow certain people in."

"What if I tried to bribe him?" Octavia asked. "Surely peacocks have some weakness that I can exploit."

Fredrick chuckled. "I am sure your plan will be diabolical, but shouldn't we depart for Vauxhall Gardens?"

"Yes, as long as we look at the pavilions first," Octavia said. "I tire of walking through their gardens. It doesn't excite me."

"Very few things do, Sister," Fredrick joked.

Harred stepped forward and offered his arm to Octavia. "May I escort you to the coach?"

"Thank you," Octavia replied as she accepted his arm. "What do you think peacocks think about?"

"I don't rightly know," Harred admitted. "I have never really thought about it."

A line between Octavia's brow appeared as she said, "In order to think like a peacock, I must become a peacock."

Fredrick glanced heavenward. "What nonsense are you spouting?"

"I am just thinking out loud," Octavia replied.

"Perhaps you can keep your outlandish thoughts to your-self or you are going to make Harred think you are going mad," Fredrick teased.

Harred grinned. "I think I would very much like to see how Octavia intends to become a peacock."

Octavia offered him a private smile. "That is why I like you…" The moment the words were spoken, she pressed her lips together and a faint blush formed on her cheeks. He had a feeling that she hadn't meant to say those words out loud. But he was glad that she had. It gave him hope that she might one day have affection for him.

As he escorted Octavia to the coach, they didn't speak and Harred missed the sound of her voice. How could he miss something that he heard so frequently? But he did. He knew it was something that he would never tire of.

Once Octavia was situated on the bench, Harred sat across from her. He thought the silence had gone on long enough so he said, "It is a beautiful day to go to Vauxhall Gardens." Had he truly just commented on the weather?

"It is," Octavia agreed as she turned her attention to the open window.

Fredrick claimed the seat next to his sister and it was only a moment later that the coach began to move.

For most of the trip to Vauxhall Gardens, they all seemed to retreat to their own thoughts, and Harred couldn't help but wonder what Octavia was thinking. It shouldn't matter to him, but it did. Greatly.

The coach came to a stop near the entrance of Vauxhall Gardens, and the footman stepped off his perch to open the door.

They all exited the coach and approached the main gate to pay the entrance fee. Once they started walking down the main path, Harred turned towards Octavia and asked, "Which attraction is your favorite?"

"That is like asking if I have a favorite biscuit," Octavia said. "I just love all of them so much."

"You love biscuits?" Harred asked.

Octavia laughed. "Very much so. Don't you?"

Harred shrugged. "I never gave it very much thought," he said. "I enjoy biscuits, but I am not sure if I love them."

"I don't love them as much as Anette does, but I do enjoy a good biscuit," Octavia said. "Food makes me happy."

"What else makes you happy?" Harred asked. He truly wanted to know.

"My family makes me happy and my friends," Octavia replied. "They lift me up and support me when I need it the most."

"I am happy that you have that support."

Octavia grew quiet. "It has been very difficult watching my mother suffer as she has, but I am fortunate that I am not alone in this, no matter how many times I have to remind myself of that," she said. "The constant presence of grief isn't what concerns me the most. It is the worry that this grief will never leave me, making me learn to coexist with it."

"I will admit that it is not easy to deal with grief, but it is much more bearable when someone can help carry the burden, if only for a moment," Harred remarked. "There will be good days and bad days, but it will get better. It must."

"I'm sorry," Octavia murmured. "I do not mean to make light of the situation, considering my mother is still alive, and your parents are..." Her words stopped.

"Are not," he said, finishing her thought. "It is all right. Grief is not exclusive to death. It comes in all shapes and forms, and I promise it will show up when we least expect it."

"I have a good life, and I have no right to complain," Octavia shared in a soft voice.

Harred stopped on the path and turned to face her. "Voicing your fears and concerns is not complaining. It is coping with what life has thrown at you. There is no shame in being honest with yourself and with others. It is what makes you human."

"I'm afraid I struggle with that since I do not like showing my emotions."

"Then you must change that," Harred said. "Society wants you to believe that showing a crack in your emotions is a weakness, but I believe it is a strength."

Octavia looked doubtful as she held his gaze. "You make it sound so easy."

"Then I must have said it wrong," Harred joked. "I am excellent at giving advice, but I do struggle with taking my own."

"Perhaps we can agree to be honest with each other on what we are feeling," Octavia suggested.

Harred nodded, knowing that nothing would make him happier. He wanted Octavia to always feel comfortable enough with him to speak the truth. "I can agree to that."

Octavia glanced over her shoulder and said, "It would appear that Fredrick is rather interested in the gardens."

Fredrick. How had Harred completely forgotten that his friend had accompanied them? He had been so distracted by Octavia that everything else had been a blur.

In a hushed voice, Octavia said, "I do worry about Fredrick. He is home from the war, but I wonder if a part of him never returned."

"He seems fine. Has he said anything?"

"No, and that is the problem," Octavia remarked. "He seems like his old self, but I worry that it is just an act that he is showing the world. He knows what is expected of him and he is just complying."

Harred glanced over at Fredrick, who was standing a short distance away as he admired a tall plant. "You may just be reading too much into it."

Octavia didn't look convinced. "Perhaps," she muttered.

"You are a good sister," Harred said.

With a huff, Octavia responded, "I think Fredrick and Roswell might disagree with you. They think I am a little too 'hoydenish.'"

"Why? Because you are not conforming to what Society expects of you?" Harred asked. "I think that is one of the things I admire most about you."

Octavia cocked her head. "You admire me?"

"Surely you must know that," Harred replied. "You are unlike any other woman I have ever known."

"Is that a good thing or a bad thing?" Octavia asked lightly.

How Harred wished that they were alone so he could tell Octavia just how much he truly admired her. Would she welcome his advances? He truly hoped so. He wasn't about to let her go without a fight. She was the reason he had started smiling again.

As he debated on what to say, Fredrick shouted, "Sniper!"

The words had just left Fredrick's mouth when he charged towards them, knocking them to the ground, just as the sound of a rifle discharging echoed throughout Vauxhall Gardens.

Octavia lay on the ground, stunned. She wasn't quite sure what had just happened and her hip hurt where it had made contact with the hard path.

Fredrick's voice came from somewhere next to her. "Are you hurt?" he half-asked, half-demanded.

She looked at him and saw that his face was etched with worry. "I don't believe so," she replied as she moved to sit up.

"I need you to be sure because we need to leave this place. Now!" Fredrick glanced over his shoulder. "We must leave before the rifle is reloaded."

The panic in Fredrick's voice let Octavia know of the gravity of the situation. There wasn't time to lollygag. They had to leave, but her brother was more concerned about her. This would not do. She needed to focus on the task at hand.

Fredrick extended his hand to her. "Are you able to walk?"

Octavia allowed her brother to assist her in rising. "I can run, if that is required."

"Walking will do just fine, but it might be at a brisk pace," Fredrick said as he withdrew his hand. "Follow me and do exactly as I do."

Harred came to stand next to her. "Are you sure you are all right?" he asked, the concern evident in his voice.

"I am," she replied. "It isn't the first time that my brother has knocked me to the ground."

"Truly?"

She shook her head. "No, I was joking. Fredrick has never been so rough with me before, but it was for a good cause."

Harred put his hand up, indicating she should go first. "We need to catch up to Fredrick, and quickly."

Octavia noticed that Fredrick was a short distance away and he had an impatient look on his face. She hurried to catch up to him and was pleased that Harred followed closely behind.

Fredrick turned and started zigzagging along the path, not making a lick of sense. But Octavia did as she was told and followed him.

Once they arrived back at the coach, Fredrick helped her in before claiming the seat next to her. Harred sat across from her and watched her closely.

"Are you sure you are well?" Harred asked.

Octavia decided to make light of the situation so she said, "I did fall on my hip, but I do not think it will affect my child-bearing."

Fredrick frowned. "Are you truly joking at a time like this?"

"I am," Octavia defended. "Now that we are safe, it is the perfect time to make a joke. You two are far too serious for my liking."

"I wish you would be serious for once," Fredrick chided.

Octavia nudged his shoulder with hers, causing him to let out a groan. She glanced down and saw that there was blood on the sleeve of her gown. It was only then that she realized Fredrick had been shot and his jacket was saturated with blood.

"You are hurt!" she exclaimed.

"It is merely a flesh wound," Fredrick responded through gritted teeth. "It hadn't started hurting until you touched it."

Shifting in her seat, she said, "We need to get you home and send for the doctor."

"You do not need to concern yourself. This isn't the first

time that I have been shot," Fredrick revealed. "I will have my valet remove the bullet, assuming I wasn't shot through and through."

Octavia could see the sweat on Fredrick's brow and the clenching of his jaw to know that he was in more pain than he was letting on. "I do think it would be best if a doctor examined you," she pressed.

"What will a doctor do?" Fredrick asked.

"He could give you something to ease the pain," she replied.

Fredrick shook his head. "I won't take anything that will dampen my senses. Not again. I do not like how medicine makes me feel," he declared. "I will be fine. Just leave me be."

Octavia pressed her lips together, not ready to concede. She couldn't just let her brother suffer in silence.

Harred spoke up. "I do believe your sister is right in this case. You should have a doctor look at that wound in case it needs stitching."

"My valet served with me in the war, and he is far more competent with a needle and thread than a doctor," Fredrick shared. "I understand your concern, but it is unfounded."

Octavia opened her mouth to debate that point, but Fredrick continued. "The issue we should be discussing is the brazen attempt on Harred's life."

"How did you know there was a sniper?" Harred asked.

"I saw the light reflecting off the rifle," Fredrick revealed. "I got used to surveying my surroundings, looking for any sign of snipers, on the Continent."

Harred ran a hand through his hair. "I am most grateful for that, especially since you saved my life."

"It was nothing," Fredrick said, brushing off his praise. "I am glad that I saw the sniper before it was too late."

The coach hit a rut in the road and Fredrick let out a groan. Octavia wished there was something she could do that would help her brother, but she was at a loss as to what she could do. She felt helpless, and she did not like that feeling very much.

Fredrick brought his hand up to his shoulder and left it there. "Do you think Lord William would have hired a sniper to kill you?"

"I don't rightly know," Harred replied. "Greydon seems to believe that Lord Drycott could be behind these attempts on my life. To me, both seem unlikely."

"Someone is obviously trying to kill you," Fredrick said. "We just have to figure out who is behind these attacks."

"How do you propose we do that?" Harred asked. "I tried to talk to William about it but he just dismissed my concerns."

"That is because you asked him. I promise that he wouldn't be dismissive with me," Fredrick said.

Harred pinched his brows together. "You don't mean to interrogate him, do you?"

Fredrick brought his hand back down to his lap. "Someone just shot me. I intend to get answers and I won't rest until I do."

"That didn't answer my question," Harred said.

"I know, but that is because you don't need to know," Fredrick stated. "The time to ask politely is over."

Octavia could hear the terseness in her brother's voice and it worried her. When he became determined, nothing would stand in his way.

As she went to voice her concern, her brother said, "Not now, Octavia. I do not have time for a lecture."

"I am not going to lecture you," Octavia stated.

"Aren't you?" he asked. "Because I see the look in your eyes. You think you know what is best for me."

Octavia stared at her brother in exasperation. "Why are you being so vexing?" she asked. "I am trying to help you."

"I do not need your definition of help," Fredrick said.

The coach came to a stop in front of their townhouse and

the coach dipped to the side as the footman stepped off his perch.

Once the door was opened, Fredrick stepped down and offered his hand back to assist Octavia out of the coach.

Octavia looked at her brother's proffered hand and asked, "Will I hurt you if I take your hand?"

"I am fine, Octavia," Fredrick sighed, wiggling his fingers. "Just take my hand."

Tentatively, she slipped her hand into his and allowed him to assist her in exiting the coach. She removed her hand as soon as she stood next to him.

Harred came to stand next to her and asked, "May I escort you inside?"

"Don't you think you have done enough?" Fredrick growled.

Octavia shot her brother a stern look. "That was entirely uncalled for," she chided, coming to Harred's defense. "We will excuse your outburst since you are obviously in pain."

"No, Fredrick is right," Harred said. "I was the reason why he was shot and it is best if I stay away, at least for the time being."

"I do not accept that," Octavia argued.

Fredrick placed his hand on her elbow. "We should get inside before we garner any attention," he ordered. "Our coach will take you home, Harred. Good day."

"Fredrick—" Octavia started.

Her words were stilled when Harred placed his hand on her sleeve and leaned in. "This is not a goodbye. I can promise you that," he said softly.

Octavia's breath hitched at his words and she couldn't help but wonder about the meaning behind them. Dare she hope that he cared for her, just as she cared for him? Her heart was turning towards him, but it didn't frighten her. Rather, it felt like her heart had found a home in his.

"You forget yourself," Fredrick stated in a firm voice.

Harred straightened and took a step back. "My apologies," he said, but he didn't sound repentant at all. "I believe I will walk home. It shall do me some good."

"I do not think that is a good idea," Fredrick stated. "It would be best if you took the coach and remained off the pavement."

Harred opened his mouth to no doubt object, but Octavia spoke up first. "I agree with Fredrick. I can't stand the thought of you being in harm's way."

He considered her for a moment before saying, "Then I shall take the coach, but only because I wish to ease your mind."

"Thank you," Octavia said.

After Harred stepped into the coach, it was only a moment later that the driver urged the team forward.

Octavia watched as the coach rolled down the street, finding great relief that Harred was safe for the time being. She couldn't quite believe that someone had tried to kill him today... again. It was becoming far too frequent of an occurrence.

Fredrick's voice drew her attention. "We should get inside."

"Do you think Harred will be all right?" she asked.

"Harred is a smart man. He won't take any unnecessary risks at this time," Fredrick replied.

Octavia turned towards her brother with pursed lips. "You didn't answer my question."

"I know, but I do not wish to lie to you. I don't know what the future holds and someone is determined to see Harred dead," Fredrick said.

"You must stop that from happening," Octavia asserted.

Fredrick gave her a knowing look. "You care for Harred, don't you?"

Octavia felt her back grow rigid at his words. She didn't

dare reveal the depths of her feelings to her brother. "He is my friend."

"I daresay that he is more than your friend," Fredrick pressed. "I can see it in your eyes. You have fallen for Harred."

She should have known that her brother would have seen right through her. He always did. But that didn't mean that *she* was ready to admit her feelings.

As she thought of what she should say to end this line of questioning, her brother put his hand up. "I won't press you... for now. But think on what I said."

Octavia knew that she was in far more trouble than she had realized. She had not only fallen for Harred, but her heart was now involved.

Chapter Sixteen

The morning sun streamed through the windows as Harred sat at his desk in his study. He'd had a restless night of sleep as he replayed the moments of the attack at Vauxhall Gardens. If Fredrick hadn't noticed the sniper when he did, he might be dead. He shuddered at that thought. What had he done that was so grievous that someone wanted to kill him?

His brother did have the means and the opportunity to kill him, but would he do such a thing? It just sounded so preposterous. He didn't share a close relationship with William, but he would like to think his brother wasn't a murderer.

But what of Lord Drycott? Was Greydon right about him? Would he truly resort to murder over a bill in the House of Lords? That seemed like such a drastic measure.

Harred glanced down at the ledger and sighed. He hadn't gotten much work done this morning, and he doubted he would fare much better as time went on. When had his life gotten so complicated? But he already knew that answer. It was the moment his parents had died, leaving him to pick up the pieces. He was trying his best, but he felt like he was failing.

The only thing that kept him going was Octavia. It was

only after he'd met her that he felt his heart begin to beat again. The light of her soul pierced through the darkness that he had let consume him. She'd brought him back to life by showing him that there was still good in this world.

But now he had to convince her that he was the man for her. How was he supposed to do that when someone was trying to kill him? Quite frankly, he wanted her nowhere near him, yet at the same time, he didn't want to let her out of his sight. It was quite the conundrum he was facing.

His study door opened and his brother staggered into the room. "Your lordship," William grumbled as he performed an exaggerated bow.

"Botheration," Harred muttered under his breath.

William approached the desk and sat down on a chair. "I need to speak to you," he said, his words slurring. "I need your help."

"My help?" he asked. "What could you possibly need me for?"

"Sir Percy isn't releasing Ruth's dowry and I need to annul the marriage," William said. "Go to the House of Lords and request that it is done."

"An annulment is nearly impossible, and I'm afraid I do not have enough influence in the House of Lords to do such a thing," Harred admitted.

"Father would have enough influence," William stated.

Harred frowned. "Yes, Father did, but he is not here anymore. I am, though."

"But you are useless to me."

Leaning back in his seat, Harred asked, "Did you just come here to insult me? If so, you may as well leave."

William looked tired with his bloodshot eyes and slumped shoulders. "I made a mistake," he admitted.

"Just one, or many?" Harred mocked.

"Do you truly intend to kick me when I am down?" William asked.

Harred held up his hand. "My apologies. Please proceed."

William relaxed into his seat. "I should never have married Ruth and now I am stuck with a wife that I don't want."

"Well, you have a wife now," Harred said. "What do you intend to do about it?"

"I don't know. I acted hastily and my life is even worse than it was before," William expressed. "I just thought marrying would be the solution to all of my problems."

"A word of advice…" He paused, waiting for his brother to object. When no objection was forthcoming, he continued. "The way you treat your wife defines what type of man you are. Are you kind? Loving? Or do you intend to neglect her, making both of you miserable in the process?"

William looked crestfallen. "I don't know the first thing about being a husband."

"Father taught us by how he treated our mother," Harred said. "It is my hope that one day I can emulate his example."

"But I don't even know Ruth."

"Then get to know her," Harred said. "By all accounts, she appears like a pleasant enough young woman who is just striving to earn your approval."

William rubbed his forehead with his hand. "She is a pretty little thing, but she is only a merchant's daughter. Why did I think it was a good idea to bring her into our world?"

Harred resisted the urge to lean over his desk and hit William over the back of the head for saying something so entirely stupid. "Ruth is a part of our world now, and you need to stop insulting her at every opportunity. She may be the daughter of a merchant, but that shouldn't matter how you treat her. A wife is your equal, in every sense of the word."

"But—"

He cut his brother off. "There are no 'buts' about it. How you treat Ruth is how you can expect Society to treat her."

"How can you be so accepting?" William asked.

223

Harred lifted his brow. "How can you not be? Mother taught us to be kind to everyone, no matter their walks of life."

William dropped his hand to his side. "It would be so much easier if I just had Ruth's blasted dowry. Instead, Sir Percy holds all the power."

"I am sure he just wants to ensure his daughter is being taken care of," Harred mused.

"Yes, but he wants me to consult with her," William declared. "Can you imagine? A woman should not have an opinion."

Harred stared at his brother in disbelief. Could his brother truly be this much of a jackanapes? "I disagree. I want a wife who voices her opinion."

"Why?"

"I do not want my wife to hide a part of herself. I want to know everything about her, including her likes and dislikes."

William looked at him like he was mad. "We have a difference of opinions on what we both expect from a wife."

"That is where you are wrong. I expect nothing from my wife. I just want her to be happy."

"She will be happy being a marchioness. Isn't that enough for your wife?" William asked.

With a shake of his head, Harred said, "You have a lot to learn about women, but I am not the one to teach you." He pointed up at the ceiling. "You have a wife that can help you."

William followed his gaze and admitted, "I don't even know where to begin."

"You could start by apologizing to Ruth for your terrible behavior," Harred suggested. "You might even have to grovel."

"Me? Grovel?" William asked. "I think not!"

Harred knew his brother was an idiot, but he decided not to press him on his backwards opinions of how matrimony was supposed to be. They had more pressing issues that needed to be resolved. "Where have you been sleeping?"

William had the decency to look ashamed. "I have been staying with a friend across Town," he shared.

Harred suspected that William wasn't being entirely truthful, but he decided it was best not to press him. "You may come home, assuming you behave," he said. "I will expect you to treat your wife courteously."

William abruptly rose from his seat and walked over to the window. As he stared out, he said in a soft voice, "I miss Mother and Father."

"As do I," Harred responded.

"Father would tell me what I needed to do to get me out of this mess that I find myself in," William stated.

Harred studied his brother and saw the pain that was etched on his face. It appeared genuine, which was something he hadn't expected from William. "Father is not here, but I am."

"Yet you aren't helping me."

"I am trying, but you aren't listening to what I am saying," Harred said. "Father's biggest mistake was fixing all your problems. It is time you own them and face them head on."

William turned around and stared at him. "I prefer when Father took care of them. It was easier; it was familiar."

"Then how will you ever learn?"

"I don't want to learn!" William shouted, tossing his hands up in the air. "I want to go back to the way it was when Father and Mother were alive. I am tired of living without them."

Harred understood William's outburst. He felt the same way. But what he didn't realize was how much William was hurting. They had never discussed their shared pain.

Rising, Harred came around his desk and approached his brother. "We can't go back. We must move forward."

William closed his eyes firmly, as if he were holding back

tears. "I am so sick of trying," he admitted. "I can't do it anymore."

"You can, and you will," Harred encouraged. "When life seems the bleakest, you must look for a reason to have hope."

"What hope do I have?" William asked as he opened his eyes. "I have nothing."

Harred placed a comforting hand on his brother's shoulder. "You have me, Brother. I won't abandon you."

"Yet you kicked me out of our townhouse," William muttered.

"That was for your own good," Harred defended. "You were out of line by the way you treated your wife."

William leaned his shoulder into Harred's hand. "I just want this pain to go away. Nothing I am doing is working."

"You are looking for happiness in all the wrong places."

"But it is what I know."

Harred hoped his voice conveyed the compassion he felt for his brother's situation. "Happiness does not mean we don't have problems, but it is the result of how we deal with them."

"Pardon me for saying so, but what problems do you have?" William mocked.

"Well, someone is still trying to kill me," Harred said as he watched for William's reaction.

William's eyes widened slightly. "Who is trying to kill you?"

"That is what I am trying to figure out," Harred replied, dropping his hand to his side. "Someone took a shot at me at Vauxhall Gardens yesterday."

"It wasn't me!" William exclaimed.

Harred wanted to believe him, but he still had his doubts. William's reaction had seemed sincere, but he couldn't risk fully trusting him. It would be best to keep him at arm's distance- for now.

"I know," Harred lied. He felt bad for lying to his brother, but it was the only thing he could think of doing at a time like this.

William walked over to the decanter and held it up. "Why is this empty?" he asked. "It never is empty."

Harred decided it was best not to speak about the arsenic that Greydon had found in it. "I will speak to Mitchell about it."

"See that you do," William said as he placed the decanter down. "I am going to lay down for a while."

As William departed from the study, Harred sat down and reached for the ledger. He needed to focus on work, but his mind would not cooperate. Now that William was home, he would need to be more diligent, knowing one wrong move might be his last.

With a book in her hand, Octavia sat next to her mother as she slept in her bed, snoring softly. Her mother would be mortified to know that she was snoring, but Octavia didn't care. To her, it was a peaceful sound, one that she would miss when her mother was gone.

She lowered the book to her lap and studied her mother's thin, pale face. The end was coming, and Octavia was dreading it. A part of her was relieved that her mother would be out of pain, but she felt guilty for even thinking about such a thing.

She wondered what would become of her. Could she handle the days, the weeks and even the months ahead of her? She wanted to believe she was strong enough, but she wasn't sure. Harred believed her to be, and she was desperately trying to prove him right. But what if he was wrong?

An image of Harred came to her mind, and she allowed herself to dwell on it. He was so much more than just a handsome man. His eyes told a story of who he truly was. Kind. Brave. Loyal. And she trusted him, wholeheartedly.

There had been many people that had come into her life, but never had someone made such an impact as Harred had. With one glance, he made her believe things about herself that she had once thought impossible. She wanted to be the person he thought she was.

Her mother's eyes blinked open. "Hello," she said softly.

"Hello," Octavia responded.

Slowly, her mother moved to sit up in bed and rested her back against the wall. "Can you get me a cup of tea?"

Octavia rose and handed her the teacup that was on the table. "Here you go, Mother."

Her mother stared back at her blankly. "Do I know you?"

Nothing could have prepared her for what her mother had just asked, despite knowing it would inevitably happen.

The doctor had told her that there was no point in arguing with her mother and to instead try to act as if it didn't bother her. But she couldn't just leave it alone. "I am your daughter, Octavia."

A line between her mother's brow appeared. "No, that doesn't sound right. I do not have any children that I am aware of."

"Please try and remember," Octavia pleaded in a soft voice.

"I'm sorry, but I am not who you think I am," her mother responded.

Tears flooded Octavia's eyes and she vehemently blinked them back. "Excuse me for a moment," she said as she fled from the room.

As she stepped into the hall, she placed her back against the wall and let the tears fall down her cheeks. Roswell had warned her about the pain associated with not being remembered by their mother but she hadn't understood until it had happened to her.

How could her mother not remember her? She knew it wasn't her fault, but it felt awful to be forgotten.

Fredrick's concerned voice came from down the hall. "Whatever is the matter?" he asked.

"She has forgotten me," Octavia replied in between breaths.

He approached her and opened his arms out wide. She rushed into them and threw her arms around him, sobbing into his chest.

"It will be all right," Fredrick said as he attempted to comfort her. "Mother means nothing by this. Surely you know that."

"I do, but I had hoped it wouldn't have come to this," Octavia said.

Fredrick leaned back and looked her in the eyes. "Mother doesn't love you any less. Her mind is just slipping and we need to be patient."

Octavia bit her lower lip. "I know, but may I just cry for a little bit longer?"

His eyes held compassion. "You can cry for as long as you need to," he informed her. "I have nowhere else to go."

"I am not hurting your shoulder, am I?"

"You are not, and even if you were, it wouldn't matter."

"Thank you," she replied as she laid her head on his chest.

As her head rested against his chest, taking comfort in the steady rhythm of his heart, he gently informed her, "Although, Harred is waiting for you in the drawing room."

"Harred is here?" she asked.

"He is," Fredrick replied. "I invited him for dinner and perhaps a game or two after. I thought you might enjoy that, considering you have been moping around all day."

Octavia took a step back. "I have not been moping about," she argued.

"Forgive me, but it seemed a lot like moping." He paused and grew somber. "Tell me what I can do to help you."

"I could use a biscuit," she joked.

His lips twitched slightly. "I will see what I can do. Anything else?"

Octavia could hear the sincerity in her brother's voice and knew that he was trying to help ease her pain. "I don't need anything."

Fredrick considered her for a moment before saying, "I think you do, and he is downstairs waiting for you."

Unsure of his meaning, Octavia asked, "Pardon?"

"You, my dear sister, are messy, complicated and vexing, but I love you," Fredrick said. "I want you to be happy."

Octavia held his gaze as she asserted, "I am happy."

Fredrick pointed towards her eyes. "I see the sadness creeping in and it worries me. So much so that I decided to help you."

"How exactly did you help me?"

He leaned forward and kissed her forehead. "You will see, and then I will undoubtedly be your favorite brother."

"I don't know. Roswell married my dearest friend. Where is your wife?"

Fredrick shuddered. "I don't need a wife, at least not in this case." He gestured towards the corridor. "You mustn't keep Harred waiting."

She reached up and placed her hands on her cheeks. "I must look a fright."

"You look lovely," her brother said. "I will be down in a moment. I just wanted to speak to Mother before I join you for dinner."

Octavia didn't need to be told twice. She was excited to see Harred and she found herself hurrying down the corridor. Once she descended the stairs, she stopped at the large mirror that hung in the entry hall.

She took a moment to study herself in the mirror and saw that her eyes held a slight redness to them. But would Harred even notice? She hoped not. She didn't feel like explaining what had upset her. It might start her crying all over again.

As she stepped into the drawing room, she saw Harred was standing by the window and he was looking out over the gardens. His hands were clasped behind his back and his expression was etched in concentration.

She decided it was time to make her presence known. "Hello, Harred." She smiled, hoping to distract him.

He unclasped his hands and turned to face her. Without hesitation, he closed the distance between them and stopped in front of her. "What is wrong?" he asked, the concern evident in his features.

Octavia should have known he would have seen through her facade. "I just came from my mother's room and she…" Her voice hitched. Dare she continue and risk making a fool of herself?

Harred placed a hand on her sleeve. "She what?" he prodded gently.

She could feel the tears pricking at the back of her eyes. "She… uh… didn't remember me."

Her words had barely left her mouth when she found herself wrapped up in his arms. "I am sorry, my dear," he whispered.

Octavia allowed herself to relax into his arms and she found great comfort there. There was something familiar about being in his arms, something that felt very much like being home.

After a long moment, Harred dropped his arms and he took a step back. "I do apologize for my brazen actions—"

"Do not apologize, please," she said, speaking over him. "You did nothing wrong."

Harred watched her with a tenderness that she had never witnessed before and she realized that no one had ever looked at her like that. For the briefest moment, she felt cherished, loved.

"I am sorry about your mother. I cannot even imagine what you are going through," he said.

"It is hard," she admitted, "but I shall manage."

"If there is anything I can do, please do not hesitate to ask."

She offered him a smile, but she knew it was a weak one. She was appreciative of what he was trying to do, but she just wanted to return to his arms. They had a way of comforting her that no words could do.

With a glance at the door, she said, "Thank you for coming to dinner. It will be nice to have you here."

"It is my honor," Harred responded.

"Our cook made mutton." The moment the words left her mouth she wished she could take them back. Why would he care about mutton?

He smiled, and she was briefly distracted by the warmth of it. "I love mutton."

"Good, perhaps you can take some home with you." Could she not stop rambling? No doubt that Harred had his own cook and didn't need to return home with their mutton.

Harred didn't comment on her obvious discomfort. "That is kind of you to offer, but I do not want to deprive you of your mutton."

Octavia pressed her lips together, hoping she could think of something clever to say. She had exhausted the conversation about mutton. What must he think of her?

"You look lovely this evening," Harred said as he perused the length of her. The way he said his words she knew he was in earnest, making her feel beautiful.

"Thank you," Octavia responded as she ducked her head to hide the blush that was forming on her cheeks.

Fredrick's voice came from the doorway. "Carson just informed me that supper is ready. Shall we adjourn to the dining room?"

Harred held his arm out to her. "May I escort you, my lady?"

As she placed her hand on his, she murmured her thanks. Perhaps the words wouldn't be so elusive to her now that Fredrick had joined them. She truly hoped so. Even she couldn't stand the thought of speaking about mutton again.

Chapter Seventeen

Harred was sitting next to Octavia at the dinner table as he ate the mutton. She had been right. It was delicious, but that is not why he had accepted the dinner invitation. He had wanted to spend more time with Octavia. He cherished every moment he spent with her.

He glanced at her and admired her beautiful face. He didn't think he would ever tire of looking at her.

Fredrick's voice broke through his musings. "Don't you agree, Harred?"

Harred shifted uncomfortably in his seat as he realized that he had been caught staring by his friend. "I apologize, but my attention was elsewhere."

Octavia looked over at him. "Are you thinking about how delicious the mutton is?" she asked with a twinkle in her eyes.

He chuckled. "I am not, but you were right. It is rather delicious."

"I am often right about a lot of things," Octavia joked. "I just wish that Fredrick would listen to me more."

Fredrick smirked. "Harred is just being nice. You are no more right than Freddy is a beloved pet."

Octavia waved her fork in the air. "How dare you!" she exclaimed with a dramatic flair. "I would have you know that lots of people tell me how right I am."

"Please do not make up people again in an attempt to prove your point," Fredrick said.

Lowering her fork, Octavia responded, "I did not make anyone up, but the recollection of the events could vary."

"That is a polite way of saying that you are wrong," Fredrick teased.

Octavia smiled. "I guess we will never know."

"We do know," Fredrick pressed. "You live in a fictitious world and you are the only one that has access to it."

"It is a glorious world," Octavia acknowledged.

Fredrick shifted his amused gaze towards Harred and addressed him. "I feel as if I must apologize for my sister… again."

"There is no need to apologize," Harred said. "I still believe that your sister is a delight."

Octavia perked up. "Did you hear that, Brother?"

"I have ears, do I not?" Fredrick asked. "But I must wonder if Harred is drunk."

Harred held up his glass. "I assure you that is not the case since I have only drunk lemonade this evening."

"Someone might have laced the lemonade," Fredrick mused.

Octavia laughed. "You are just upset that Harred isn't agreeing with you. But your point is flawed."

Fredrick put his hand up. "I can see that I am outnumbered, but I stand by my original argument."

"My brother can never admit that he is wrong," Octavia said.

"That is a family trait," Fredrick countered.

Harred sat back in his seat as he listened to the siblings bantering back and forth. How he enjoyed listening to them.

Their words were laced with love, leaving little doubt how much they cared for one another.

What had gone wrong in his life that he didn't share a close relationship with his brother? They were so different and had always been at odds with one another. Perhaps if he had made a more valiant effort they wouldn't be where they were now.

Harred leaned to the side as a footman came and collected his plate. He went to address Fredrick as he asked, "How is your shoulder?"

"My valet stitched me up, and it will be as good as new," Fredrick replied. "Have you heard from your brother?"

"I have," Harred replied. "William returned home this morning and we had a long, frank conversation."

"I would be leery of him, especially at this time," Fredrick counseled.

Harred nodded. "I agree. I just don't want to believe that he could be behind the attempts on my life. He is my brother, after all."

Fredrick's eyes held compassion. "The people closest to us have the power to hurt us the most."

"Hurt, yes, but murder?" Harred asked. "William has made some terrible choices in the past, but I hope that even he has some limits."

The butler stepped into the room and announced, "Lord Rushcliffe would like a moment of your—"

The moment the words left his mouth, Greydon stepped into the room. "Pardon for the interruption, but I saw no reason to wait in the entry hall while I was announced."

Fredrick rose from his seat and gestured towards a chair. "Would you care to sit down and join us for dessert?"

"I suppose I could spare a moment," Greydon said as he pulled out the proffered chair. "I have discovered something of importance."

"Which is?" Fredrick asked.

Greydon turned his attention towards Harred. "Does the name Mr. Carswell mean anything to you?"

With a shake of his head, Harred replied, "No, that name has no significance to me."

"Interesting," Greydon muttered. "That was the man that Lord William shot during a duel over his sister."

Harred was utterly stunned by the news. "William was in a duel?" he questioned.

Greydon's gaze remained somber. "I take it that he didn't tell you, nor did your father."

"My father knew?" Harred knew he sounded like an absolute fool, but how had he not known that his brother had been in a duel? That was something that should have been discussed.

"Who do you think paid off Mr. Carswell's family to make it all go away?" Greydon asked.

Harred asked the one question that he dreaded knowing the answer to. "Did William kill this Mr. Carswell?"

"Not at first," Greydon replied. "But then an infection set in around the wound and he died a very painful death."

"Yet my brother didn't say anything about how he killed a man," Harred stated in an incredulous tone. "When was this?"

"Shortly before your parents died," Greydon revealed. "My informants told me that Lord William did not take it well. He started spending more time at the gambling halls and drank excessively. Some of the gambling halls even turned him away because he became too much to handle."

"Why didn't he tell me?" Harred asked. "I could have helped him."

"People don't always think rationally when they are dealing with grief," Fredrick attempted. "It sounds as if he is still dealing with the repercussions of his actions."

"There is more," Greydon said.

Harred huffed. "How can there be more?"

"Mr. Carswell left behind a wife and two young girls," Greydon shared. "By all accounts, it appears that Lord William has taken Mrs. Carswell on as a mistress. He visits her rather frequently and was there for the past few nights."

He didn't think his brother could sink so low but William continuously surprised him. And not in a good way. How could he take the wife of the person he killed as his mistress? Did he have no shame?

Greydon accepted a plate from the footman and picked up his fork. "Mrs. Carswell lives in Cheapside and I confirmed that Lord William is paying her rent."

"How did you determine that?" Harred asked.

Greydon smirked. "I asked nicely."

Harred doubted that, but he appreciated what Greydon had done. His brother was worse off than he had previously thought. If his brother had killed before, what would stop him from killing again?

Fredrick must have read his thoughts because he said, "It was a duel; not an execution. Mr. Carswell challenged him to the duel and your brother accepted. Other than a questionable lack of judgment, Lord William is not guilty of anything."

Octavia interjected, "Are duels not illegal?"

"They are, but only if you get caught," Greydon replied. "In this case, the late Lord Kendal made it all go away by paying off the family."

Harred leaned back in his seat and heaved a sigh. "Do I even know what my brother is capable of anymore?"

After Greydon took a bite of his pudding, he said, "I can't say for certain that your brother isn't behind the attacks on you, but it is evident that he is reeling from the effects of the duel. And it did not help that your parents died so quickly after."

Harred needed to be alone as he collected his thoughts. He rose and muttered, "Excuse me for a moment."

Once he stepped into the corridor, he placed his back against the wall and let out a few deep breaths. His brother had killed someone. How could he reconcile that?

Octavia's voice came from the doorway. "Lord William is still your brother."

Harred straightened from the wall and turned to face her. "I know, but I don't know him anymore. What was he thinking?"

She approached him and stopped in front of him. "Does it matter now?" she asked. "Lord William needs you now, more so than ever."

"He killed a man, and is now sleeping with his widow," Harred grumbled. "He is past hope."

"Do you truly believe that?" Octavia asked, her eyes searching his.

Harred lowered his gaze since he was fearful of what she might see in his eyes. "I don't know what to think anymore."

Octavia placed her hand on his sleeve. "I know the man you are and you won't abandon your brother. Not now."

"I can't help him," Harred admitted, bringing his gaze back up. "I tried, but it is too late."

"I am not saying that I condone your brother's behavior, but you will never regret straying on the side of kindness."

Harred slipped his hand over hers. He needed the strength that only her touch could provide. "You don't know what you are asking of me."

"I know precisely what I am asking of you," Octavia said. "But if you don't help your brother, you will one day come to regret it."

He winced, knowing that she was right. He hadn't abandoned his brother yet. How could he do so now?

"I will try," Harred said. And that was the truth. That was

all he could agree to, not knowing if William would even want his help.

Octavia smiled, and he knew that everything would be all right. A single smile from her could make him utterly undone. It was terrifying to think of how much power she had over him. But he didn't mind.

Fredrick stepped into the corridor and glanced down at their hands with disapproval. "Time is up, Octavia," he said.

Harred removed his hand and took a step back. "I think it would be best if I retired for the evening."

Octavia's smile dimmed. "I thought we could play some parlor games after our dessert."

Not wishing to disappoint Octavia, Harred said, "I am not opposed to a game or two."

"Good luck trying to get out of here at a reasonable hour," Fredrick remarked. "Octavia is very competitive and won't let you stop as long as she is winning."

"That is not entirely true," Octavia attempted. "I occasionally let you win because I feel bad for you."

"I win on my own merit," Fredrick said.

Octavia's lips twitched. "If you say so, Brother."

"I have long suspected that you cheat, but I can't prove it," Fredrick said with amusement in his eyes.

"That is only because you constantly lose," Octavia bantered back.

Fredrick gestured towards the dining room. "Let's eat our dessert before we settle this once and for all in the game room."

"Very well," Octavia said as she stepped into the dining room.

As Harred went to follow her, Fredrick placed a hand on his shoulder and stopped him. "Do avoid being so familiar with my sister or I will have no choice but to challenge you to a duel." His voice was hard and held a warning.

"I understand," Harred responded.

LAURA BEERS

Fredrick dropped his hand and the warmth returned to his voice. "Good, I am glad that we understand one another."

Harred watched as Fredrick disappeared into the dining room before he let out the breath that he had been holding. How in the blazes was he going to press his suit with Octavia when Fredrick was always around?

Octavia tried to ignore the blatant look of disapproval on her companion's face. Mrs. Harper was determined to press her point, despite Octavia never asking for her opinion in the first place.

"I think this is a terrible idea," Mrs. Harper declared, her hand waving in front of her. "We should turn this coach around and go home."

"There is no reason to."

Mrs. Harper scoffed. "A young lady should never call on a gentleman. What you are doing is disgraceful."

Octavia sighed. "I am not visiting Lord Kendal," she explained for what felt like the umpteenth time. "I am calling upon Lady William."

"Who happens to live with Lord Kendal," Mrs. Harper stated with a shake of her head. "Just think about what people would say if they saw you enter Lord Kendal's townhouse."

"I do not care what people think." Which wasn't entirely true, but she didn't want her companion to think she was softening towards her argument.

"But you must!" Mrs. Harper exclaimed. "If you don't abide by the rules of Society, you will become an outcast. Perhaps you will even have the misfortune of becoming a spinster."

"There are worse things," Octavia argued.

"Worse than becoming a spinster?" Mrs. Harper asked. "Name one."

Octavia knew that she might come to regret this, but she was tired of her companion's haughty attitude. "Being trampled by a coach. Traveling in a hot air balloon and having it fall out of the sky. Being kicked in the head by a donkey."

Mrs. Harper frowned. "You are an impertinent child."

"Furthermore, I would rather be a spinster than lose an arm," Octavia said. "Because if I lost an arm, everyone would point at me and call me the 'one-armed lady.' They might even throw trash at me."

"Good heavens, what an imagination you have," Mrs. Harper stated.

The coach came to a stop in front of Lord Kendal's townhouse, thankfully ending their conversation. The footman stepped off his perch and went to inform the butler of their arrival. Once the main door was opened, the footman returned to the coach and opened the door.

Octavia exited first and promptly headed towards the main door. The butler was standing to the side and greeted her politely. "Please come in, my lady," he said.

"Thank you," she responded.

Mrs. Harper had followed her into the entry hall just as she let out a yawn. "My apologies, but I did not sleep well last night."

Octavia bit her tongue and she tried to refrain from remarking on what Mrs. Harper had just said. Her companion never slept well and was constantly falling asleep in the most inopportune places. But, quite frankly, she didn't mind. She didn't think she needed a companion.

Mrs. Harper continued. "I believe I will remain out here in the entry hall and close my eyes for a moment. You don't need me, do you?"

"No, I don't," Octavia replied. Which was the truth. It

would be much easier to converse with Ruth without her companion in tow.

The sound of laughter drifted out from the drawing room and Octavia found herself being drawn to it. The first voice sounded like Ruth, but she didn't recognize the male's voice.

As she approached the drawing room, the butler spoke up from behind her. "Do allow me the privilege of announcing you."

Octavia nodded. She didn't want to give Mrs. Harper another reason to lecture her. The good thing was that she was fairly confident her companion would fall asleep the moment she sat down. She always did, except when she was in the coach and she thought she had being right on her side.

After the butler announced her, Octavia stepped inside of the drawing room and saw Ruth and Lord William. They were sitting on the same settee and they both wore smiles on their faces.

Octavia was confused. They appeared to be enjoying one another's company, but what had happened to cause such a radical transformation?

Lord William rose and bowed. "Good morning, Lady Octavia."

She dropped into a curtsy. "Good morning, my lord," she greeted.

He turned back towards his wife. "If you will excuse me, I will leave you and Lady Octavia to it."

Ruth's smile grew more, if that was even possible. "That is most kind of you, William," she responded.

After Lord William departed from the room, Octavia gave her friend an expectant look. "Pray tell, what has transpired between you and your husband?"

"Isn't it wonderful?" Ruth gushed.

"It is, but how?" she asked.

"Lord William apologized for his behavior and he told me that he wants to start over," Ruth replied.

Octavia knew that people could change, but generally it didn't happen that quickly. Which made her wonder what Lord William was about. "Do you think it is genuine?"

Ruth's smile dimmed. "Of course he is being genuine. Why do you ask?"

She sat down next to Ruth. "I do not mean to be a naysayer but I question his motives."

Apparently, Octavia said the wrong thing because Ruth visibly tensed. "His motives?" she repeated. "Have you considered that William made a mistake and is man enough to own it?"

Octavia could hear the terseness in Ruth's voice but she wasn't ready to back down. She feared that her friend was blinded by feelings for her husband. "I just think you should consider—"

Ruth abruptly rose, stilling her words. "I think you should go."

"Pardon?"

"William apologized and I forgave him," Ruth said. "What happened was in the past, where it will remain."

Rising, Octavia responded, "But he said some terrible things to you."

"He explained that he was under a great deal of pressure and he promised that it won't happen again," Ruth shared.

Octavia arched an eyebrow. "What kind of pressure did Lord William say he was under?"

"My father is being entirely unreasonable about my dowry and we are going to speak to him later today. Together."

"Do you think he is more interested in obtaining your dowry than a relationship with you?" Octavia asked.

Ruth frowned. "You know nothing about love. Why should I take advice from you?"

"Love?" Octavia asked. "Who said anything about love?"

"I will get Lord William to love me," Ruth said with a determined look on her face.

Octavia let out a sigh. "Love is freely given. You cannot force such a thing."

"I can." Ruth walked over to the door and stopped. "I trust that you can see your way out."

She didn't even have a chance to respond before Ruth disappeared through the door, leaving her alone.

She wondered what had just happened. Was she wrong to voice her concerns over Lord William's abrupt change? It just seemed too convenient.

Regardless, it was time to leave. She had been dismissed by Ruth and she had no desire to tarry where she wasn't wanted.

As she stepped into the entry hall, she saw Harred descending the stairs.

A smile came to his lips at the sight of her. "Hello," he greeted. "What a pleasant, unexpected surprise to see you."

Octavia returned his smile. "I came to call on Ruth," she informed him.

"Is she not in the drawing room?" he asked, coming to a stop in front of her.

"No, we spoke but she didn't like what I had to say," she admitted.

He seemed surprised by her admission. "I can't imagine that to be true."

Octavia lowered her voice and asked, "Have you noticed anything unusual between Ruth and Lord William?"

"Yes, I have," Harred replied. "By all accounts, my brother is appearing enamored with his wife."

"Does that not seem odd to you?" she pried.

Harred glanced over his shoulder before saying, "I am questioning my brother's intentions. I must assume it is to gain access to Ruth's dowry."

"That is what I fear as well," she said. "Poor Ruth wants to believe it is genuine, though."

With a glance at her sleeping companion in the corner, Harred asked, "What do you propose we do?"

"Can you speak to your brother?"

"I do not believe that will do any good. He doesn't listen to me."

Octavia blew out a puff of air. "Ruth is upset with me for daring to bring it up. I don't think she will listen to reason on this one."

"We will figure it out… together."

She quite liked the sound of that.

He stepped closer to her, but still maintained a proper distance. "I am sad that we do not get to play the part of husband and wife any longer."

"Are you?" she asked. "I thought it would be rather burdensome for you."

"Quite the opposite, in fact," Harred said, his eyes holding her transfixed. "There is no one else I would rather be in a fake relationship than with you."

Octavia felt the same way, but she didn't dare admit that. If she did something so foolish, he would see right through her. And he would know that she had developed feelings for him. Feelings that were not reciprocated.

Mrs. Harper snorted and her eyes flew open. "Good heavens, did I fall asleep again?" she asked as she stretched her arms.

Harred stepped back and created more distance between them. "If you have no objections, may I call upon you later today?"

"I have none," Octavia promptly replied. She felt a blush crawl up her neck at the rush of her words. Dear heavens, she was being far too brazen.

"Wonderful," Harred said.

Octavia remained rooted in her spot as she stared at Harred. She knew it was impolite to stare but she couldn't quite seem to help herself. She wanted to memorize every curve of his face.

Mrs. Harper rose from her seat. "We should be going, my

lady," she urged. "You do not want to take up too much of Lord Kendal's time."

Her companion's words broke the spell that had come over her and she turned her attention towards Mrs. Harper. "Yes, you are right."

Harred bowed. "Enchanted as always, Lady Octavia."

She dropped into a curtsy and murmured her goodbyes. How she wished she could tarry with Harred. The thought of staying with him forever was very appealing. But that was not an option. He had his life and she had hers.

As she walked towards the door, Harred's voice stopped her. "Lady Octavia."

"Yes?" she asked.

Harred closed the distance between them and reached for her hand. He brought it up to his lips and kissed the air above it. "I know you came to see Ruth, but just seeing you lifted my spirits."

"It was my pleasure," she said, pleased that she found her voice. His touch was causing her heart to do inconvenient things.

He held her hand a moment longer than what was considered proper before he released it. "I will be seeing you shortly."

"I hope so," Octavia said.

Mrs. Harper cleared her throat. "Shall we, my lady?" she asked, impatiently.

Octavia knew it was time to leave, no matter how much she didn't want to. "My lord," she acknowledged before she walked out of the townhouse.

She didn't speak as she went to sit in the coach and Mrs. Harper sat across from her. The moment the door closed, her companion said, "Well, that was entirely inappropriate. Lord Kendal should never have kissed your hand."

"I thought it was sweet."

"That is the problem," Mrs. Harper said. "You seem to lose rational thought when you are around Lord Kendal."

Octavia didn't feel like being lectured... again. Her hand still tingled from Harred's touch and she closed her eyes, reliving the moment. With every touch, every glance, she was falling more and more in love with Harred.

Chapter Eighteen

Harred reviewed the accounts as he sat at his desk in the study. He was biding his time until he could call on Octavia. It had been a pleasant surprise to see her earlier today and it had lifted his spirits. He had wanted to press his suit but he was unable to do so since Octavia's companion had been rather eager to leave. What he wouldn't give for just a moment alone with her.

He hoped that she did care for him as much as he did for her. But that might just be wishful thinking on his part. Either way, he wasn't about ready to give up. He would fight for Octavia. She was a woman worth fighting for.

William stepped into his study and performed an exaggerated bow. "Mitchell informed me that you wanted to see me, your lordship."

"I could do with less theatrics from you," Harred said.

"And I could do without you ordering me about," William countered. "But we are stuck with one another."

Harred should have known that their previous conversation wouldn't have solved all of their problems. But he had hoped it would have at least softened William towards him.

William stepped further into the room and dropped down

onto a chair that faced the desk. "What do you want, Brother?"

He decided to be honest with his brother, not caring if it stoked his anger. "I am concerned about your relationship with Ruth."

"You are?" William asked. "Were you not the one who told me that I needed to work on repairing my relationship with Ruth?"

"I did, but—"

William spoke over him. "I did exactly what you said, and it is still not good enough for you," he said, his voice rising. "You are unbelievable."

Harred leaned forward in his seat. "I just want to ensure your intentions are honorable."

"Who cares what my intentions are?" William asked. "Ruth and I are getting to know one another, and it wasn't as cumbersome as I thought it would be."

"Your wife is…"

"Is none of your concern," William said, finishing his thought. "Furthermore, I am not interested in hearing your opinion on anything."

Why did Harred think his brother was capable of changing? As much as he wanted to lecture his brother on his relationship with Ruth, he knew it would be best to move on. They had something much more important to discuss.

As he held his brother's gaze, Harred asked, "Why didn't you tell me that you were in a duel with Mr. Carswell?"

William grew rigid. "That is none of your business," he snapped.

"Isn't it?" Harred asked. "You fought in a duel and Father paid to cover it up. How is it not my business?"

"Leave it," William growled.

"I'm afraid I can't do that, especially since you have taken Mrs. Carswell as your mistress," Harred said. "Have you no shame? You are sleeping with the widow of the man that you killed."

William jumped up from his seat and advanced towards the desk. "You don't know what you are talking about."

"Enlighten me, then," Harred responded.

"I will do no such thing. My business is my own and I would ask you to stay out of it," William demanded as he leaned over the desk.

If his brother was trying to intimidate him into silence, it wasn't going to work. "I'm sorry, but your actions could disgrace our family," Harred stated. "I want you to end things with Mrs. Carswell before anyone else finds out what you have done."

William narrowed his eyes. "You think you have everything figured out, but you don't. You know nothing."

"I know enough," Harred responded. "You stayed with Mrs. Carswell for the past few nights and you visit her frequently."

In a huff, William stepped away from the desk and walked over to the drink cart. He picked up the empty decanter and slammed it down. "Why in the blazes hasn't Mitchell replenished the brandy?"

"I told him not to since I discovered arsenic in it," Harred explained.

William scoffed. "How would you even know there was arsenic in it?" he asked. "You are not that clever."

Harred thought his brother's response was rather telling. William couldn't care less about the danger associated with arsenic or that someone wanted Harred dead. But if William had placed the arsenic in the decanter, would he have been so quick to take a drink from it?

Leaning back in his seat, Harred said, "Thank you for that, but do we have an understanding?" he asked. "You need to do right by your wife."

"I am doing right by my wife since I need her dowry. If I

can woo her, it will go a long way with the negotiations with her father."

"Why not woo her because it is the right thing to do?"

William looked at him like he was a simpleton. "I can do both at the same time, can I not?" he asked. "Regardless, you will be happy to know that Mrs. Carswell is not my mistress."

"You expect me to believe that, considering you call upon her constantly?"

William furrowed his brow. "How would you know such a thing?" he asked. "Are you following me?"

"I asked a friend to look into it for me, and he discovered your relationship with Mrs. Carswell," Harred explained.

"Who is this friend?"

"It matters not, but he has worked as a Bow Street Runner in the past."

William pursed his lips together and stared off into the distance. "Just when I think you wouldn't do something so despicable, you go and surprise me."

"You left me little choice in the matter," Harred said. "You and I don't speak, at least not about what is important."

William closed the distance between them, stopping a short distance away. "You wish for me to confide in you, do you?" he mocked.

"No, but I wish for you to tell me the truth."

"For what purpose?" William asked. "Nothing you say will change anything between us. You think you are better than me and lord it over me."

"I do no such thing."

William's eyes flashed with annoyance. "You are sitting there, judging me, but you don't know what I have been through. What I am still going through."

"Why won't you tell me then?"

"Because," William started, tossing his hands up in the air, "I don't want to talk about it. It is in the past, where it will remain. I just want to forget that the blasted duel ever happened."

"But it did happen, and you can't outrun that."

"I can try," William said.

Harred crossed his arms over his chest. "How is that working for you?" he asked. "I only ask because you seem miserable at the mere mention of Mr. Carswell's name."

Some of the fight drained out of William as he held Harred's gaze. "How is it fair that I killed Mr. Carswell and I get to go on living as if nothing happened?" he asked.

"Was it a fair duel?" Harred asked.

William shifted his gaze away. "According to the gentlemen that acted as our seconds, it was, but you know what a good shot I am," he said. "I deliberately tried not to kill him, but his wound got infected. How could I plan for such a thing?"

"You couldn't have," he agreed. "But your actions afterwards define what type of man you are."

William hung his head. "I killed a husband and a father, leaving his family penniless," he admitted. "All my disposable funds have gone to support them."

"I thought Father paid off her family?" Harred asked.

"He did, but Mrs. Carswell was forced to pay off all of her husband's debts, leaving her with only a roof over her family's head."

"What you are doing is admirable but doesn't explain why you took Mrs. Carswell as your mistress."

His brother's head snapped up. "Are you daft? She is not my mistress. I have been providing for her and her children. That is all. I would never…" His words trailed off. "How could you think I would be capable of such a thing?"

Harred put his hands up. "If she isn't your mistress, why did you stay at her home?"

"Because I had nowhere else to go," William shouted. "Or did you forget that you kicked me out of our home?"

LAURA BEERS

If his brother wanted him to feel the slightest ounce of guilt for what he did, William would be sorely disappointed. "You know the reasonings behind why I did that."

William's nostrils flared. "I do, but how could you so easily turn your back on your own brother?"

"You left me little choice."

"Yes, but I suspect it was because I spoke harshly to your precious Lady Octavia more than anything," William said.

Harred reared back slightly. "Lady Octavia is not mine."

William gave him a knowing look. "Are you sure about that?" he asked. "You seem rather enamored with her."

Had he been so transparent that William had seen through him? Harred decided it was best if he was honest with William about his feelings since he was hoping to get his brother to confide in him. "I do care for Lady Octavia, but I did not do it for her."

His brother didn't seem convinced by the frown that marred his features. "You can lie to yourself all you want, but it is obvious to everyone around you."

"I do intend to pursue her, assuming she will have me."

"Good," William said. "Lady Octavia would make a fine wife for you."

"You have no objections?"

William shrugged. "I have many, but I doubt it would change your mind. I just hope Lady Octavia brings you the happiness you deserve."

There was a sadness to his brother's voice that was undeniable, prompting Harred to say, "You deserve to be happy, too."

"No, I don't," William responded. "That ship sailed long ago."

"It isn't too late to hope for happiness."

William looked at him with disbelief. "Since when did you get so sappy?" he asked. "I take it that this is Lady Octavia's influence."

256

"Lady Octavia has opened my eyes to many things," Harred admitted.

His brother's shoulders slumped. "Any chance of happiness for me fled the moment I killed Mr. Carswell. Now I have a lifetime to live with what I did, and it is pure misery."

Unsure of what to say, Harred remained quiet. He was at a loss for words. He wanted to cheer his brother up, but he knew that advice would fall upon deaf ears.

"Am I free to leave?" William asked.

"You always had a choice in the matter," Harred replied.

William straightened himself to his full height. "Did I?" he asked. "If you will excuse me, I have a wife that I must woo."

"For what it is worth, I find it admirable that you are caring for Mrs. Carswell and her children," Harred said.

"Thank you, but it is the least I can do."

"Does Ruth know?"

William shook his head. "No, and you are not going to be the person that will tell her. It is my business and I expect you to stay out of it."

"I think that is a mistake—"

His brother cut him off. "I did not ask for your opinion, did I?"

Harred opened his mouth to argue his point but his brother departed from the study without saying another word. Would William ever learn? No good would come from keeping secrets from his wife, or anyone, for that matter.

Octavia was hiding. She knew she should be with her mother, but she didn't think she could take the heartache of not being remembered again. So she sat in the drawing room- like a coward- and attempted to work on her needlework, but her heart wasn't in it. The only noise came from Mrs. Harper, who was snoring softly.

She looked up at the ceiling as she reminded herself that her mother's mind was slipping, and it wasn't her fault. But this was her mother. Her whole world. And she couldn't stand the thought that her mother didn't remember her.

Her brother stepped into the room and eyed her with concern. "Why are you hiding in the drawing room?"

"I am not hiding," she lied. "I am working on my needlework."

"Mother is asking for you."

Octavia perked up. "Mother remembers me?" she asked.

Fredrick approached her and sat down on the settee next to her. "I can't help but notice that you have been avoiding her since yesterday."

She lowered her gaze. "Was it so obvious?"

"It was to me, but I understand why it is."

"You do?" she asked, bringing her gaze back up.

Fredrick nodded. "I remember the first time that Mother forgot who I was. It hurt, and I struggled with it. How could a mother forget her own son?"

"How did you reconcile it?"

"Mother is trying her best, and we need to meet her where she is," Fredrick replied. "She isn't going to get better and we need to cherish the time we have left with her."

Octavia leaned over and placed her needlework on the table. "I will admit that I wasn't prepared when Mother forgot me."

"No one ever is," Fredrick said. "But you will regret it if you waste your time on needlework instead of spending it with Mother."

"I know, but I am bonding with my companion," Octavia joked.

Fredrick shifted his gaze to Mrs. Harper and said, "It is astonishing how much she can sleep through."

"I have come to find her snoring soothing."

"That is odd, Sister," Fredrick teased.

Carson stepped into the room and announced, "Lady William Woodville has come to call. Are you accepting callers, my lady?"

Octavia was surprised that Ruth was here, considering how they had left things the last time she had called on her. But she wasn't about to turn her friend away over a misunderstanding. "Please send her in," she said.

Fredrick rose in anticipation of their guest.

As Ruth stepped into the room, she had a look of unease on her face and she was gripping her reticule tightly in her hand.

"Thank you for agreeing to see me," Ruth said, stopping near the door.

Fredrick bowed. "It is a pleasure to see you," he greeted.

Ruth dropped into a low curtsy. "My lord."

Turning towards Octavia, Fredrick said, "If you will excuse me, I have work that I need to see to, but I hope to go riding later today."

"I would like that very much," Octavia acknowledged.

Fredrick offered them both a pleasant smile before he departed the room.

Ruth remained by the door and she looked utterly nervous. Octavia decided she needed to set Ruth at ease or else this conversation would go nowhere.

Gesturing towards a chair, Octavia asked, "Would you care to sit, Ruth?"

"I would, thank you." Ruth glanced at Mrs. Harper as she lowered herself down onto the chair. "I have come to apologize. I was completely out of line yesterday and I feel awful."

"You are kind to apologize, but, if anything, I should be the one who apologizes to you," Octavia started. "I had no right to pry into your business."

"You weren't wrong and that is why I reacted so terribly. I

didn't want you to be right. I just wanted my husband to want me."

Octavia couldn't help but wonder what Ruth wasn't saying, causing her to ask, "What has Lord William done now?"

Ruth sighed as she relaxed her posture. "I am unable to get a good read on him. One moment he is attentive and kind, and the next…" Her voice stopped. "He is aloof. It is exhausting trying to keep up with his emotions."

"Give it time," Octavia encouraged. "You hardly know one another."

"That is what I keep telling myself, but I just wanted an easy relationship like you and Harred have."

With a shake of her head, Octavia said, "You are mistaken. Harred and I do not have a relationship."

"Forgive me, but I thought you two had an understanding of sorts."

"No, we are just friends."

Ruth looked baffled as she pressed her lips together. "Does he not call on you frequently?"

Octavia thought it would be best to reveal the truth of why Harred came around so often. "We were pretending to be married for the sake of my mother," she explained. "My mother's mind is slipping and we didn't have the heart to tell her I wasn't married."

"Oh, I see," Ruth murmured, but she didn't look convinced by the explanation.

Octavia wasn't quite sure what else she could say to persuade Ruth, considering she didn't know what was truly going on between Harred and her. They were more than just friends, but they had no understanding. Not that she would be opposed to one.

In need of a distraction, Octavia reached for the teapot on the serving tray and asked, "Would you care for a cup of tea?"

"Actually, I was hoping we could go to Gunter's," Ruth

suggested. "I haven't been yet since I arrived in London and I would love some of their delicious ice."

"I am never opposed to a trip to Gunter's."

Ruth smiled broadly. "It shall be my treat, but I should warn you that I like to try the different flavors."

"I always have the intention of trying a new flavor, but I usually stick with a lemon ice. It is comfortable, familiar."

"Well, I hope to change your mind," Ruth said, rising. "Should we wake your companion?"

Octavia rose. "I don't need a companion since you can act as one for me, assuming you don't mind."

"Not at all. It is nice to not have to follow all those silly rules now that I am married," Ruth remarked. "I was not fond of my companion at all. She was my distant cousin but she was a stickler for propriety."

Mrs. Harper let out a slight snore and her eyes flew open. She glanced between Octavia and Ruth and said, "Dear heavens, I must have dozed off again."

"You awoke at the perfect time," Octavia informed her. "Lady William and I are departing for Gunter's."

Her companion stood up. "I shall join you."

"That won't be necessary since Lady William can act as my chaperone. She is married, after all," Octavia said.

"Very well," Mrs. Harper conceded, sitting back down. "I will go up to my room and rest until you return."

Octavia was grateful that her companion relented so easily. "Shall we?" she asked Ruth.

As they walked towards the main door, Ruth shared, "Harred was gracious enough to allow me to use one of his coaches."

"That was nice of him," Octavia acknowledged.

"It was," Ruth agreed. "He has been nothing but kind to me since I arrived on his doorstep. Sometimes I wonder how Harred and William are related. They both are so incredibly different."

"That they are," Octavia readily agreed.

They exited the townhouse and stepped into the coach. Once the footman closed the door, they started the short drive to Gunter's.

Ruth glanced out the window as she said, "Thank you for joining me today. It is nice to get out of that townhouse, even for a moment."

"Did Lord William not wish to join you?"

"I didn't ask him," Ruth admitted. "He wasn't home when I left and I didn't dare ask where he went."

Octavia could hear the sadness in Ruth's voice and knew that his absence was taking a toll on her. But she was at a loss as to what she could say to comfort her.

"I don't dare complain, though. I married the son of a marquess and my status has been elevated," Ruth said. "I should be grateful for what I have been given."

Octavia asked the one question that had been plaguing her thoughts as of late. "Are you happy?"

Her friend grew quiet. "Yes… no… I don't know," Ruth confessed. "I want to be happy, but William is making it rather difficult."

"Your happiness should not be defined by others," Octavia counseled. "Only you can decide if you are happy."

Ruth offered her a sheepish smile. "My father grew up penniless, and he had to fight to marry my mother. No one thought he was good enough for her. But, slowly, he built his empire and proved his worth," she shared. "Unfortunately, my father never made time for my mother since he worked all the time, and they drifted apart."

"I am sorry to hear that."

"After my mother passed away, my father told me that his biggest regret was that he hadn't been there for my mother. He had been so focused on chasing fame and fortune that he had failed to see what was right in front of him."

Ruth continued. "I am not ready to give up on William. I refuse to accept this is how our story will go."

"I do not believe that William is past hope," Octavia responded. "With time, he may come around and realize what he has right in front of him."

"I hope so," Ruth said. "For what is the purpose of having what I always wanted, if I don't have anyone to share it with?"

Octavia bobbed her head. "I was most fortunate to have a mother and father who adored one another. I was raised with an abundance of love in my home."

"That sounds perfect," Ruth said softly.

"It is what I aspire to have in my own home," Octavia shared.

Ruth gave her a curious look. "Would you object terribly to Harred pursuing you?"

Octavia pressed her lips together as she thought on how much she should reveal. She would love it if Harred pursued her, but did she admit it to his sister-in-law?

"It is all right if you don't wish to answer," Ruth said.

"No, it is all right," Octavia responded. "I am not opposed to Harred pursuing me, but you mustn't tell him that I said that."

The words had just left her lips when the coach came to an abrupt stop, causing Octavia to fall off her bench.

"What just happened?" Octavia asked as she righted herself.

A moment later, the door was thrown open and a stocky man pointed a pistol at Octavia. "Lady Octavia, you are coming with me!"

"I think not," Octavia said as she sat back on the bench.

The man cocked his pistol. "I do not have time for your insolence. I was ordered to retrieve you. No one specified if I couldn't shoot you first."

Ruth spoke up. "I have money. Lots of money. I will give it

to you if you leave Octavia alone," she attempted, the fear evident in her voice.

"Tempting, but no," the man declared. "Come along, my lady."

Octavia didn't want to leave the safety of the coach, but she was running out of time. She figured that this man would make good on his threat and shoot her.

The man reached in and grabbed her arm, yanking her forward. "I am tired of asking nicely. You have no choice in the matter."

Octavia fumbled as she stepped down onto the pavement, but the man kept his hand firmly on her arm. Glancing up, she counted two other attackers as they held the footman at gunpoint.

As she was being forcefully led to another coach, Octavia tried to resist but it was no good. The man was much stronger than her and her resistance was futile.

Octavia was tossed into the coach, landing with a thump in the center. The man followed her inside and sat on the bench.

"The bench is far more comfortable than the ground, my lady," he mocked.

She sat up and moved to sit on the bench. "Why are you doing this?" she asked just as the coach started picking up speed.

The man shrugged. "For the money."

"My brother will pay you whatever you wish if you return me home," Octavia said.

"I don't think so," the man said as he tucked the pistol into the waistband of his trousers. "I don't think my pistol is needed anymore, do you?"

The coach sharply turned a corner and Octavia reached out to steady herself. "Who paid you to abduct me?"

"You shall find out soon enough."

With a glance at the drapes that covered the window, she asked, "Where are you taking me?"

The man looked uninterested. "You ask far too many questions."

"Not really. I have only asked three."

"That is three too many in my opinion," the man growled. "Now, be a good girl and shut your mouth before I do it for you."

Octavia didn't dare ask another question, but one thing was for certain- this man had vastly underestimated her and her brother. Neither one would stop fighting until she returned home. Until then, she just had to bide her time.

Chapter Nineteen

Harred had just changed out of his riding clothes when someone pounded on his bedchamber door. The valet crossed the room and opened the door, revealing a red-faced footman.

"What is the meaning of this?" the valet asked.

The footman didn't respond to the valet but instead turned his attention towards Harred. "Lady William needs to speak to you at once, my lord."

Hearing the urgency in the footman's voice caused him to ask, "Did something happen to her?"

"No, but it is best if you hear it from her and not me," the footman replied, shifting uncomfortably in his stance.

Harred knew he wasn't going to get much more from the footman so he exited his bedchamber and hurried down the corridor. What could have caused his footman to have acted so strangely?

As he descended the stairs, he saw Ruth was pacing back and forth with a panicked look on her face, causing him to feel uneasy.

"Ruth," he called out.

She stopped pacing and ran up to him. "Harred, something terrible has happened," she rushed out.

His heart sank. "Did something happen to William?"

"What? No, William is fine, at least I think he is," Ruth replied. "It is Octavia. Someone abducted her."

The news hit Harred like a punch to the gut, leaving him reeling. In a voice that was far more steady than the turmoil he felt inside, he asked, "What happened?"

"We were driving in a coach to Gunter's and it abruptly stopped. A man opened the door and pointed a pistol at Octavia and ordered her out of the coach," Ruth informed him in between breaths. "I tried to stop him by offering him money but he refused it. Who refuses money?"

He placed his hands on her shoulders in an attempt to comfort her. "What happened next?"

"The man tossed her into another coach and it raced off," Ruth replied. "We tried to follow them, but the coach was moving too fast. There was nothing that we could do."

Harred had so many questions for Ruth. He needed to know everything about what had transpired. "What can you tell me about the man?"

Ruth bit her lower lip. "He was big and scary. And he smelled awful."

"Can you describe the smell?"

"Like excrement," Ruth replied as she scrunched her nose.

That hardly helped him, but he hoped Ruth could expand on what she witnessed. "Did he say or do anything that was unusual?"

Ruth's brow knitted in concentration. "When he opened the door, he pointed the pistol at Octavia and called her by name. How would he know who she was?"

"I don't know, but I am going to find out," Harred said, dropping his hands to his sides. "Did you tell anyone else about what happened?"

She shook her head. "No, I came here straightaway. I didn't know what else to do."

"Good, I will handle telling Octavia's family," Harred said.

"I do not want you to leave this townhouse for any reason for the time being."

Tears flooded Ruth's eyes. "I am sorry that I couldn't stop Octavia from being abducted. What will become of her?" she asked with a sob.

"Go have a cup of tea and try to remain calm," Harred encouraged. "Panicking will not help the situation."

"Are you going to send for the constable?"

"Not yet," Harred replied. "I know someone who can help me far better than a constable. He will help me get Octavia back."

Ruth reached out and touched his sleeve. "Please be careful," she said. "The man that abducted Octavia had a devilish glint in his eyes."

He was touched by her concern, but he would move heaven and earth to get Octavia back. "Do not concern yourself with me. I will be fine."

The main door opened and William stepped into the entry hall. His eyes narrowed when he saw Ruth's hand was on Harred's sleeve.

"What is the meaning of this?" William demanded.

Ruth quickly withdrew her hand and stepped back. "My apologies," she said, lowering her gaze. "I shouldn't have been so familiar."

William puffed out his chest as he glared at Harred. "Is this why you have been so concerned with my wife's welfare? You wish to have a go with her?"

Harred wasn't going to dignify his brother's question with a response, but he did have a few questions for him. "Where have you been?"

"Out," William answered. "Are you not going to answer my question?"

"Define 'out,'" Harred replied.

William huffed. "I don't answer to you, Brother. Or did you forget that?"

Harred was tired of William's pompous attitude and he was done playing nice. He advanced towards William and grabbed the lapels of his brother's jacket before shoving his back against the wall.

"Do you know where Octavia is?" Harred demanded, leaning into him.

William stared at him with wide, disbelieving eyes. "Why would I know such a thing?" he asked.

"Then where were you, and I want the truth," Harred said.

With a reluctant glance at Ruth, William replied, "You know where I was."

Heaven help him, Harred believed his brother, but that didn't mean he wasn't still responsible for Octavia's abduction. It just meant that he hadn't abducted her himself.

"If I find out that you had anything to do with Octavia's abduction, I will ensure you spend the remainder of your days in Newgate," Harred stated in a firm voice.

William's mouth dropped. "Octavia was abducted?" he asked. "And you think I had something to do with it?"

"I don't know what to think right now, but I am not ruling out anyone, including you," Harred said.

"I know we don't always get along, but you have to believe me. I am telling the truth. I would never hurt a woman," William stated.

Harred glared at his brother. He truly hoped his brother was telling the truth, but the man had lied to him before. "We shall see," he said before he released his brother and promptly departed from his townhouse. He now had the unfortunate task of informing Fredrick that his sister had been abducted.

He started walking down the pavement towards Fredrick's townhouse but it quickly turned into a run. He saw the curious looks that were being cast his way from people that he passed on the pavement and he gave them little heed. Who cared what they thought of him? He was far more concerned about Octavia at the moment.

In what felt like an eternity, but was probably only mere moments, he arrived at Fredrick's townhouse and pounded on the door, which was promptly opened.

"May I help you, my lord?" the butler asked.

Without waiting to be invited in, Harred stepped inside and demanded, "I need to speak to Lord Chatsworth at once."

Fredrick appeared in the doorway of a room off the entry hall. "Whatever has happened?"

Harred knew there was no easy way to say this so he just decided to say what needed to be said. "Octavia has been abducted."

In an instant, Fredrick's jaw clenched and he looked dangerous. "Tell me what happened," he ordered.

"Ruth and Octavia left to go to Gunter's and someone intercepted their coach. A burly man held Octavia at gunpoint and made her leave in another coach."

"Did the man say anything about who hired him?" Fredrick asked.

"Ruth did not mention that, but she did say that he refused the money she offered to leave Octavia be," Harred replied.

A maid approached Fredrick and held out a piece of paper. "This was just delivered for you, my lord," she announced. "It was delivered to the servants' entrance by a street urchin."

Fredrick accepted the note and read it. He lowered it to his side and revealed, "The note says that if I want to see my sister alive, I am to bring you to the northwest entrance of St. James's Park tonight at midnight."

"Then we must go," Harred said.

His friend put his hand up. "Hold on," he stated. "If you

go, you most assuredly will be killed and there is still no guarantee that her abductor will return her to me."

"But can we risk not going?"

"Oh, I will be going with Rushcliffe, but you won't be going anywhere near St. James's Park," Fredrick replied.

Harred wasn't about to stand by and let his friends fight his battles for him. "I want to go," he stated firmly.

"This is not the time to play hero," Fredrick said. "Someone is intent on seeing you dead and they won't stop until they accomplish that feat."

"So you want me to do nothing?"

Fredrick nodded. "Now you understand." He turned towards the butler. "Bring the coach around front and do so quickly."

The butler tipped his head. "Yes, my lord," he replied as he departed to do his bidding.

"I will bring Octavia back. You do not need to worry," Fredrick said.

Harred trusted his friend, but he loved Octavia. And he wasn't about to sit at home and do nothing to help her. "I am coming with you."

"I don't think that is wise—"

He cut his friend off. "I am going, and that is final."

Fredrick looked as if he were going to object, but instead he said, "I understand your urgency, I truly do, but there is a chance this could go very poorly for you."

"As long as Octavia is in danger, I refuse to just sit back and do nothing," Harred declared.

"Very well," Fredrick responded, "but you will do exactly what Rushcliffe and I tell you to do. Quite frankly, if it came down to Octavia's life or yours, I would choose her."

Harred grew solemn. "That is precisely what I want you to do. My life has no meaning without Octavia in it."

Fredrick placed a hand on his shoulder. "If you survive

this, I hope you have the courage to tell Octavia how you really feel about her."

"I intend to."

"Good, but we mustn't dwell on that now. We have far more important things to discuss," Fredrick said.

The butler stepped back into the entry hall and announced, "The coach is out front, my lord."

They both didn't need to be told twice and they quickly headed towards the coach. Once the coach was rolling down the street, Fredrick glanced out the window. "Please say that you are a better shot than when we were younger."

"I have improved," Harred said.

"Have you ever shot anyone?"

"I have not."

Fredrick's eyes held something he couldn't quite decipher. Remorse, perhaps? "It is not something you should ever do lightly," he said. "Every death will stay with you, pricking at your very soul, until you begin to wonder what type of person you truly are."

It was evident that Fredrick spoke from experience and he didn't dare ask any questions about what he must have gone through during the war. It wasn't his place to do so. But it definitely had taken a toll on him.

As quickly as those emotions entered his friend's eyes, they disappeared and he continued. "Whoever took Octavia made a big mistake. Whatever he does to my sister, he will suffer a similar fate. I can promise you that," Fredrick declared.

Harred found himself to be exceedingly anxious, knowing nothing could be done for Octavia until midnight. What kind of conditions was she forced to endure right now? Was she cold? Frightened? How he wished he could be there to hold and comfort her. He would tell her it would be all right and he would do whatever it took for her to return home, even sacrificing his own life.

Harred didn't bother to wait for the footman to open the door after the coach had come to a stop in front of Lord Rushcliffe's townhouse. He had no time for such luxuries since time was of the essence.

The moment his foot was on solid ground, he headed towards the main door and pounded on it.

Fredrick's voice came from behind him. "You need to calm down."

"Calm down?" Harred repeated in disbelief. "Why aren't you more upset? Your sister has been abducted."

"I am well aware of that, but going off half-cocked is going to solve nothing. If anything, it will make the situation worse."

"Well, I can't just stand by and do nothing."

"We are doing something," Fredrick asserted. "You must trust me if you want to keep Octavia safe."

Before he could respond, the door opened and the butler asked, "How may I help you?"

"We are here to see Lord Rushcliffe," Harred said with urgency in his voice.

The butler gave them a look of regret. "I'm sorry, but that is impossible. Lord Rushcliffe is having dinner with family. If you would come back later—"

Harred placed his hand on the door and shoved it open. "No, we must speak to Lord Rushcliffe now!"

The butler staggered back. "If you do not leave at once, I will be forced to send for the constable."

"Good," Harred replied as he stepped into the entry hall. "Rushcliffe! Where are you? I must speak to you at once!"

Fredrick placed his hand on Harred's arm. "This is not the way to get Rushcliffe's attention," he warned.

Harred knew he was acting irrationally but he needed

Greydon's help and he needed it now. He would do whatever it took to get Octavia back, including making a complete and utter fool of himself.

Greydon's voice came from a doorway off the entry hall. "What is the meaning of this, Kendal?" he demanded.

"I need your help," Harred rushed out.

Fredrick shook his head. "We need your help, and I'm afraid it is rather urgent. Do you have a moment to speak to us?"

Greydon frowned. "Why is it so imperative that you speak to me right now?"

"Octavia has been abducted," Fredrick revealed. "And the only way to get her back is to trade Kendal for her at midnight."

A gasp came from behind Greydon. "Poor Octavia," Enid said as she appeared by her husband. "You must save her."

Greydon nodded before he addressed his wife. "I am sorry about dinner."

Enid waved her hand in front of her. "Octavia is much more important," she stated. "I shall go back and keep your father company."

"Thank you, my love," Greydon said as he kissed her on the cheek.

"Just promise me that you will return home to me," Enid responded with a seriousness in her voice.

"Always," Greydon promised. "You won't be getting rid of me that easily."

Enid gave him a playful shove. "Go and save my friend. But I should warn you that I won't let your dessert go to waste."

Harred shifted in his stance as he tried to quell the growing irritation inside of him. They had more important matters to discuss than dessert.

After Enid disappeared back into the room, Greydon gave

Harred a knowing look. "You need to go home and let us handle this."

"Absolutely not!" Harred exclaimed. "I can't just stand by and do nothing."

"You are too emotional, and that could get you or Octavia killed," Greydon said.

Harred put his hands out and asserted, "I am a part of this, whether you want me to be or not."

Greydon exchanged a look with Fredrick before saying, "Very well, but you will do precisely what Fredrick and I tell you to do. Any variance could have dire consequences."

"I can do that," Harred agreed.

Gesturing towards a corridor, Greydon said, "We can speak freely in the study."

No one spoke as they headed towards the study in the rear of the townhouse. Once they arrived, Greydon closed the door behind them and crossed his arms over his chest.

"Tell me everything," Greydon ordered.

Harred opened his mouth, but Fredrick spoke first. "Octavia was riding with Lady William in a coach and someone intercepted it. They abducted Octavia at gunpoint and fled with her in another coach."

"Was there a ransom note?" Greydon asked.

Fredrick slipped his hand into his jacket pocket and removed a piece of paper. "There is," he confirmed as he handed it to Greydon.

Greydon read it before he asked, "Who delivered it?"

"A street urchin," Fredrick replied.

Crumpling the note in his hand, Greydon said, "Whoever abducted Octavia is determined to kill Kendal."

"That is what I concluded as well," Fredrick remarked.

Greydon bobbed his head. "We need to come up with a plan to retrieve Octavia, without turning over Kendal."

"How is that possible?" Harred asked.

With a smirk, Greydon replied, "Everything is possible with the right preparation."

Harred ran a hand through his hair. "If it comes down to it, I will gladly trade myself for Octavia's safe release."

"I know, and that is what this person is hoping for," Greydon said.

Fredrick turned towards Harred. "Do you think Lord William would go to such drastic lengths to see you dead?"

Harred shrugged. "William seemed genuinely surprised that Octavia had been abducted. I want to believe he isn't capable of such a thing," he said. "Besides, if he truly wanted me dead, he could have done so when I slept."

"That would be too suspicious," Greydon remarked. "If he did such an act, he wouldn't inherit the title and estate. No, it would be much more underhanded."

"My brother is lazy. I can't imagine he would orchestrate such an elaborate crime," Harred reasoned.

"Greed can be a powerful motivator," Fredrick said.

Harred dropped down onto the settee. "It can't be my brother."

"I don't think you want it to be your brother," Greydon remarked. "But he does rub shoulders with disreputable people. He could have easily recruited a group of ruffians to help him with this."

"You are right. I want to believe the best in my brother," Harred admitted.

Greydon placed his hands on the back of a wingback chair and leaned into it. "There is also Lord Drycott. He has means, and motive."

"I can't imagine Lord Drycott would do such a thing over a bill," Harred said.

"If that bill passes, it will ruin him," Fredrick reminded the group. "If not him or William, then who?"

"Until a few days ago, I wouldn't have thought anyone would want me dead," Harred admitted.

"We need to draw this person out," Greydon said.

"I agree, but how do you propose we do such a thing?" Fredrick questioned.

Greydon pushed back on the chair and straightened to his full height. "I don't rightly know, but we have a few hours to think of something."

"I feel as if we are missing something here," Fredrick said. "Who else would benefit from Harred's death?"

"All I can think of are Lord William and Lord Drycott," Greydon responded.

"There must be someone else," Fredrick pressed.

Greydon walked over to the window and looked out over the gardens, appearing deep in thought. After a long moment, he asked, "Who else knows that Harred is in love with Octavia?"

Harred's mouth dropped but he quickly recovered. "I never said that I loved Octavia."

"You didn't have to," Greydon responded. "It is obvious in the way you speak of her. You say her name with such reverence that it would be impossible for someone not to interpret."

"Have I been so obvious in my affection for her?" Harred asked, glancing between them.

Fredrick chuckled. "Why do you think I was pushing you towards each other? You both care for one another."

"I do not presume to know what Octavia feels for me," Harred said. But he felt elated by Fredrick's words.

Greydon pressed his lips together before asking, "Do you have any tenants that despise you or a business deal that went bad?"

"No," Harred replied. "I try to be fair with all of my tenants and my man of business handles all of my business deals."

"Yet someone wants you dead," Greydon pointed out. "And I think the answer lies with Octavia."

Fredrick interjected, "What if we pretended to hand over Kendal, but lay in wait and ambush the abductors first?"

"That is too risky," Greydon said. "Octavia could be shot in the process. No. We need to turn over Kendal if we want to save Octavia."

"If that is the only way," Harred stated. He wasn't afraid of dying if it meant that Octavia would be spared.

"It is, but I have an idea," Greydon shared. "There are risks associated with it and you would be in harm's way for a short time."

"I will do whatever you will have me do. I just want to ensure that Octavia walks away, unharmed," Harred responded.

"Don't worry, we will keep Octavia safe," Fredrick said. "But I daresay she would never forgive me if something happened to you in the process."

Greydon crossed the room and sat down next to Harred. "It starts with you turning yourself over to the enemy and hoping they won't kill you right away…"

Chapter Twenty

Octavia sat in the darkened coach as it traveled along the road. She was watching her captor as he stared out the window. She knew she should be afraid, but she wasn't. Fredrick would save her; she was sure of that. But what did they want with her?

She had spent the past few hours in an abandoned warehouse in the rookeries, where the rats had scurried around her feet. But she hadn't let her discomfort be known. She didn't want to give them that satisfaction.

One of her other captors had let it slip that the man who had abducted her was named John. She studied his features. Her captor didn't look like a John, she thought. He looked more like a Judas or a Simon. Either name would be far more terrifying than John.

John closed the drapes and turned his attention towards her. "We are almost there."

"Where?"

"Does it matter?" he asked. "If everything goes according to plan, you will be home soon and you can put this all behind you."

Octavia wanted answers so she pressed, "Are you just going to let me go?"

John chuckled. "No, it is not that simple," he replied. "You are far too valuable to just let go."

"Did you request a ransom from my brother?"

"In a way."

"I don't understand."

The humor left John's face. "I preferred it when you were quiet."

"And I preferred it when I wasn't abducted, but here we are."

With narrowed eyes, John said, "You are a cheeky little thing. How does your brother handle you?"

Octavia felt her back grow rigid at that ridiculous remark. "My brother does not 'handle' me. Furthermore, he is not concerned with me voicing my opinion."

"It is vexing."

"So say you," she retorted. "I have been told that I am a delight."

John placed his hand on the butt of the pistol that was tucked in the waistband of his trousers. "I tire of this conversation. You will remain quiet or there will be consequences."

Octavia knew it would be best if she remained quiet, but she couldn't help herself. There were too many questions that she needed answered. "You would truly shoot me for talking?"

"If it got you to stop."

Octavia cocked her head. "Why are you doing this?"

"I already told you, for the money."

"Yet you wouldn't take Lady William up on her offer for more money," she remarked. "If it was all about the money, as you said, you could have walked away without abducting me."

John huffed. "Lady William would have never given us that money since she would need to ask her husband for permission."

"You do not think that Lady William can speak for herself?"

"Frankly, it doesn't matter now," he replied. "Soon, I will be paid and I can rid myself of your incessant chatter."

Octavia shifted on the bench before asking, "Who is paying you?"

"It doesn't matter to you, now does it?"

"You are wrong. It does matter to me since this person paid to have me abducted."

John retrieved his pistol and pointed it at her. "Stop talking," he ordered.

Now if Octavia was smart, she would follow his command and leave it be. But she refused to be cowed by this man. "May I ask one more question?"

He looked at her in disbelief. "I am pointing a pistol at you. Does that not concern you?"

"It does, but this isn't the first time someone has pointed a pistol at me," she replied.

"I could shoot you."

"You could, but you wouldn't do something so foolish."

John looked amused by her words. "And why is that?"

"You do not want to do anything to upset my brother," Octavia said. "He is fiercely protective of me and he will enact revenge if I am harmed."

Puffing out his chest, John remarked, "Your brother doesn't scare me."

"He should," Octavia stated. "He is not a man that you want to trifle with. Neither of my brothers are. But Roswell is on his wedding tour or else he would be plotting his revenge right now."

John smirked. "Your brothers probably have never gotten their hands dirty before. What would they have done?"

Octavia smiled, knowing she was privy to a secret. "My brothers are far more dangerous than you."

He let out a bark of laughter. "I didn't realize you had such a vivid imagination."

She decided it would be best not to elaborate because she thought it was better if the man kept his preconceived notions. No matter how wrong they were. It would be for their benefit when Fredrick came to rescue her.

"I have been watching you for a while," John started, "and I have noticed nothing that would indicate that Lord Chatsworth is a threat to me."

"Why have you been watching me?"

"One is always well-versed with his target," he replied. "It is how I knew that Lord Kendal's weakness was you."

Octavia furrowed her brow. "I am not his weakness."

"You are. He is enamored with you."

"I do not believe that to be true."

John considered her for a moment before saying, "You truly don't know how he feels about you?"

She grew silent, not knowing what to say. She hoped what he was saying was true, but she didn't want to get her hopes up. After all, John had abducted her. Why would she think he would tell her the truth?

"I did the impossible. I got you to shut your mouth," John mocked. "Well, you might be saddened to hear that Lord Kendal is going to die tonight."

Her eyes grew wide. "What? Why?" she asked.

"I don't know the reasonings nor do I care," he said. "Our job ends when we kill Lord Kendal."

Panic welled up inside of her as she rushed out, "I am rich. I will pay you whatever you want to leave him be."

"I don't want your money," John spat out.

"Why is my money not good enough for you?" she pressed.

He flicked his wrist. "Once we have Lord Kendal, you will be returned to your brother. Consider yourself lucky."

"Please, you don't have to do this," she pleaded.

In a swift motion, John slapped her across the cheek. "Stop talking!" he ordered. "Nothing you say will change anything."

Octavia's cheek throbbed but she refused to show any sign of weakness to her captor. And she wouldn't let Lord Kendal sacrifice himself for her. She wouldn't be able to live with herself if he did.

The coach came to a stop and John muttered, "Finally." He opened the door and stepped out. "Get out here."

She did as she was commanded and exited the coach. As her eyes roamed over the path, she recognized this place as St. James's Park. She had been here many times before.

John gripped her arm tightly. "Just do what I say and you will survive this," he said.

Octavia knew there was no point in pleading with him to stop this madness and just walk away with his life. Her abductor was far too stubborn.

She turned her head to see the other two of her captors, both with pistols in their hands. They barely spared her a glance as they kept their gazes on an approaching coach that was slowly making its way along the path.

The coach came to a stop a short distance away and the door was tossed open. Octavia watched as Fredrick emerged first and was followed by Harred, causing her heart to drop at the sight of him. What was he doing here? She hoped he wasn't going to try to be a hero by sacrificing himself.

John pressed the pistol to her temple. "Remove your pistols and drop them to the ground," he ordered.

Fredrick retrieved a pistol and lowered it to the ground as instructed. He winked at her as he rose, and she suddenly felt better. Her brother would make this right. He just had to.

Harred put his hands up and said, "I did not bring a pistol with me."

John shifted his weapon to point the pistol at Harred. "Of

course you didn't, my lord," he mocked. "Shall we get this over with?"

Fredrick spoke up. "Before I hand over Lord Kendal, I demand to know who hired you."

"You demand, do you?" John asked in an amused voice. "What gives you that right to ask such a thing?"

"It is only fair for you to tell us since we did as we were told," Fredrick replied.

John tightened his hold on her arm. "What if I just shot your sister?" he asked. "Would you stop asking ridiculous questions then?"

Fredrick's next words came out more as a warning. "Anything you do to Octavia, the same will be enacted on you. I promise you that."

"You do not frighten me," John said. "You are just an earl. What do you know about making good on threats?"

"I served in the Army under Wellington," Fredrick replied. "I saw things that you couldn't even comprehend."

"Regardless, that will not help you here. Just hand over Lord Kendal and we can end this," John commanded.

"No," Fredrick said.

John's brow shot up. "No?" he repeated. "Are you mad?"

Fredrick pointed at her abductor. "I count three of you and you are vastly outnumbered, outmanned and outgunned."

"There are only two of you, and we are all pointing pistols at *you*," John pointed out. "Why should we believe you?"

"Did you even bother to scout the area before you arrived?" Fredrick asked.

John glanced over at the woodlands that surrounded the path. "There was no need to. We are just here to exchange Lady Octavia for Lord Kendal. No one needs to be a hero here."

Harred interjected, "Yet you assumed we would come alone?"

"For your sake, you better have," John replied. "I could just as easily kill Lady Octavia as I could hand her over to her brother."

Octavia glanced at her other two abductors who were holding pistols aimed at Fredrick and Harred. They both had looks of uneasiness on their faces as their gazes darted towards the woodlands. There were plenty of places to hide just off the path, and she assumed they had made that assumption as well.

John shoved the pistol into Lady Octavia's side and she let out a cry of pain. "Once Lord Kendal is in our hands, we will turn over Lady Octavia."

Fredrick shook his head. "That isn't going to work for me. I want you to release my sister and you may leave with your lives."

"Our lives?" John scoffed. "Surely you are not that delusional."

"I don't play games, especially when it comes to my sister's safety, and this is your only warning," Fredrick stated.

One of her other abductors said in a hushed voice, "Perhaps we should walk away."

"Nonsense!" John exclaimed. "Lord Chatsworth is just all talk. He is just trying to scare us. Nothing more."

"I would listen to your comrade," Fredrick urged. "He seems like the smartest one of you three."

John pointed the pistol at Lord Kendal and cocked it. "It might be best if I just kill Lord Kendal and be done with it."

———————— ◆ ————————

As Harred stared at the pistol, he felt no fear. He should. But he didn't. Whatever happened, he knew this was not the end. He trusted the plan that Greydon had set into motion.

Fredrick stepped in front of Harred, blocking him from the shooter. "You don't want to shoot this man," he said.

"Yes, I do," the burly man replied. "Once I kill him, I can collect the money and this will all be over."

"Unfortunately, the moment your finger twitches on that trigger, you will be shot by one of the snipers that are posted in the woodlands," Fredrick revealed.

The man's eyes nervously darted towards the woodlands. "You are lying."

"Am I?" Fredrick asked. "Do you truly want to find out if I am telling the truth?"

Greydon stepped out from behind a tree and pointed a pistol at the man's back. "You are surrounded by men that owed me a favor, and it would be best for you to put your pistols down."

The other two abductors lowered their weapons to the ground and ran towards the woodlands, disappearing within.

"They won't be getting far," Greydon said.

The lone abductor tightened his hold on his pistol and shouted, "You were supposed to come alone. That was the deal."

"We had no deal," Fredrick stated. "You made a big mistake by abducting my sister. I cannot let that go unanswered."

Indecision crossed the man's face and Octavia must have seen it, too. She slammed her foot into the top of the man's boot and yanked her arm away.

While Octavia started running towards her brother, the man pointed his pistol at her back, causing Greydon to discharge his pistol into the back of the man's leg.

The abductor dropped to the ground, howling in pain, as he held his wound tightly. "You shot me!" he shouted.

Octavia ran into her brother's open arms and he warmly embraced her. "You are safe now," Fredrick said. "No one will hurt you now."

Greydon approached Octavia's abductor and stripped him of his pistol.

Fredrick leaned back and met Octavia's gaze with disapproval etched on his features. "What were you thinking?" he asked. "I had it handled."

With a stubborn tilt of her chin, Octavia responded, "I was thinking that I was tired of having a pistol pointed at me."

Harred placed a hand on her sleeve. "I, for one, am immensely grateful that you were able to get away from your attacker safely."

Octavia gave her brother a smug smile. "Did you hear that, Brother?" she asked. "Harred thinks I did the right thing."

"No, he never said that," Fredrick countered. "I'm wondering if your hearing was affected by being abducted."

Greydon cleared his throat, drawing their attention. "As touching as this moment is, we need to speak to this man before we get him to a doctor."

"You are right," Fredrick said. "Please proceed."

Greydon crouched down by the man and ordered, "Now, you are going to tell me who is behind this."

The man winced in pain as he asked, "Why would I do that? You shot me."

"You left me little choice when you aimed your pistol at Lady Octavia's back," Greydon said.

The man scoffed. "I wasn't going to shoot her."

"I somehow doubt that," Greydon responded. "Perhaps we should start at the beginning, shall we? If not, I will shoot your other leg."

In a panicked voice, the man said, "I don't know who hired me."

"Do you expect me to believe that?" Greydon asked as he aimed the pistol at the man's other leg.

"Someone slipped a piece of paper under my door and told me that I would be paid two thousand pounds if I killed

Lord Kendal," the man rushed out. "I tried tampering with his carriage, but he survived. Every attempt after that was thwarted as well. It's as if the man has nine lives."

Fredrick approached the man with Octavia tucked by his side and asked, "Did you place the arsenic into Lord Kendal's decanter?"

"I didn't poison anyone with arsenic," the man claimed. "I am not stupid enough to try to break into a lord's house."

"Yet you are stupid enough to try to murder the lord," Fredrick pressed.

"It was for two thousand pounds! I would murder my own mother for that much money," the man declared. "It beats working at the docks for hours on end."

Harred came to stand next to Octavia and inquired, "How did you recruit the others for the job?"

"That was easy," the man replied. "I offered to pay them to help me. We were going to be rich, but you ruined that for us."

Greydon glanced up at Fredrick. "Do you believe him or should I shoot him just in case?"

"I just have one more question," Fredrick started, "once you killed Lord Kendal, how were you going to get paid?"

"The money was to be delivered to my room at the boarding house," the man replied.

"What if the person reneged on the deal?" Fredrick pressed.

The man looked at Fredrick like he hadn't considered this a possibility. "Why would they do that?"

Greydon rose and said, "I have heard enough. We should get him to a doctor before we transport him to Newgate."

"Newgate!" the man shouted. "Why are you taking me there? I didn't kill anyone."

"By your own admission, you tried to kill Lord Kendal, multiple times, and you abducted Lady Octavia," Greydon replied. "Newgate is the perfect place for you to be."

The man put his hand up. "Wait!" he shouted. "If I tell you everything I know, will you let me go free?"

"What more do you know?" Fredrick asked.

"I don't know much, but I can help you set a trap for him," the man attempted.

Greydon clucked his tongue. "As tempting as that is, I have no desire to work with someone like you."

As the man tried to plead his case with Greydon, Harred caught Octavia's eyes and asked, "How are you faring?"

Octavia stepped out of Fredrick's arms and replied, "I am well." Her words were not very convincing.

Harred wanted to pull her into his arms and hold her. But it wasn't his place to do so... yet. He had every intention of winning Octavia's heart. He just needed more time.

Greydon assisted the man in rising. "It is time for us to go," he said. "I don't want him to bleed out before we get him to Newgate."

Once Greydon had placed Octavia's abductor in the coach, he moved to sit across from him and closed the door.

"Should one of us go with Greydon?" Harred asked.

Fredrick shook his head. "There is no need. Greydon can handle himself with an injured assailant." He turned back towards the coach. "Shall we return home?"

"I think that is for the best," Octavia agreed. "It is rather chilly out here."

Harred quickly removed his jacket and slipped it over her shoulders. "I hope this helps."

She gave him a grateful look. "That is kind of you," she said.

Fredrick assisted his sister back to the coach and claimed the seat next to her. Harred sat across from them and it wasn't long before the coach departed.

Octavia met Harred's gaze and asked, "Did you know that these men were planning on killing you?"

"I did," Harred replied.

"Then why did you come?" she asked.

Harred gave her a weak smile. "I had to come to ensure you were safe," he said softly.

Fredrick cast him a frustrated look. "We tried to tell him that his presence wasn't needed- or wanted- but he didn't seem to listen to us."

Octavia's face softened. "I appreciate the gesture, and I am glad that you weren't killed."

"As am I," Harred agreed.

Shifting in her seat, Octavia addressed her brother. "Who else did you enlist to help?"

Fredrick grinned. "Between me and Lord Rushcliffe, we had a small army of people that were willing to help, including two snipers who were well-placed in the trees. I wasn't about to let anything happen to you."

"You took your time though," Octavia teased. "I wanted to be home before supper but instead I ate some stale bread in an abandoned warehouse. No thanks to you."

"Poor Octavia," Fredrick joked.

"It was awful," Octavia declared. "And do not get me started about the rats that were scurrying around the floor."

Harred felt himself relax now that Octavia was out of harm's way. He hadn't realized how tense he had been during the whole ordeal, but it was over now. She was safe, and that was all that mattered.

Octavia lifted her brow as she turned to face him. "What is so funny?"

"Pardon?" Harred asked.

"You are smiling," she pointed out.

"Am I? I hadn't noticed," Harred responded.

Fredrick gave him a pointed look. "Typically, one does not look amused when someone is sharing their story of survival."

With a slight shrug, Harred said, "I guess I am just happy that Octavia is safe and she is here with us. Right here. Right now."

"Thank you, Harred," Octavia responded. "I think my brother could learn from you. He is forever teasing me but he should be grateful that I am always around."

The coach came to a stop in front of Harred's townhouse and Fredrick opened the door for him. "Goodnight, Harred," he said.

Harred remained rooted in his seat as he addressed Octavia. "May I call upon you tomorrow?" he asked.

"I would like that very much," Octavia replied with a hint of a smile playing on her lips.

He opened his mouth but Fredrick spoke first. "Goodnight, Harred," he repeated. "It is late, and I do not have the energy to deal with you for a moment longer."

Octavia swatted at her brother's sleeve. "Do be nice," she encouraged. "Someone tried to kill him tonight."

"Yes, and it was because of me that he is still alive," Fredrick pointed out.

Harred thought it best if he took his leave. He politely tipped his head as he said, "Goodnight, Octavia. Fredrick." He exited the coach and hurried up the steps towards the main door.

When he stepped inside, he was immediately met by William and Ruth.

"Are you all right?" William asked. "Were you able to save Octavia?"

Harred bobbed his head. "I am perfectly fine and Lady Octavia is on her way home with her brother."

Ruth brought a hand to her chest and let out a sigh. "What a relief. I have been so worried about you both."

"If you will excuse me, I would like to retire to bed," Harred said. "It has been a long day."

William surprised him by stepping closer and giving him a firm embrace. "I am glad that you are all right, Harred," he said before he released him and walked off.

The amazement must have shown on Harred's face

because Ruth explained, "William was particularly upset over the events of the evening."

Harred didn't know why but he found great relief in that. They still didn't know who was behind everything, but surely it couldn't be William. Not if he had reacted in such a fashion. Could he?

Chapter Twenty-One

The following morning, Harred sat at his desk as he attempted to review the accounts but his mind kept straying towards Octavia. He wanted to offer for her, but he couldn't do that, not while someone was trying to kill him. He refused to put her in harm's way... again.

The door opened and his brother stepped into the room. "Do you have a moment to talk?" William asked.

Harred placed the paper onto the desk and replied, "What would you care to talk about?"

William looked unsure, which was in stark contrast to how he usually acted. "I have done some thinking and I want to apologize."

Now his curiosity was piqued. William had never been known to be one to apologize, well, for anything. "What do you want to apologize for in particular?"

"For everything," came his brother's reply. "I have made a real muck of my life and I realize that I need to change."

Harred leaned back in his seat as he gauged his brother's sincerity. "Where did this change of heart come from?"

William walked over to the chair that faced the desk and sat down. "Everything came crashing down when I realized that you thought I was behind the attacks on your life," he revealed. "At first, I blamed you for thinking something so preposterous. But then it hit me. I was to blame, not you. It was my behavior that allowed you to think such a thing."

His brother continued as he held his gaze. "We may not always get along, but I do not want you dead. You are the only family that I have left."

Touched by his brother's words, Harred said, "I do believe you."

William looked relieved by his admission. "I am happy to hear you say that," he sighed. "I may not always appear to be listening, but I do hear your words. Frankly, you remind me of Father in so many ways, and I know he would have been proud of you."

"Our parents would have wanted us to rely on one another," Harred said. "Let's not disappoint them."

William nodded. "I hope one day to be the person that you have become, but I find that change is difficult for me."

"It is for everyone, but it is the silent battles that you must overcome. The ones that no one even realizes that you are fighting."

His brother considered him for a moment before saying, "I just wish I could see the future and know that everything will work out for me."

"That would be nice, but the fun is in the journey."

Rising, William said, "I am meeting Ruth for breakfast. Would you care to join us?"

"No, thank you. I have enough work for two lifetimes here," Harred replied.

"If the offer still stands," William started, "I would like to accept the job to help run the estate."

Harred could not have been more surprised by his brother's change of heart. "You would?"

"It might take some time before I get Ruth's dowry and I

have plenty of time on my hands," William replied. "But if you would prefer that I didn't—"

Speaking over him, Harred said, "I would be honored to work with you."

William smiled. "Very good."

A knock came at the door before Ruth stepped into the room. "Good morning," she greeted. "I have come to collect my husband for breakfast."

Harred had risen when Ruth stepped into the room. "Good morning," he responded.

Ruth came to stand next to William and he leaned down to kiss her on the cheek. "Hello, Wife," he said.

A shy smile came to Ruth's face. "Hello, Husband."

It was evident that his brother was making progress on wooing his wife. Which was a good thing. They both deserved to be happy.

The butler stepped into the room and met Harred's gaze. "Lord Chatsworth and Lady Octavia would like a moment of your time, my lord," he announced.

"Send them in," Harred ordered. He was pleased by the prospect that Octavia was here to see him.

A moment later, Fredrick and Octavia entered the room. Harred briefly admired how beautiful Octavia looked in her pale yellow gown. Her brown hair was pulled back into a low chignon and she looked the epitome of perfection. He hoped, and not for the first time, that one day he could convince her to be his.

Fredrick put his hands up. "I am glad that everyone is here because Octavia and I figured out who is behind the attacks on Harred."

"You have?" Harred asked.

Octavia bobbed her head. "There was one more person that would benefit from Harred's death. It was someone that we hadn't even considered."

William spoke up. "Who is that?"

"Ruth," Octavia replied.

Ruth's eyes went wide. "I beg your pardon?" she asked. "You think I was behind these vicious attacks on Harred?"

"It all makes sense," Fredrick said. "You had the means to pour arsenic into the decanter and the motive, and you were the only one who could have lured Octavia out of her townhouse to be abducted."

"This is preposterous. What motive could I possibly have?" Ruth asked.

"At first, we couldn't think of one, but then your words came back to me. You wanted a title to prove that you are worthy of Society's esteem," Octavia said.

Ruth furrowed her brow. "I have William's title. That is all I have ever wanted."

"But it wasn't enough, was it?" Octavia asked. "You wanted to be a marchioness and have a higher rank than the young women from your boarding school."

Turning her attention towards Harred, Ruth asked, "You don't believe this nonsense, do you?"

Harred wanted to believe that Ruth wasn't capable of such terrible crimes, but he wasn't about to dismiss what Fredrick and Octavia were saying. He trusted them and wanted to hear them out before he came to his own conclusions.

As Harred debated about his reply, Fredrick interjected, "You were a merchant's daughter and you spent time on the docks. It wouldn't be a stretch for you to figure out which of your workers would be capable of murder."

Ruth brought her hand up to her chest. "You think I would lower myself to have someone murdered, especially someone that has been nothing but kind to me?"

Greydon's voice came from the doorway. "I do," he said as he held up a bag. "And this bag of arsenic we found in your bedchamber is all the proof that I need."

William took a step back from his wife with a disbelieving look. "Why did you have arsenic in your bedchamber?"

Ruth rushed out, "The arsenic is for the rats in my bedchamber. Nothing more. You have to believe me."

"But I don't," William said. "How could you?"

Tears came to Ruth's eyes as she frantically glanced around the room. "Why does no one believe I couldn't do this?"

Greydon stepped further into the room. "It is over, and those fake tears are not going to save you," he said. "The constable is on his way to arrest you, and you can try to convince the magistrate of your innocence."

Ruth reached up and wiped away the tears that were streaming down her face. "You only believe I am capable of such a thing because I am a merchant's daughter."

"That has nothing to do with it," Greydon said.

"No matter what I do, I will never be good enough for this family," Ruth declared. "I would have always been an outcast because of my lowly status."

Harred had heard enough and he was convinced that Ruth had been behind these crimes. But he didn't understand why she would do such a thing. "Why, Ruth?" he asked.

Ruth took a step towards him but stopped. "Harred, how could you think I was behind this? You of all people——"

He cut her off. "Our time is short. I would prefer the truth, please."

"The truth?" Ruth asked as she blinked back her tears. "I was treated cruelly by everyone because I was only a merchant's daughter. It didn't matter how rich my father was. I was never going to be good enough for the *ton*."

"But we could have taken on the *ton* together," William said.

"Together?" Ruth huffed. "You were too busy spending time with your other family to even notice me. I tried to get you to love me, but you always looked past me. Even you, by your own admission, thought I was beneath you."

"That was at the beginning. It changed after we kissed," William attempted.

Ruth's eyes grew cold. "I never cared for you. You were just a means to an end. What I wanted was to be a marchioness. Can you imagine the power that I would have wielded in Society? Then I could have proven everyone else wrong."

"Ruth..." William's voice stopped. "How could you?"

"How could *I*?" she shouted. "Did you know that my so-called friends at my boarding school would put manure onto my bed? They claimed that is where I deserved to sleep. They tortured me, and no one did anything because of who their parents were. That is when I knew I had to become one of them so I could beat them at their own game."

A tall, burly man stepped into the room. "I have heard enough," he said. "I am Constable Randall and I will gladly escort Lady William to Newgate."

Ruth took a step back. "No, you can't do this to me. I am a lady."

"I don't care who you are, my lady," the constable said. "You broke the law and will be tried for your crimes."

"What about the crimes that were committed against me?" Ruth asked defiantly. "Does no one care about those?"

The constable approached her and reached for her arm. "You are under arrest for the attempted murder of Lord Kendal."

Ruth yanked her arm out of his grip. "No, I won't go. This has all just been a terrible misunderstanding." She turned her attention towards Harred. "Please, don't do this. I didn't really mean to kill you. I was just confused."

Harred saw the fear in Ruth's eyes but it was of her own making. "William and I will ensure you are given a fair trial," he informed her.

Ruth's eyes darted over the room until they landed on William. "Are you going to let the constable take me?" she asked. "If so, you will never get my dowry."

"I don't care about your dowry," William responded. "You tried to murder my brother. That is not something I can ever accept."

Turning her attention towards Harred, Ruth looked desperate as she said, "My father is rich and he will pay you whatever you want if you don't let me get arrested."

"Enough of this," the constable said as he grabbed her arm. "It is time to transport you to Newgate."

"But I haven't had breakfast yet," Ruth cried out.

The constable led her towards the door as he replied, "They will feed you in Newgate."

"You can't treat me like this! I am a lady now!" Ruth exclaimed, digging her feet into the ground.

"I don't care if you are the Prince Regent, you are going to jail," the constable stated.

After the constable had forcefully removed Ruth from the study, Harred turned his attention to Octavia and asked, "How was it that you came to suspect Ruth?"

"Her own words are what convinced me," Octavia said. "She tried to pretend the past didn't affect her, but she told me that she was going to start fighting back. Which made me realize that she was the only one that would truly benefit from your death."

"Aside from me," William pointed out.

"Yes, but Harred never quite believed that you were responsible," Fredrick said. "And I trust my friend."

"I should be grateful for that," William acknowledged.

Greydon tucked the bag of arsenic into his jacket pocket. "If you will excuse me, I need to go make a statement to the magistrate."

"How did you know to search Ruth's bedchamber?" Harred asked.

"When Octavia's abductor mentioned he worked at the docks, I recalled Lady William's father was a merchant and spent plenty of time there," Greydon replied. "It wasn't inconceivable to me that Lady William might have used those connections to advance her position in high Society."

William dropped down on the chair. "My wife is not who I thought she was," he muttered. "How was I so easily fooled?"

"We were all fooled by her," Fredrick said, "but Octavia figured it out. I am beginning to think she may have spy senses as she claims. She even concocted her own invisible ink."

"It worked?" Octavia asked, her eyes brightening.

"Yes, but we can discuss that later," Fredrick replied. "Don't you need to speak to Harred about something?"

Octavia clasped her hands together, exclaiming, "I do, but I can't wait to tell our cook that we were triumphant."

With a wry smile, Fredrick added, "And there goes the spy sense. A true spy never utters a word. Now don't you have something to do; something far more important than discussing invisible ink?"

Octavia exchanged a meaningful look with Fredrick, a silent communication that Harred couldn't quite decipher.

Turning towards Harred, Octavia asked, "Would you mind terribly if you took me on a tour of your gardens?"

Harred was not a fool. He would gladly spend time with Octavia, especially if it meant he got her alone for even a moment. "Nothing would make me happier," he replied. And that was the truth.

As he approached Octavia, Fredrick remarked, "I will be watching from the window. Do try to behave yourselves."

Harred held his hand out to Octavia. "Shall we, my lady?"

Octavia accepted his arm and Harred knew the time had come for him to confess his love to her. And he hoped he didn't make a fool of himself. However, even if he did, it would be worth it if she agreed to be his wife.

It was time. Octavia had gotten Harred alone and she was going to confess how she truly felt for him. Fredrick thought it was utter madness on her part, but she had to at least try. She knew Harred cared for her, but she could no longer go on the way they were. She loved him far too much to settle with just being friends with him.

As they walked along the path, Octavia tried to think of how she could start off the conversation but, for once, she was at a loss for words. What could she say that wouldn't scare him off?

Harred's voice broke through her musings. "You seem rather quiet."

"Do I?" she asked as she let out a nervous laugh. "I suppose I have a lot on my mind."

"I can only imagine, especially since Ruth was your friend."

Octavia bobbed her head. "She fooled me into believing she was something she was not, and I can't believe I didn't see it earlier."

"Why would you have?" Harred asked. "You have always managed to see the best in people. It was no different with Ruth."

"It must be a relief that you know that Lord William wasn't behind the attempts on your life," Octavia remarked.

Harred grew solemn. "He came to me this morning and apologized for his behavior. He couldn't believe we had gotten to a point where I would believe he was capable of such a thing. His demeanor was so different from the way he usually is that I believed him."

She nudged her shoulder against his. "We are alike in more ways than one. You also see the good in people."

"Yes, but it wasn't until I met you that I started doing that."

"I find that hard to believe."

Harred's eyes left hers and roamed over the gardens. "It is a beautiful day, is it not?"

Octavia inwardly groaned. This was not going well. It appeared that Harred had run out of things to say to her and was now commenting on the weather.

"It is rather nice touring your gardens without worrying about an evil peacock that is determined to attack me every time I set foot in his domain," Octavia said.

"You poor thing," Harred teased.

Octavia pressed her lips together before saying, "I never did get to thank you for what you did for my mother. It was rather nice playing pretend with you."

"How is your mother faring?"

Her eyes grew downcast. "Not well. She is struggling to remember even the simplest of things and she is growing more paranoid of the servants."

Harred slipped his hand over hers and said, "You are not alone in this. I am here for you. All you have to do is but ask."

"I know and I am most grateful for that." But she wanted more from him.

"I don't know how you can endure what you do and still have a reason to smile," he remarked. "You are extraordinary."

Octavia felt buoyed by his comment. Perhaps he did care for her, maybe even love her? After all, he always said the most kind things about her.

Harred stopped on the path, his boots grinding on the gravel as he turned to face her. "Octavia, I am glad that we have this opportunity to be alone. I have been meaning to talk to you about something."

"As do I," she admitted.

"Would you care to go first?"

No.

But she could do this. She just needed to muster up the strength to tell him how she felt. The time to be bold was now.

Octavia cleared her throat. "I… uh…" Her voice trailed off. It was much harder than she thought to declare her feelings. And why was that? She knew he wouldn't laugh at her, but the fear of him not reciprocating her affection petrified her.

Harred must have sensed her discomfort since he suggested, "It might be best if I go first, assuming you have no objections."

She nodded slowly. "I have none."

Harred's eyes never wavered from her face as he shared, "I rather enjoyed playing the part of your husband but I grew tired of it."

"Oh, I see," she murmured, not knowing what else she could say. She was disappointed that he hadn't enjoyed the role as much as she had.

In a gentle voice, he continued. "After a while, I realized that I wanted to stop pretending and truly be your husband."

Octavia's heart took flight. "You did?"

The way Harred was watching her made her heart skip a beat and had her knees go a little weak. "Before I met you, I didn't think I would ever find love. Or that anyone would be able to fill the void in my heart. But all that changed when I met you. You broke down my barriers, and touched my soul, making me whole." He paused. "But I have a problem."

"What is that?"

With a tender smile playing on his lips, he replied, "I have come to realize that I am hopelessly, desperately in love with you, and I can't go on without you by my side. I love you, Octavia. I have for a long time now, and I was hoping you would do me the privilege of becoming my wife."

Octavia felt tears well up in her eyes, but she made no attempt to stop them. These were happy tears.

But Harred failed to recognize that. "Did I say something wrong?" he asked with concern in his voice.

"No, you did everything right," she rushed to assure him. "It was perfect."

"Then why are you crying?"

She smiled through the tears. "I do not think I have ever been so happy in my entire life as I am right now," she admitted.

"Does this mean you will marry me?"

"Yes!" she exclaimed. "I would marry you today, tomorrow or any day you would like. Whatever day you choose, it cannot come soon enough for me."

Harred moved closer and cupped her right cheek. "I love you, my dear," he said. "You have made me the happiest of men."

Octavia stared up at him, fearing that her heart might burst from happiness. Was that even possible? "I love you, too."

"I wanted to tell you so many times, but I was afraid you didn't feel the same," Harred admitted.

"I was worried about the same thing."

Harred smiled, and in that smile, she saw her future. "It sounds like we prolonged our own agony," he said.

"Did you know that Fredrick foresaw this happening?" she asked. "That is why he has encouraged us along."

"Your brother is a wise man, but do not tell him that I said that. He is already cocky enough," Harred remarked.

"That he is," she agreed.

His finger started tracing along her bottom lip, distracting her terribly. "May I kiss you?" he asked.

It took everything she had to nod. She couldn't formulate words, not when he was looking at her like that. It was the way that every woman wanted to be looked at by the man she loved.

Harred leaned closer until his lips brushed against hers. "Octavia," he whispered. "I have dreamed of this for so long."

Then he kissed her. It was soft, gentle, and she found herself lost in his touch, trusting him completely. This was everything that she had ever wanted. She didn't have to pretend with him anymore. Her heart now beat with his, and they would never be apart.

He broke the kiss but remained close. "That was better than I ever imagined," he said, his warm breath on her lips.

"It wasn't bad. But I think if we practiced more, it would be much better," she joked as she flashed him a coy smile.

Harred looked amused by her response. "I would be a fool to turn down that offer."

Fredrick's irate voice came from behind them. "Your time is up," he said. "You will release my sister, Harred!"

Harred dropped his arms and moved to create distance between them. "Octavia has agreed to be my wife," he announced.

"What wonderful news," Fredrick muttered. "I don't need to challenge you to a duel- at least this time."

Octavia placed a hand on her hip. "Promise me that you won't shoot my fiancé for any reason," she said.

Fredrick frowned. "I can't promise that. If he becomes too familiar with –"

She spoke over him. "Even if he is too familiar," she stated. "If you can't promise that, then I shall abduct Harred and take him to Gretna Green tonight."

"Typically, it is the man that absconds with the woman," Harred pointed out.

She arched an eyebrow. "You are not helping, Harred."

Harred put his hands up in front of him. "My apologies. Please proceed with your threat. It is very frightening."

"Fine, I will not shoot your fiancé for any reason," Fredrick conceded. "But can I at least engage in fisticuffs with him?"

Octavia pretended to consider her brother's words. "I will allow fisticuffs," she said, knowing full well that Fredrick wouldn't make good on his threat.

Fredrick offered his arm. "Shall we go inform Father of the news?"

As Octavia placed her arm on Fredrick's sleeve, she replied, "We must tell Mother as well. I know she might not remember it but I have to try."

"I think that would be the right thing to do," Fredrick agreed.

Fredrick started leading Octavia away from Harred and she realized there was one more thing she had to do. "Wait!" she exclaimed.

"What is wrong?" Fredrick asked as he stopped on the path.

With quick steps, Octavia hurried back to Harred, went up on her tiptoes, and pressed her lips firmly against his.

"Octavia!" Fredrick shouted.

She released Harred and said, "You must promise to call upon me later."

"Nothing could stop me," Harred responded.

Spinning on her heel, Octavia felt almost giddy as she declared, "Now we can depart."

Epilogue

It had been three weeks since Harred had declared his love to Octavia and had offered for her. Three long weeks. And Fredrick had done everything in his power to ensure that they hadn't had a moment alone with each other.

That is why Harred was resorting to such tactics as he stood outside of Octavia's bedchamber window- in the middle of the night- with a handful of small rocks. He just wanted the opportunity to speak to her before their wedding tomorrow.

He reared his hand back and tossed one of the rocks towards her window. *Clank.* He waited for a moment before he took aim again.

After his third attempt, the window opened and Octavia stuck her head out. "Good heavens, what are you doing?"

"I am here to serenade you," Harred declared.

"Are you mad?" Octavia asked. "You might wake Freddy, or worse, Fredrick. Either one would chase you out of our gardens."

Harred smiled. "I am madly in love with you and I am willing to risk their wraths just to spend some time with you."

Octavia's face softened at his words. "We are getting married tomorrow and then we will never have to be apart."

"I am counting down the moments."

The window next to Octavia's opened and Anette stuck her head out. "Harred?" she asked. "What are you doing here?"

"I am here to speak to Octavia," he replied.

"At this hour?" Anette spoke over her shoulder as she said, "It is Harred. He is here to speak to Octavia."

A moment later, Roswell appeared by his wife's side. "If you two don't quiet down, you are going to wake the whole household."

"We are talking softly," Octavia said.

Roswell chuckled. "I do not think you could ever speak softly. You are, and always have been, a loud talker."

"I am not!" Octavia argued.

"My point exactly," Roswell said.

Anette swatted at her husband's arm. "Leave Octavia alone. She is getting married tomorrow."

"Yes, and she should be sleeping," Roswell remarked.

Harred interjected, "I just wanted a chance to speak to Octavia without Fredrick standing watch."

"I don't blame you. He has been a bit overbearing lately," Roswell agreed. "But it was only to ensure you two behaved."

Octavia leaned further out of the window and addressed Anette. "Where is Mr. Fluffy?"

"He is asleep on the bed," Anette responded. "He refused to wake up, even for this entertaining show."

"It is not a show," Harred muttered.

Roswell shook his head. "I am regretting getting Anette a puppy. Mr. Fluffy is like a ball full of energy and he never stops chewing."

"But I love Mr. Fluffy," Anette said.

This was not going well, Harred thought. He had come to serenade Octavia, not discuss Mr. Fluffy.

Octavia must have sensed his growing irritation and asked, "Do you mind giving me and Harred some privacy?"

"You have five minutes and then I am going to wake Fredrick myself," Roswell said.

Another window opened and Fredrick appeared, much to Harred's chagrin. "Don't bother," he grumbled. "I am already awake."

Harred looked heavenward. Could this night get any worse?

"What are you doing, Harred?" Fredrick demanded.

Anette spoke up. "He has come to speak to Octavia."

"At this hour?" Fredrick asked.

"That is precisely what I said," Anette remarked. "But I think it is sweet. We should let them speak privately."

Roswell looked amused. "I would prefer to sleep and not hear their chatter."

"Go home, Harred," Fredrick ordered. "I do not have the energy to deal with whatever this is. Besides, Octavia will see you at the chapel tomorrow."

"No, he is going to serenade me first and then he can leave," Octavia stated firmly.

"I would like to witness this," Roswell said as he leaned against the window frame.

Anette turned towards her husband and asked, "Why haven't you serenaded me?"

"Because I can't sing or play an instrument," Roswell replied. "It is your fault. You married me, knowing I lacked those abilities."

Fredrick's frustrated voice interrupted their conversation. "There will be no performance tonight. We don't want to wake anyone else."

Harred had failed to get Octavia alone and he decided it was best if he left. "Fredrick is right. I should go."

"So soon?" Octavia asked.

"Yes, but I assure you that I will be early at the chapel tomorrow," Harred replied.

The moonlight hit Octavia's face as she smiled and her

whole face appeared to light up. "I loved seeing you, even if it was for just a moment," she said.

Harred stared at Octavia longer than what was considered proper, but he didn't care. He loved Octavia and, tomorrow, they would be wed. The only thing that was irrevocably his in the world was the love and appreciation that he felt for Octavia. With her by his side, he could do anything. He was sure of that.

Roswell asked his wife in a low voice, "Do you think they are having a staring contest?"

"They are in love," Anette replied. "Leave them be."

"Are we this sappy?" Roswell inquired.

Fredrick rushed to say, "Yes."

"Only a brother would be truly honest with me," Roswell joked as he disappeared from the window.

Harred bowed. "Until tomorrow, my love," he said.

"Are you truly leaving without singing me a song?" Octavia asked with a slight pout on her lips.

"He can sing to you tomorrow," Fredrick stated. "I have heard him sing, and it is not something I wish to hear again."

Octavia came to his defense by saying, "Harred has a lovely voice, even Mother thinks so."

"I think it would be best if I waited," Harred admitted.

Fredrick bobbed his head. "Finally, that is the first sensible thing that Harred has said all night."

"Be nice to Harred," Octavia encouraged. "He will be family come tomorrow."

A screeching noise could be heard in the distance and Harred knew his time was up. All this noise had attracted Freddy's attention.

Octavia must have heard it, too, because she urged, "I would leave quickly before Freddy finds you and attacks."

Harred didn't need to be told twice. He didn't really want to fend off a peacock this evening. "Goodnight, my love," he said before he turned to leave.

"I have my money on Freddy," Fredrick shouted.

As Harred hurried towards the gate, he was relieved to see that Freddy was nowhere to be seen. Then he looked up.

Freddy was in the tree and was staring down at him with his black, beady eyes.

Harred froze, unsure of what he should do. Should he make a run for the gate or stare the peacock down? How he wished he had learned more about peacocks. That information would have come in handy at a moment like this.

He decided to throw caution to the wind and run.

Harred lunged for the gate and unlatched it. He started running on the pavement and didn't stop until he was nearing his townhouse.

While he stopped to catch his breath, he realized that this evening hadn't gone as he had planned. But it was all right. He had seen Octavia and that was enough for him.

He finally understood what true love was. It meant that he cared for Octavia's happiness more than his own. For it only worked if he was by her side. Forever living and loving their way through anything.

The End

Next in series...

Miss Emilia Hembry had a remarkable twist of fate when an unexpected inheritance changed her life for the better. However, now she must navigate through high Society- something she knows little about. The fear of failure is not far from her mind as she tries to accept her newfound position.

Fredrick Westlake, Earl of Chatsworth, had a chance encounter with Miss Hembry and felt compassion for her plight. He offers to help, all while dealing with his own demons. He still struggles with returning from the war as one of Wellington's spies and leaving his comrades behind. He puts on a brave face, but he is miserable, weighed down by his past.

As Emilia and Fredrick are brought together, they form an unlikely friendship, finding solace in each other's company. But when Fredrick is pulled back into the spy world, he begins to question what it is that he wants out of life, especially when he finds himself experiencing a love he never believed he deserved. But will his past shatter any hope of a future together?

About the Author

Laura Beers is an award-winning author. She attended Brigham Young University, earning a Bachelor of Science degree in Construction Management. She can't sing, doesn't dance and loves naps.

Laura lives in Utah with her husband, three kids, and her dysfunctional dog. When not writing regency romance, she loves skiing, hiking, and drinking Dr Pepper.

You can connect with Laura on Facebook, Instagram, or on her site at www.authorlaurabeers.com.

Made in the USA
Coppell, TX
20 October 2024

38968994R00177